Praise for Pete Hamill's
The Christmas Kid

"Hamill, a master raconteur, mines his own roots in an enchanting new anthology.... And while they are fiction, not reportage, they are grounded in the writer's personal experience with real people.... Each story is a tone poem. Don't even skip the dedication, a litany of characters whose nicknames alone conjure up Mr. Hamill's 'Brooklyn hamlet.' Two constants endure in the old neighborhood: change and an endless stream of stories."

—Sam Roberts, *New York Times*

"Pete Hamill is New York City's citizen chronicler.... Vivid characters such as 'Wonderful Kelly' and 'Facts McCarthy' abound.... Hamill's skill as a reporter is evident here. His simple descriptions and careful observance record a place and time that is physically no more but is imprinted on the DNA of the city.... Hamill's great love is New York City and his mission is to open a portal to the vanished world that lies beneath and alongside the modern trappings of today's New York. He succeeds."

—Patricia Harty, *Irish America*

"Hamill is a seasoned journalist who can be counted on to write fiction with heart and old-fashioned human charm.... Hamill knows the toughness of city streets but also the warmth and richness to be found in the lives of the denizens of those streets.... With their universality of theme and directness of style, the stories speak to all readers."

—Brad Hooper, *Booklist*

"Famed writer Pete Hamill's latest book is a lesson for the Brooklyn newcomer clueless to what life was like before yuppies flooded the now highbrow neighborhood. *The Christmas Kid* is composed of thirty-six short tales depicting a bygone era when bloody street fights, heartless murders, and torrid love affairs were all part of everyday life on and around the Seventh Avenue strip."

—Simone Weichselbaum, *New York Daily News*

"Lost treasures from a time gone by, brimming with affection for old New York.... The stories remain surprisingly timeless, full of regular joes, gangsters, lost souls, and the cold, cold rain. There's plenty of nostalgia, remembrances of that awe-inspiring feeling of the world being new, but also the harsh reminders of New York's hard times, not least the wave of heroin and crack that swept the city in that time.... A fine collection." —*Kirkus Reviews*

"Hamill's words paint a vivid nostalgia, a love letter to the borough of Brooklyn from a time when you could find the Dodgers, longshoremen on the waterfront, and kids playing in the street." —Will Yakowicz, *Park Slope Patch*

"Hamill writes like the great Sugar Ray Robinson could

punch: with incredible power, style, and grace....With *The Christmas Kid,* Hamill cements his place as one of the greatest American writers who ever lived. This collection reads like a panoramic novel of a lost world. It's a place filled with vitality and nostalgia. The people inhabiting these pages deal with love, loss, and fate as best as they can. This is an impossible collection to put down once you start it. It's Pete Hamill at the absolute top of his game....In page after page, you see the work of a master craftsman....As people who love words and literature, we are lucky to have Pete Hamill, who is a national treasure. This is a book you must have in your collection."   —Tom Callahan, *Bookreporter*

"The title story of Hamill's collection is a Brooklyn Christmas tale that hits just the right nostalgic chord....He strikes a tonal balance between cozy reminiscence and sharp, immediate sadness....With its various moods, Hamill's collection mirrors the city itself, especially during the holidays. Tragedies and frustrations occur daily, as they always do here. But New York City's numerous small communities also thrive."   —Alexia Nader, *PolicyMic*

"Hamill has honed his nostalgia for a midcentury Brooklyn populated by immigrants, cops, and wiseguys."
      —Yvonne Zipp, *Washington Post*

"A collection of thirty-six street-smart short stories....A veteran columnist at his best....If you like O. Henry, you'll appreciate Hamill."   —Bob Minzesheimer, *USA Today*

"This collection reveals Hamill's skill in recreating the Brooklyn he grew up in, with baseball, the neighborhood bar, the characters that come home to their own small culture held within the microcosm of the neighborhood after the Depression. There is a loyalty, a safety within the confines of their lives.... Well written, compelling, and bringing back a time when small stores were communities, small people became large, with Brooklyn as the background for a world that held compassion and caring within its streets and characters." —Ava Rogers, *The Review Broads*

The Christmas Kid

The
Christmas Kid

And Other Brooklyn Stories

Pete Hamill

BACK BAY BOOKS
LITTLE, BROWN AND COMPANY
New York   Boston   London

Copyright © 2012 by Deidre Enterprises, Inc.
Reading group guide copyright © 2013 by Deidre Enterprises, Inc., and Little, Brown and Company

Back Bay Books / Little, Brown and Company
Hachette Book Group
237 Park Avenue, New York, NY 10017
littlebrown.com

Originally published in hardcover by Little, Brown and Company, October 2012
First Back Bay paperback edition, October 2013

Back Bay Books is an imprint of Little, Brown and Company. The Back Bay Books name and logo are trademarks of Hachette Book Group, Inc.

The publisher is not responsible for websites (or their content) that are not owned by the publisher.

The Hachette Speakers Bureau provides a wide range of authors for speaking events. To find out more, go to hachettespeakersbureau.com or call (866) 376-6591.

Library of Congress Cataloging-in-Publication Data
Hamill, Pete,
  The Christmas kid: and other Brooklyn stories / Pete Hamill.—1st ed.
    p. cm.
  ISBN 978-0-316-23273-9 (hc) / 978-0-316-23274-6 (pb)
  1. Brooklyn (New York, N.Y.)—Fiction. I. Title.
  PS3558.A423C48 2012
  813'.54—dc23   2012027288

10 9 8 7 6 5 4 3 2 1

RRD-C

Printed in the United States of America

This book is for—*in no particular order*—*the people from my* Brooklyn hamlet: Tim Lee and Jack Daugherty, Patty Rattigan, Georgie Loftus, Dick Ganley, Frank and Red Cioffi, Geordie Stewart, Harry Kelly, Buck Vermilyea. It's for Mr. and Mrs. Mike Caputo and their kids, Junior, Sonny, and Babe. It's for Ann Sharkey and Mae Irwin, Carrie Woods and Cliff, for Mae, Marilyn, and Jackie McEvoy, Dottie and Pete DeRossi, Harry Kerniss, Walter Wagner, Jack O'Loughlin, and Sam Brody. It's for Billy Begley, Hoppo Chambers, Gil and Kenny Hope, Mike and Sonny Fischetti, Mr. Greenberg, Mr. B., Mr. Fortunato, Mr. Gutter, Mom and Pop Sanew. It's for Jim Brady, Wimpy Vento, Noona Taylor, for Billy Delaney, Vera, Paul, and Sara DeSaro, Harold Sicker. It's for Marion and Dom, Cookie, Tommy, and Laura Ventriglio, Billy Rossiter, Jimmy Lanzano, Raymond Dix, Harry D'Arcy, Eddie Prybys, Nit-Nat DelVecchio, Billy Boy Sirico, Joe Kelly and No-Toes Nocera. It's for Catherine and Rosie Rogan, Roberta Perrin, Mary Cottingham, Betty Kayata, Mary Christopher, Marilyn Lawless, Lorraine Hines, Betty Gahan, Dotty and Betty Long, Rosemary Malden, Jeanie Miller,

Kathleen Quigley, Mary Lou Speck, Maureen Crowley, and Pat Colligan. It's for Aggie, Bobby, and Tommy Lenihan. It's for Josephine Wares. It's for Georgie Lee. It's for Dotty Condril and Dotty Meserole. It's for Eddie Farrell, Tommy, Danny, and Eddie Mills, for Ray Garvey, Tweetsie Farrell, Jimmy Houlihan, Mike Lee, Bill Powers, Jake Conaboy, Richie Kelly, Ralph Squicciarini, Jackie Heegan, George Planco, Duke Baluta, John Yard, and Eddie Cush. It's for Danny Gorman, Downtown Ronnie, and Donald O'Connor. It's for Shrovelhead, Ray Grillo, Icebox McNiff, Mousey Malone, Lefty Murray, Blackie the Cop, Pinhead Lupinsky, Bubba Lee, the Fryars, the Spillanes, the Kanes, the Egans, the Wallaces, the Donnellys. It's for Pat Fenton. It's for Steve Jerro, Joe Attara, Eddie Lauterbach, Gerard McGrath, Harold, Tommy, and Billy Gates. It's for Jerry and Whitey Mackie, Jimmy Blatz, Howdy Doodie. It's for Joe Whitmore and his daughter, Pat, for Dinny Collins, for Jimmy and Peter Budgell, for John Duffy and Jim Shea, Unbeatable Joe, Mr. Semke, Jackie Metcalf, Ronnie Zeilenhofer, and Alvera the Bush. For Nat the Laundryman, Teddy from the fruit store, and Mr. Glass the glazier. For Vito Pinto, Boopie Conroy, Johnny Rose, Jack McAleavey, Mickey Horan, Eddie Griffin, Eddie Norris, Fabulous Murphy, Hot Dog McGuinness, and Joey Corrar. It's for Willie Sutton. It's for Toddo Marino.

All were residents of my Brooklyn shtetl. All remain alive as long as some of us are alive.

Contents

About These Stories   3

The Christmas Kid   9

The Price of Love   26

A Death in the Family   32

Wishes   38

The Love of His Life   44

Good-bye   51

Changing of the Guard   57

Footsteps   63

A Poet Long Ago   69

The Car   76

Just the Facts, Ma'am   82

6/6/44   89

The Trial of Red Dano   95

Leaving Paradise   101

Lullaby of Birdland   107

The Boarder   114

The Men in Black Raincoats   120

The Radio Doctor   131

The Challenge   137

A Hero of the War   143

The Final Score   149

Gone   155

You Say Tomato, and…   161

'S Wonderful   167

The Warrior's Son   173

The Second Summer   179

The Sunset Pool   186

The Lasting Gift   193

The Man with the Blue Guitar   200

The Hitter Bag   206

Trouble   213

The Home Country   219

The Waiting Game   226

The Home Run   232

Up the Roof   239

The Book Signing   251

Acknowledgments   273

Reading Group Guide   277

...I had my existence. I was there.
Me in place and the place in me.

—Seamus Heaney, "A Herbal"

The Christmas Kid

About These Stories

Most of these tales were first published on Sundays by New York's *Daily News* in the early 1980s. The original notion was to bring short fiction back into a newspaper, in the tradition of O. Henry in New York, Alberto Moravia in Rome, Kafū Nagai in Tokyo, and many others in many countries. These tales are set in Brooklyn, the large, dense, beautiful borough where I was born and grew up. I will carry the place with me to my grave.

Many of these stories are charged by the city's most enduring emotion: nostalgia. Two factors still drive that emotion: the rapidity of change in New York and the immigrant roots of almost all its inhabitants. You go away for a month, and when you return your favorite coffee shop is being gutted to make way for another jeans shop. You ache for people gone, and places, and music, for lost loves, absent friends, vanished games, departed baseball teams. Immigrants might have been hurt into exile, as my parents were in the 1920s from Ireland, as millions are in today's America, but they still yearn for old roads, familiar smells, special foods, for songs, for language, for old games, for parents and aunts and uncles, for homes where they knew every inch of each room, even in the dark. Whatever brought them to New York—bigotry, hunger, oppression, war—the Old Country was still the place where they once ran barefoot in the grass. Everyone's present also contained a past. Then. Now.

The Brooklyn neighborhood where I grew up is now called the South Slope. When I was young it was an unnamed wedge between the brownstones of Park Slope and the solid lower-middle-class houses of Windsor Terrace. The inhabitants were almost all immigrants and their children: Italians, Irish, and a smaller number of Eastern European Jews. They were virtually all blue-collar workers, many engaged in the commerce of the port: loading and unloading cargo, transporting it to distant places. Others worked in construction, as ironworkers, wire lathers, masons, carpenters. Many (my father among them) worked in factories, including the huge redbrick mass of the Ansonia Clock factory at 12th Street and Seventh Avenue. The Factory, as we all called it, was erected in 1881 (the same year as the Gunfight at the O.K. Corral), and in 1982, when all the jobs were gone and I was writing these stories, it was converted into an excellent co-op, with a grand, cobblestoned courtyard. It's still there.

There were saloons on almost every corner between 9th Street and 15th Street, some of them born as speakeasies during Prohibition. My father's favorite was Rattigan's, on the corner of 11th Street and Seventh, and it appears in more than a few of these tales. Like all the others, Patty Rattigan's wonderful saloon served as an employment agency ("I just heard they're hirin' at American Can..."), a refuge, a music hall ("Give us a song, will ya, Billy?"), a debating society ("Hey, no politics, no religion, ya got it?"), and a social club. When someone died, they took up collections to help pay for the burial. Women were allowed into the back room, but not at the bar, and that back room was often full of people after weddings, graduations, and funerals. There were bad guys in the neighborhood, a street gang called the Tigers, along with various bookmakers and loan sharks. But most of the people were decent, including the Mob guys. Woe to the punk who hurt a child or an old person. If the cops didn't find him, the Mob guys would. Even they believed in rules. So did the crowd at Rattigan's. Most sins were forgiven as long as you always paid your debts, voted the straight ticket (the Democratic Party), and never, ever crossed a picket line.

Most adults in the neighborhood had come through the Depression and the war. Their most important four-letter word was work. They never envisioned having something as grandiose as a career; that was for their children. But work meant they could put money on the bar on a Friday night and still have something left in the morning. On holidays, graduations, christenings, Bar Mitzvahs, they could even buy gifts for their kids. As a child, I often heard their mantra: a day's work for a day's pay. Work gave them pride. With any luck, they would work until they died. And the world would stay the same. Peace. Steadiness. Even some happy endings.

The world didn't remain the same. The Korean War meant that we had not seen the end of war. Young men who were thirteen when World War II ended were now being drafted and trained to kill for their country. If most Brooklyn veterans of the first of those wars used the GI Bill for housing benefits, the Korean veterans began using it for higher education. I was one of them, but I was certainly not alone. Everywhere in our country the tradition of following your father into his union started to end. But there were other huge changes underway. The arrival of television. And, much worse, the spread of heroin. In a neighborhood where none of us owned anything worth robbing, locks appeared on all the doors.

Years later, when I was a young newspaperman at the *New York Post,* my editor, Paul Sann, once stopped at my desk in the city room and handed me a collection of the stories of Sholem Aleichem. "Read this," he said. "It's about your tribe, too." And so it was. Tevye the Dairyman was Murphy the Milkman. There were few saints, many sinners, some small heroes, a few cold villains. I understood then that in our world, each neighborhood was a kind of shtetl, an urban hamlet, complete with its own lore and legends and heartbreak.

But change never stopped. I wrote most of these tales in a city without personal computers, cell phones, tweets, digital cameras, or iPads. A world where "friend" was not yet a verb. The sources of the stories were varied: chance encounters on the Brooklyn streets, phone calls at the newspaper, letters from old classmates. My press card took me many places and to many stories. A court officer at a trial would stop me in the hall during a recess and tell me a tale. At a murder scene a detective would take me aside and tell me what happened to so-and-so from the Tigers. I'd visit grieving friends sitting shivah, or gathering at a wake, and once I was back out on the sidewalk, the tales came in a stream.

They are flowing still. I hope somebody is writing them down.

—*Pete Hamill*

The Christmas Kid

I

IN THAT LOST CITY of memory, the wind is always blowing hard from the harbor and the snow is packed tightly on the hills of Prospect Park. They are skating on the Big Lake and the hallways of the tenements are wet with melted snow and the downtown stores are glad with blinking lights and the churches smell of pine and awe. And when I wander that lost Christmas city, I always think of Lev Augstein.

He was to become our Christmas kid. But he came among us one day in summer, a small, thin boy, nine years old, speaking a language we had never heard. His eyes were wide and brown and frightened, and he wore short pants that first day, and he stood on the corner near the Greek's coffee shop, staring at us as we finished a game of stickball. When the game was over, my brother, Tommy, asked him to play with us, but the boy's face trembled and he backed up, his eyes confused. Ralphie Boy handed him the Spaldeen and the boy shook his head in refusal and said something in that language and then ran away on toothpick legs to 11th Street.

"He don't speak English," Ralphie Boy said, in an amazed way. "He don't even speak Italian!"

Within days, we learned that the new kid was from Poland, which we located with precision in our geography books. Poland was wedged between Germany and Russia, and the language he spoke was called Yiddish. We also learned that the boy was living with his uncle, a cool, white-haired man named Barney Augstein.

"If he's related to Barney," my father said at the kitchen table, "then he's the salt of the earth."

Barney Augstein was one of the best men in that neighborhood, and one of the most important. He was the bookmaker. Each day, dressed like a dude, smiling and smoking a cigar, Barney would move from bar to bar, handling the action. Until Lev arrived, Barney lived alone in an apartment near the firehouse, and they said in the neighborhood that long ago, he had been married to a Broadway dancer. She had left him to go to Hollywood, and this gave Barney Augstein an aura of melancholy glamour. Ralphie Boy, Eddie Waits, Cheech, and the others all agreed that any nephew of Barney Augstein was okay with us.

We learned that the new kid's name was Lev. Ralphie Boy showed Lev how to hold a Spaldeen, throw it, catch it, hit it, and the rest of us taught him English. We told him the names of the important things: bat, ball, base; car, street, trolley; house, roof, yard, factory; store. Soda. Candy. Cops. Lev stood there while we pointed at things and he named them, proud when he got the word right, but trembling when he got it wrong. "I hate when he does that," Ralphie Boy said one morning. "It's like a dog that got beat too much." And we noticed two things about him. He never smiled. And he had a number tattooed on his wrist.

"A number on his wrist?" my mother said one night. "Oh, my God." She was silent for a while, then glanced out the window at the skyline glittering across the harbor. "Well, make sure you take care of that boy. Don't let anything happen to him. Ever."

The summer moved on. Lev put on weight, and Barney Augstein bought him clothes and Keds and a first baseman's mitt. We tried to explain all of life to him, particularly the Dodgers. Lev listened gravely to the story of the holy team, and if he didn't fully comprehend, he certainly tried. He recited the litany: Reiser, Reese, Walker…

"He play baseball good?" Lev said, pointing at a picture of Reiser in the *Daily News*. "He play stickball good?"

"Good?" Ralphie Boy said. "He's like Christmas every day."

"Christmas every day?" Lev said.

11

II

One afternoon, Barney Augstein came around with Charlie Flanagan. They were best friends, though Charlie was a cop. Their friendship was one reason Augstein could work openly as a bookmaker in the neighborhood without being arrested. My father said their friendship went back to Prohibition, when they lived on the Lower East Side and worked as guards on the whiskey runs to Canada. Now Charlie lived alone. He and Barney went to the fights together, and bought their clothes from the same tailor, and even went to Broadway shows. We were sitting on the cellar board of Roulston's grocery store when they came over together.

"Listen, you bozos," Augstein said. "One of yiz has been teachin' my nephew bad woids, and I want it to stop."

"Nah," Ralphie Boy said.

"Don't gimme 'nah,'" Augstein said. "I'm warnin' yiz. If yiz keep teaching Lev doity woids, I'll have yiz t'rown in fronta da Sevent' Avenue bus. Ya got that?"

"Dat goes for me, too," Flanagan said. "Barney wants his nephew to be a gent, not a hat rack like you guys. So teach the kid right. And if I hear he gets in trouble, I'll lock yiz all up."

They turned around and walked across the street to Rattigan's Bar and Grill, a couple of cool older dudes in sport shirts. They were laughing.

III

The trouble started around Labor Day weekend, and it all came from Nora McCarthy. She lived up the block from Rattigan's, almost directly across 11th Street from Barney Augstein's house. She was in her forties, a large, box-shaped woman with horn-rimmed glasses, and she was awful. Everybody's business was her business, and when she wasn't working at the Youth Board, a job she'd received from the Regular Democratic Club, she was policing private lives. My father called her Nora the Nose. Now she had begun investigating Lev Augstein. On Labor Day weekend, when we were feeling forlorn about the imminent return to school, she came over to us after a game.

"What's this new boy's name?" she said, pointing at Lev.

"Why?" Ralphie Boy said. "What business is it of yours?"

"I live in this neighborhood!" she snapped. "I have a right to know when strangers show up. Particularly if they live with a known criminal. And particularly if they are young. Young people are my job."

We all made rude noises and laughed. But Lev did not laugh. He looked up at Nora McCarthy, at her severe hairdo, her coarse skin, the mole on her chin, the square, blocky hands, the hard judgmental lines that bracketed her mouth, and he sensed danger. He backed away, but Nora McCarthy grabbed his wrist. She moved her thumb and saw the tattooed number and then she smiled.

"You're a Jew, aren't you?" she said. "You're one of those DPs. Those displaced persons. Aren't you?" She gave Lev's wrist a tug. "But I bet you don't have any papers. You got that look. That scared look. Tell me the truth."

Lev pulled away, but she held on. And then Ralphie Boy came around behind her and gave her a ferocious kick in the ass, and she let go, and then we were all running, Lev with us, and we didn't stop until we were deep in the bushes of Prospect Park. We sat there, aching from the run, and then laughing at what Ralphie Boy had done. Lev didn't laugh. He didn't know a lot of English but he sure knew what Nora the Nose meant when she said the word "Jew."

That night, my father came home angry because he'd run into a furious Nora McCarthy. He hated giving the Nose even a slight edge and wanted to know why we'd done what we did. We told him. He started laughing hard, and gave us each a hug and told us to dress quickly because we were going to Barney Augstein's to see a fight on Barney's new television set. We walked up 11th Street in the chilly evening to Barney's. Across the street, Nora McCarthy was at the window, inspecting the block. My father walked over, spit in her yard, and yelled up at her: "Benny Leonard was a Jew!" I didn't know who Benny Leonard was, but I knew from the way he said it that if Benny Leonard was a Jew, then being a Jew was a great thing. Nora McCarthy closed the window.

Barney Augstein's living room was packed. Charlie Flanagan was mixing drinks in the kitchen. A woman named Bridget Moynihan was cooking a beef stew. In the living room, seated in a large chair, there was a lean, sun-tanned, dark-haired man with an amused look on his face.

Lev brought me over and said something in Yiddish to this man, and the man shook my hand politely, while Lev told me that the man was his Uncle Meyer.

"Nice to meet you, sport," Meyer said to me. "You take care of this kid, okay? He's been through a lot." He looked down at a diamond pinkie ring. "His mother, his father, the whole goddamn family, except him. They all got it. Know what I mean?"

Then he turned his attention to the TV, talking about Willie Pep with Charlie Flanagan, and about Ray Robinson with Barney Augstein, and then about baseball, and somehow the talk got around to Pete Reiser.

"Pete Reiser," Lev said. "Like Christmas every day."

"Now, *there's* a smart kid," said Meyer, and they all laughed. Meyer and Barney argued for a while about the fight on TV, and then Meyer produced the fattest roll of bills I'd ever seen. "Put your money where your mouth is," Meyer said, and smiled.

"Come," Lev said, and led me to his room. It was very small—a bed, a bureau, a chair. But it felt like a library. There were stacks of comic books everywhere, grammar books, two fat dictionaries. And drawings that Lev had made: Batman, the Green Lantern, Captain America, Donald Duck. There were other drawings, too; buildings with spirals of black cloud issuing from chimneys; barefoot men with shaved heads and gray pajamas; watchtowers; barbed wire.

"You're an artist," I said.

"An artist?"

"Yeah, an artist."

"Pete Reiser is an artist?"

"Yeah," I said. "In a way."

"Like Christmas every day," Lev said. "An artist."

IV

Fall arrived. The days shortened. Most of us went to the Catholic school, but Lev enrolled in public school, where Ralphie Boy became his protector. Ralphie Boy had been kicked out of Catholic school.

"The kid is scared all the time," Ralphie Boy told me. "I gotta teach him how to fight."

Every day now, the woman named Bridget Moynihan was coming to Barney's house. She was about forty and lived with her mother and had a plain, sweet face. Barney hired her as a housekeeper, to make sure Lev ate properly and washed himself and always had clean clothes.

"I tried," Barney said to my father one day. "But I just got no talent for being a mother. This kid is family, you know. I'm his only living relative. But a mother I'm not."

They started to go to the movies together: Barney and Charlie and Bridget and Lev. They took walks, and went shopping together, too. Then at Thanksgiving, Barney prepared a big dinner. He asked us to come over after our own dinner and make Lev feel like he had a home. But Lev was in his room when we got there, and he was crying. Barney asked me to talk to him.

"Go 'way," Lev said, turning his back on me, sobbing into his pillow.

"What's the matter, Lev?"

"Go 'way, go 'way."

"You don't like turkey, Lev?" I said.

He whirled around, full of anger. "Too *much!* Is too *much!* All *food, food, food.* Too much!"

I was a kid then, but looking into the eyes of a boy who had survived a death camp, even I understood.

V

After Thanksgiving, the Christmas season began. Down on Fifth Avenue, store windows magically filled with toys and train sets and red stockings. Christmas banners stretched across the downtown streets, painted with the slogans of Christmas, about peace on earth and good will toward men. Christmas music played from the loudspeakers, and there were Salvation Army bands outside Abraham & Straus and men selling chestnuts and rummies dressed in Santa Claus costumes, ringing little bells. We took Lev with us as we wandered these streets, and he was full of amazement and wonder.

"But what is?" he said. "What is they mean, Christmas?"

"Hey, Lev, fig-*get* it," Ralphie Boy said. "You're a Jew. Christmas is for Catlicks."

"Explain, please."

A theological discussion of extraordinary complexity

then took place. Was Santa Claus a saint? Did they have Christmas bells in the stable in Bethlehem, and who made them? Did Joseph and Mary put stockings over the mantelpiece, and was there a mantelpiece in that stable? How come the Three Wise Men didn't come on reindeer instead of camels, and, by the way, where did they come from? If Jesus was the son of God, why didn't God just show up in person? It got even worse as we roamed around. But Lev stayed with it, almost burning with intensity, as if torn between the images in those store windows and the fact that he was a Jew.

"Why is not for Jews?" he said.

"Because Jesus was a Catlick, Lev," Ralphie Boy explained.

"No, he wasn't," my brother, Tommy, said. "Jesus was a Jew."

"Come *on,*" Ralphie Boy said. "Stop kiddin' around."

"I ain't kiddin'," Tommy said. "Jesus was a Jew. So was his mother and father."

"That's right," I said. "You could look it up."

"Well, when did he become a Catlick? After he *died?*"

"How do *I* know?" Tommy said. "All I know is, while he was here on earth he was a Jew."

"Ridiculous!" Ralphie Boy said.

If Lev had any doubts about the essential craziness of the goyim, they were not resolved by this version of the Council of Trent.

VI

Then Barney Augstein got sick and was taken to Methodist Hospital. There were whispered conversations about what was wrong with him, and then plans were made by Bridget and my mother and Charlie Flanagan. Bridget moved into Barney's house, and my mother and Tommy and I came over every night to help Lev with his homework, and the women decided they could give a Christmas party anyway. They would combine Hanukkah and Christmas, get a Christmas tree, hang pictures of Santa Claus around the house, but leave out all the mangers and statues of Jesus. Barney was part of the planning; he called each night from the hospital and talked to Lev and then Bridget, and later Bridget would talk to my mother.

"He wants to get the lad everything," Bridget would say. "Train sets, and chemistry sets, and a big easel so he can paint. A camera. A radio. And I have to keep stopping him, because he's gonna spoil that kid rotten."

Then on December 19, the first snowfall arrived in the city. Lev was in our house and we took him up to the roof and we stood there while the snow fell on the pigeon coops and the backyards, and obscured the skyline and the harbor, and clung to the trees, all of it pure and white and blinding. We scooped a handful from the roof of our pigeon coop, explained to Lev that it was "good packing," and started dropping snowballs into the street, hoping that we would see Nora the Nose. She wasn't there but others were, and soon Ralphie Boy was with us, too, and Eddie Waits, and

Cheech, and we were all firing snowballs from the rooftops, as skillful as dive-bombers, and Lev was with us, joining in, one of the crowd at last.

"Good packing," he shouted. *"Good packing!"*

That night, while we all slept, Barney Augstein died.

VII

They took Lev away two days later. A man and a woman in a dirty Chevy arrived at Barney's house at eight in the morning, showed Bridget their credentials, and took Lev to the children's shelter. Somewhere downtown. Where the courthouses were. And the jails. Bridget swore that she looked across the street and saw Nora McCarthy at her window, smiling. We learned all this that afternoon, when Ralphie Boy told us that Lev wasn't at school. We went up to Barney's and Charlie Flanagan was there with Bridget.

"He didn't have papers," Charlie said. "Barney got him in through Canada. The kid never had papers."

"So what'll they do?"

"Ship him back."

"To the concentration camp?"

"No," Charlie said. "To Poland."

"Well, maybe not," Bridget said. "Maybe he'll just go to an orphanage."

"An orphanage?"

We were filled with horror. Poland was bad enough, over there between Germany and Russia. But an orphanage was right out of *Oliver Twist*. I could see Lev, like Oliver on the H-O Oats box, holding a wooden bowl, his clothes in rags, asking for more gruel. That's what the book said. Gruel. Some kind of gray paste, what they always fed orphans, and I thought it was awful that Lev would have to spend all his years until he was eighteen eating the stuff. Worse, he could be adopted by some ham-fisted jerk who beat him every night. Or, even worse, someone who hated Jews. And all of us, in that moment, seemed to agree on the same thing.

"We gotta get him outta there," Ralphie Boy whispered. "Fast."

The phone rang and Charlie answered it. He talked cop talk for a while, and mentioned the State Department, shook his head, and said he couldn't adopt a kid because he was single. He hung up the phone, lit a cigar, cursed, and stared at the wall. Then he turned on us.

"All right, you bozos," he said. "Beat it."

I was halfway down the block when I realized I'd left my gloves on the kitchen table. I went back. Bridget answered the door and I hurried past her to get the gloves. Charlie was on the phone again.

"Hello, Meyer?" he said. "This is Charlie…"

He glowered at me until I left.

That night it snowed, and kept snowing the next day, and on the day after that, they closed the public schools, and we listened in the morning to "Rambling with Gambling," praying for more snow and the closing of the Catholic schools, too. The snow piled up in the streets, and we burrowed tunnels through it, and made huge boulders that blocked the cars in the side streets. The park was like a wonderland, pure and innocent and white, the leafless trees like the handwriting Lev used when he showed us his own language, and kids were everywhere—on sleighs, barrel staves, sliding down the snow-packed hills. All the kids except Lev. He was in the children's shelter, eating gruel.

Then on the afternoon of Christmas Eve, Charlie Flanagan rang our bell. My mother went out to the hall and met Charlie halfway down the stairs. There was a murmured conversation. Then she came up and told us to get dressed.

"Charlie's taking you to see Lev," she said. She gave us a present she had bought for him, a picture book about Thomas Jefferson, and down we went to the street. Ralphie Boy, Eddie Waits, and Cheech were already in Charlie's Plymouth, each carrying a present.

"Now, listen, you bozos," he said, "Don't do anything ridiculous when we see him. Got it straight? Just do what the hell we tell you to do."

We drove to downtown Brooklyn, where the government buildings rose in their mean, gaunt style from the snow-packed streets. Charlie pulled the car down a side street and parked. And in a few minutes, a Cadillac parked in front of him. He looked at his watch.

"The party for the orphans is already started," he said. "So you bozos just come in with us."

Two men dressed like Arabs got out of the Cadillac. They had headdresses on and mustaches, and shoes that curled up, and pantaloons, and flowing green-and-orange capes. One of them was the largest human being I ever saw. The other one was Meyer.

"Hello, sports," Meyer said, pulling a drag on a cigar. "Hello, Charlie."

He handed Charlie a box, and Charlie opened it and took out an Arab costume, and put it on over his suit. In a minute he, too, was a Wise Man from the East, his face covered with a false beard and mustache. We followed the three of them around the corner and into the children's shelter. There was a scrawny Christmas tree in the lobby, and windows smeared with Bon Ami cleanser to look like they were covered with snow, and cutouts of Santa Claus on the walls, and a few dying pieces of holly. A guard looked up when we walked in, his eyes widening at the sight of the three wild-looking Arabs.

"We're here for a Christmas party," the big guy said.

"Oh, yeah, yeah," the guard said. "Second floor."

We walked up a flight of stairs. The three Arabs glanced at each other, and Meyer chuckled and opened a door. They stepped into a room crowded with forlorn children, and then started to sing:

"We t'ree kings of Orient are…"

Everybody cheered and they kept on singing and patting the kids on the head, and looking angelic, and then Lev came running from a corner, right to Ralphie Boy, and hugged him and started to cry and then Ralphie Boy started to cry and then everybody was crying and the three Wise Men kept right on singing. They did "Jingle Bells" and "Silent Night" and "White Christmas." The two guards cheered, and the other kids sang along with them, and then Meyer couldn't stand it any longer and he lit a cigar, and then the other two lit up, and they were singing "Mairzy Doats," and the big guy slipped a bottle of whiskey to one of the guards and a cigar to the other, and they went into "Jingle Bells" again, and moved closer to Lev, and after a little while, we couldn't see Lev anymore. The singing went on. The guards were drinking. And then it was time to go. Meyer, Charlie, and the big guy backed out, doing one final chorus of "We t'ree kings of Orient are..." We followed them outside, waved good-bye, wished all the other kids a merry Christmas, came into the lobby, wished the guard a merry Christmas, too, and headed into the empty street.

Around the corner, Meyer stopped, lifted his whirling Arab costume, and let Lev out.

"Merry Christmas, sport," Meyer said to the kid. "Merry Christmas."

For the first time, Lev Augstein smiled.

VIII

That night, we sneaked Lev into our house, far from the eyes of Nora the Nose, and said our tearful good-byes. Then we all went down to Meyer's car. The trunk was packed with suitcases, but they wedged in a few more packages, and then Lev was driven out of our neighborhood, heading into Christmas Day, never to return. A few weeks later, Charlie Flanagan put in his papers, retired from the cops, married Bridget Moynihan, and moved to Florida to live on his pension and serve as a security boss in a certain hotel in Miami Beach. It's said that he and Bridget adopted a young boy soon after, and raised him as a Jew out of respect for the boy's uncle. Christmas was a big event in their house, but then so was Hanukkah.

I thought about Lev every year after that, when the snow fell through the Brooklyn sky and turned our neighborhood white, or when somebody told me that the snow was good packing, or when I heard certain songs from hidden speakers. I also thought about him when I met people with tattoos on their wrists, or saw barbed wire. But I didn't worry about him. I knew he was all right.

The Price of Love

In the mornings now, Levin walked the winter beach, his body buffeted by the hard sea wind, his heart blown through with emptiness. Gulls watched his progress. He plucked shells from the receding surf. He combed the sand for man-made things. He was accustomed now to the permanent grieving sadness of the summerhouses, sealed with boards and plastic sheets against the invasions of winter. On some mornings, Levin was sure he could hear laughter from their porches, remnants of summer evenings frozen in ice.

Alone, bundled in down and wool, his boots heavy, Levin walked about three miles each morning, with the Atlantic pounding the shore beside him, and then went back. He never had breakfast, and no longer read the newspapers or watched television. Across the long mornings, he worked with his hands in the small rented house, carving wood into birds and small animals and the heads of vanished friends, amazed that after so many years his hands were again capable of intricacy and control. The wood shavings helped feed the fireplace. Mozart fed his heart. He only thought about her five or six times a day.

He ate a late lunch, always in a pub called Magic's, where he liked the chili and the cheeseburgers. Nobody talked to him. He was just another middle-aged customer. If the pain came over him, as it sometimes did when he saw a waitress brush back her hair, or heard a woman's laugh, he would try to remember a melody by Mozart. This usually worked. After lunch, he would stop at the post office to pick up his mail, most of which was junk; his friends didn't know where he was, and that was all right with Levin. He didn't want to experience their pity, or have them ask for an explanation. His wife didn't love him anymore. It was as simple as that. And she had gone. That was all. He didn't want to explain that to anyone.

In the afternoon, he would polish whatever piece he had been working on that day, sitting in the large, soft chair beside the fireplace. The nights were more difficult. In those first weeks, after quitting his job, and closing his apartment, and coming out here to the beach to do things he had never had time to do, Levin's pain was most terrible at night. He would see her laughing with other men. Faceless men. He would see her cool gray eyes accusing him of misdemeanors he had not known he'd committed. He saw her empty closet. He would get up and walk around the small house then, and try to read, and lie again on the brass bed, hearing the house settling and the distant roar of the sea. And sometimes he was afraid. Thinking: I could die here, and nobody would know.

The fear of solitude slowly left him. It had been years since he'd slept alone, and for a long time he would still awaken and reach for her. But then, knowing that she was not there, and would never be there, he learned to accept her absence, and made new habits. Indifference replaced fear. And he began to look forward to the luxury of his solitary bed. I must be healing, he thought. I don't fear, I don't love, I don't hate. The wound is closed. I am alone. I am indifferent. I have survived.

And then one gray afternoon after lunch, he went to the post office and opened his box and removed the little bundle of mail. And along with the circulars and the tax forms from his accountant and the catalogs, he saw the letter. His name was written in the familiar handwriting, the round letters made by a fountain pen on a pale-blue envelope. But he did not open it, and then walked slowly back to the rented house.

He sat before the fire for a long while, dropping junk mail into the flames, until there was nothing left except the pale-blue envelope. He looked at the flames, considering whether he should simply throw the letter in with the other junk of his life. He decided not to do this, but could not open it, either. He laid the envelope on a table and went into the workroom to polish a head he'd carved of W. H. Auden. He thought about Auden's ravaged face and gentle eyes, wondering what his own face would look like after time had finished its erosions. I have time yet, he thought. Another twenty years. Maybe a few more than that. And will leave the world as alone as when I entered.

That night, he fell asleep while a heavy rainstorm lashed the village. He dreamed of Prospect Park when he was a boy, running across meadows. Then he was in the zoo, and the bars of the cages had all been removed, and the animals roamed around, free at last. They seemed almost timid in the dream. And then a panther was before him, sleek and black, with yellow eyes, and Levin was afraid. He tried to move, but his legs seemed encased in concrete. And then he was awake, and sweating, and still afraid.

He turned on the light, and lay in the damp bed listening to the steady drumming of the rain. And then he rose, pulled on a terry-cloth robe, and went out to the guttering fire to read the letter. He held it for a brief moment, jingling coins in the pocket of the robe, then opened it with a forefinger. There was a date on the upper-right-hand corner of the page, and the letter was addressed simply: "Darling." The word itself made Levin hurt.

He read the words:

This is no doubt too late. I've caused you so much pain, I suppose, that it will be a long time before you can think of me without anger. I don't blame you. This has been a hard and difficult time. In some ways, leaving you was the hardest thing I ever had to do. The pain was not all yours.

But I think now that I've been a fool. I have no excuses, but I owe you, at least, an explanation. It would be nicer if I could say that there was no other man, that I'd made an abstract decision to be free, in the best feminist way. It's true that I often felt smothered by you, oppressed by your love. If you'd love me less, I sometimes thought, maybe I could love you more. And in too many ways, I was depending upon you. You decided so many things. You controlled the money, too, which meant that in some ways you controlled me. So be it. That is the way it was.

But I didn't leave you for those reasons. I left you for a man. And now the man is gone. I'm not sure even now how it all happened, how a woman who was happily married for almost twenty years could suddenly behave like a silly girl. But it did happen. I was swept away.

But this man turned out to be a stranger. I suppose I was more impressed by the idea of him, by what I thought he was, than with the man he actually was. I'm not the first human being who has made that mistake; I won't be the last; but a mistake it was, and I made it.

Anyway, I am here. I want to see you. More than that, I want to go back to you. Perhaps all the king's horses and all the king's men can never put Humpty together again. But don't you think it's worth a try? You and I cannot wander the world without each other. Please call me.

She signed it with love, and Levin stared at the words for a while as if they were abstract forms—squiggles and circles and lines made by an inhabitant of some lost city. Then he put the letter back in the envelope and placed it on the couch beside him. His fingers rubbed the coins in the pocket of his robe. And then the fear rose in him again, as if some coat of armor had been abruptly removed. He saw her leaving him, again and again and again. He saw her with other men, always laughing. And then anger displaced fear; he cursed her, he snarled, he said terrible things.

The rain spattered the windows, and he peered through them into the darkness. He opened the front door and stepped outside. The rain lashed him, whining through the trees, drowning the lawn, soaking his robe. Levin shouted her name at the sky. Once. Twice. The wind and rain tore the words from him. He wrapped his arms around a maple tree, its wet bulk solid against his body. He cursed her again, his voice now a strangled sob.

And then he started to walk across open lawn, heading for the dark, drowned village. There was a telephone there, beside the bank. And he had coins in his pocket, to pay the price of love.

A Death in the Family

HEROIN ARRIVED IN THE neighborhood during Eddie Devlin's first winter in the navy. He went off to boot camp in Bainbridge on the day after Labor Day and came home to the snows of Christmas and, by then, all his friends were riding the white horse. They came up beside him in the bars, while Christmas music played on the jukeboxes, and offered him junk. When he said no, they moved away and smiled thin, superior smiles and left him to the beer drinkers. A line had been drawn.

"When did this start?" Devlin asked his brother Liam, who was two years younger, in his second year of high school. "Who brought this crap around?"

Liam didn't know, and Devlin's mother didn't know. His father, who was a good cop, might have known, except that

Devlin's father was dead. But others knew who brought heroin around, and they told Eddie Devlin. His name was Joe Tooks, a bone-thin, dark-haired man who drove a white Cadillac as he moved around the neighborhood. One snowy afternoon during Christmas leave, Devlin saw Joe Tooks get out of the Cadillac in front of the Athenia movie house, where the tough guys from the Leopards hung out in the summer. Joe Tooks looked immaculate in a long gray cashmere coat and matching gingerella hat, tapered dark pants, polished pointed shoes. Some of the old tough guys came over, but it wasn't summer for the Leopards anymore and they would never be tough guys again. Joe Tooks smiled and listened and shook his head. When he drove away, the old summer tough guys looked forlorn and lost.

"Stay away from the crap," Eddie Devlin told his kid brother on the day the Christmas leave was over. "And stay away from Joe Tooks."

Eddie Devlin was assigned to Florida, going to school for three months in Jacksonville, then working as a helicopter mechanic in Pensacola. For a while, he boxed on the base team, going from 165 pounds to 182, all of it muscle, and then had to quit. He was too big to box 175-pound light heavyweights and too small for the heavyweights. He worked hard as a mechanic and talked about going to college when he was discharged and becoming an engineer. He listened to Hank Williams now and Webb Pierce instead of Sinatra and Crosby; his best friend was from a town in Kentucky with a total population of 127, less than half of his tenement block in Brooklyn. When he had a summer leave due, he went to Key West instead of New York. The neighborhood seemed a long way away.

"I don't know anybody there anymore," he'd say when asked why he never went home. He didn't talk much about the letters from home, which read like reports from a distant battlefield. Charlie Barrows was dead. Sammie Pilser had died. The body of Danny Collins was found on a rooftop. Coconut was dead, too, and Jimbo Elliott and Frankie Flanagan and Junior Vittorino. There was a plague at home and the plague was called heroin. If the neighborhood was a kind of family, then the family was dying. Eddie Devlin would read the latest letter, shake his head sadly, and turn to the simpler, cleaner world of machines.

Then one December morning he was told to report immediately to the executive officer; there was a phone call from New York. He washed his hands and left the hangar, and as he moved across those tame green lawns, past the drooping date palms and the silent morning barracks, his mind filled with the spiky calligraphic images of fire escapes and gaunt tenements and the faces of the neighborhood. His stomach tightened and coiled; nausea made its move. It's Liam. Something terrible has happened to Liam.

And he was right.

A cold steady rain was falling in New York when Eddie Devlin arrived at Floyd Bennett Field, after hitching a ride on a navy transport plane. He went straight to the funeral parlor. At the wake, nobody mentioned heroin; there had been too many deaths and too much shame. But Eddie

Devlin knew, looking down on his brother's ravaged face, and his mother knew, trembling among the sweet dying flowers and the ruined candles.

"The poor boy," his mother said. "The poor little boy." In the afternoon of his second day home, Eddie Devlin went off to Prospect Park, to look at the place where they'd found Liam's body. He stood for a long time in a grove of ice-polished trees and knew what he had to do. It began to snow.

They found Joe Tooks two days later, under deep snow in the backyard of his apartment house. He was not pretty to look at. His elbows had been shot off. His left knee was gone. So was the back of his head. Most of the rest of him had been broken in the fall from the roof.

"Someone really did a job on this bum," one of the cops said, looking up at the faces in the back windows of the surrounding buildings. "I'd say we got about four thousand suspects."

The cops did their best, as news of the killing spread through the neighborhood like a stain. No, there had been no gunshots heard that night; it was snowing; snow muffles sound. No, there had been no strangers seen in the halls. Nobody knew Joe Tooks and nobody knew why anyone would kill him. It was as if no individual had killed Joe Tooks.

Eddie Devlin stayed at home, talking for long hours with his mother about his father, or gazing at the television set. The girls he used to know had married and moved from the neighborhood to the suburbs. The movie houses offered fare he had already seen at the base in Pensacola. His friends were all dead or strung out on junk. He was reading a book one night when the cops came knocking on his door.

"We'd like to talk to you about Joe Tooks," the big one said, his coat wet from snow, his eyes weary from life and felony.

"Joe who?"

They sat in the living room, the big weary cop and a small lean cop with quick eyes. They had heard he bought a gun from a certain party in South Brooklyn a few days ago, and could it be possible that the gun was used on Joe Tooks? Not that the cop would blame him, given what happened to his brother, but murder was murder. Eddie Devlin smoked cigarettes, said he didn't know what they were talking about, glanced at the falling snow. His mother offered the detectives tea. They accepted. They talked about Eddie's father, a good cop. An hour later, they got up to leave.

"Who do you think killed Joe Tooks?" the weary cop said to Eddie Devlin.

"Everybody," Eddie Devlin said.

The weary cop lit a cigar. "Yeah, well…see you around, kid. Enjoy the navy."

The next morning, Eddie Devlin packed his seabag. The emergency leave was over, and it was time to go. He urged his mother to leave the neighborhood, go out to Queens, where her sister lived, or even think about Florida.

"There's a lot of jobs down there," he said. "You could work in one of the hospitals. Enjoy the sun."

"I don't know," she said. "I've never lived anywhere else."

"Well, it's not the same anymore," he said. "It never will be what it was."

He said his good-byes, went down through the scabrous wet halls of their tenement, and came out into the bright glare of the snow-packed street. He had to walk three blocks to the subway, which would take him to Penn Station and out of the neighborhood forever. People were already at work, shoveling snow in front of the stores on the avenue, accepting deliveries from trucks, shopping. He started to walk. And then heard the voices of his other family.

"Oh, Eddie," Mrs. Vittorino said as he passed. "That was a wonderful thing that you did."

"Thanks, Eddie," Jimmie Barrows whispered.

"There was nothing else ya coulda done, Eddie Boy," Bruno Pilser said. "Godspeed."

Eddie Devlin smiled and said nothing and kept walking steadily until he reached the subway. There was a police car in front of the bakery on the corner. A cop waved. Eddie waved back. And then went down into the station without looking back.

Wishes

DAVIS PARKED NEAR THE corner of Gates Avenue and looked behind him at the tenement in the middle of the block. The old red brick was dark with the rain, the building's somber face relieved by scattered Christmas decorations in the windows. There were no decorations in the windows of the apartment at the top floor right, where his Uncle Roy lived alone. Uncle Roy: the old one, the lost one, the brother of Davis's mother. It had taken Davis two days, but now he'd tracked him down. The visit would not be pleasant. The only way to do it was quickly. He got out of the car, shielded by an umbrella, locked the door, and hurried through the rain to the building.

"Who is it?" the hoarse voice said from the other side of the door on the top floor.

"Your nephew, Uncle Roy," he said. "Tyrone Davis."

"Go away."

"I gotta talk to you, Uncle Roy. About my mother."

"I don't want to talk about her, or about nothin' else, boy."

Davis tried the doorknob. Locked. He made a fist and thumped on the door. "Come on, Uncle Roy...."

"Get lost."

"She's dead, Uncle Roy. My mother's dead." A pause. "We buried her last week."

Davis waited while Christmas music drifted up from the floors below. There was movement in the apartment, and then the door opened. God, Davis thought, he's old. The picture that Davis had grown up with, the picture leaning on the mantelpiece at home, was of a handsome young man in paratrooper jump boots, smiling, confident, bursting with life. This was a wasted, legless, gray-haired man in a wheelchair, staring at him with angry eyes.

"What happened?" the old man said quietly. Davis closed the door behind him, glancing around the small, spare, two-room apartment, with its TV set, bed, and stacked books, and tried to explain to Uncle Roy what had happened to his sister. He told him about the first heart attack, and how full of hope they'd been when she seemed all right for a year, and then how, when she was Christmas shopping the week before on Fulton Street, she'd pitched forward on her face and was gone.

"Damn," the old man said softly. "I'm sorry to hear that."

"But I wanted you to know something, Uncle Roy," the

younger man said. "She wanted to make it up with you. She wanted to be friends. She wanted you over for a visit this Christmas, and so did my wife, all of us, and all the kids. She wanted that."

"That never woulda happened," he said, bitterness suddenly in his tone.

"Maybe not. But that's what she wanted. She was sorry for what happened, Uncle Roy. Every day of her life. You must know that."

"She ruined my damned life," he said. "Her and that damned drunk boyfriend of hers..."

"She didn't run you over!" Davis shouted. "*He* did!"

"She brung him around! I told her he was no damn good and she wouldn't hear it! He came around, drunk, lookin' for trouble, and..."

The old man turned his head, his eyes welling with old angers, and wheeled himself into the second room, where the bed was neatly made. He looked out at the gray rain.

"It was a long time ago, Uncle Roy."

The old man's voice was hoarse and distant. "It was yesterday, boy."

Davis sighed. "Well, we still want you to come over to Christmas dinner, Uncle Roy. Two days from now. My house."

"Shoot. Just go away, boy."

Davis walked to the door. "Suit yourself," he said, angry now. "I'll see you sometime, Uncle Roy."

Then Uncle Roy said, "It cold out there?"

"Thirty degrees. They say the rain might turn to snow."

"Hell, it don't snow anymore the way it used to, you know. Used to be ten, twelve feet out there. We'd build forts and tunnels, tall as a house. It'd snow for days when I was a boy. Prospect Park'd look like Russia..."

"What happened?"

"Some folks say it was that Panamanian canal. You know, it changed the Gulf Stream and whatnot, and the weather with it. All the way up here, fifty years after the canal opened. Lots of folks blame the atom bomb, too. Who knows.... You want some coffee?"

And so it began. The old man talked about the great stickball games after the war, and the gang fights between the Bishops and Robins, and the music, always the music; the great times he had at jump school in the army and coming home and seeing Max Roach, who was from right there on Gates Avenue, playing at Birdland, and feeling so proud, seeing a tough smart black man playing better than anyone in the world. He talked about women, and came finally to The Woman, the beautiful one, the one he thought was so sweet, the one who left him after the accident. He talked about a lot of things.

"What do you want for Christmas, Uncle Roy?"

"What do I want for Christmas?" he said, and laughed. Then he turned away, and his face seemed oddly younger. "Get me Ben Webster for Christmas. Or Dinah Washington. Or Willie Mays. Yeah. Let me watch Jackie take a lead off third with the Duke at bat and Campy in the on-deck circle...." His face was lost in reverie now. The light in the apartment was grayer. "I want to stand at the bar of the

Baby Grand and look at the pretty girls come in. I want to go to the Apollo on a Friday night. I want the Cardinals to come to Ebbets Field in September, Musial and Slaughter, all of 'em, and we win three out of four, and then we go for the goddamn Yankees. I want to go down to Bay Twelve and eat dogs at Nathan's and find a pretty girl and swim out to the third barrel and tell her we can keep goin', all the way to Spain. I wanna stay up late with Nat Cole on the jukebox and eat eggs in Monroe's...."

The old man paused. "Or jump out of an airplane. Or run in Prospect Park, in the morning, you know? When it's hot and the grass is wet and there's like a fog there. I'd like to see California. Or Florida. I'd like my woman to come up them stairs and tell me she's sorry and she's stayin' for the last innings, know what I mean? I want to walk into the old Garden on a Friday night, with my friends, all of us laughin', and excitement in the air, just standin' in the lobby, where the statue of Joe Gans was, and we go in, and the place is packed and it's Robinson, it's Robinson, it's always Ray Robinson. That's what I want for Christmas...."

Then he simply ran down. The words wouldn't come. He stared off at the rain, his hands gripping the arms of the wheelchair. Davis came over, put an arm around the old man's shoulders, and squeezed his chilly brown hand.

"I'm sorry, Uncle Roy. I didn't mean to upset you."

"Ah, the hell with it."

"Want another coffee?"

"No. No more coffee. I'd never get to sleep later."

He moved the chair away from Davis and looked down at the street. He was quiet for a long moment.

"I'm sorry about your mother," he said finally. "I truly am." He fumbled in his pocket, brought out a pack of Viceroys, lit one. "Listen…I mean, how'd you get me over your house, anyway?"

Davis said, "I've got two teenager sons, Uncle Roy. Big strong kids. Between us, we'd get you down the stairs, and the chair, too, get you back up, too. No sweat."

The old man considered this. Davis could hear Christmas music drifting from the hall again, and down in the street he saw two kids lugging a tree through the rain. Then the old man said, "Ah, the hell with it. One thing I can't stand is bein' a bother to someone. Forget it, boy. I can't stand pity, you know what I'm sayin' to you? I don't want nobody feelin' sorry for poor ol' Uncle Roy. Forget it."

Davis said, "Okay, we'll pick you up Christmas Day, at eleven. Case closed."

"No, wait a minute, I don't want to—"

"You got no choice, Uncle Roy. We're comin' to get you."

Davis started for the door, and the old man turned in the wheelchair, the cigarette burning between his fingers.

"I ain't gettin' dressed up," he said. "Not for nothin'."

"Okay with me."

Davis was at the door now. The old man was silent.

"What do you really want for Christmas, Uncle Roy?"

The old man's eyes blinked a few times, and he ran a hand on the hidden stump of a ruined leg.

"Nineteen forty-nine," he said. "Nineteen forty-nine."

The Love of His Life

Hugo boarded the D train in Brooklyn one winter morning in 1951 and his life changed forever, although he didn't know it at the time. He was squashed against the door of the conductor's booth, reading a newspaper, when his eyes briefly wandered and came to rest on the face of a young woman. She was sitting facing him, reading a book called *And Quiet Flows the Don*. In his twenty-two winters on the earth, Hugo had never seen anyone quite like her.

"It wasn't just her face," he told me when I went to visit him many years later. "I mean, her face was amazing. Shaped like an oval, high cheekbones, clear skin, a great straight perfect nose…It was more than that. She had, like…like an *aura*."

Possessed by the force of the aura, Hugo remained on the

D train past his stop. He noticed that she had a portfolio of some kind beside her, and what seemed to be a toolbox on her lap; a model, he thought, or an artist. The aura pulsed with force, penetrating Hugo, and he suddenly knew, recklessly and intuitively, that this woman embodied everything he wanted: beauty, intelligence, warmth, humor, sensuality. He must have her. Not for a day or a week, but forever.

"She never noticed me looking at her," he told me. "But finally she folded down a corner of the page in her book, looked around as we pulled into a station, picked up the portfolio and the toolbox, and got off. I followed her. The aura..."

He walked after her through the crisp winter morning. She turned onto 57th Street, and he noticed now that she had a perfectly proportioned body, good legs, a rhythmic, confident walk. He wanted to call her, touch her arm, ask for directions or a match. He did nothing. Without breaking stride, she hurried up the stairs of a large stone building and was gone. The Art Students League. His heart thumping, late for work, Hugo hurried back to the subway.

All that day, grinding away in the financial advertising agency on lower Broadway where he worked as a copywriter, Hugo brooded about the astonishing young woman. She dominated his night thoughts in the furnished room in Brooklyn, and the next morning he waited for the same D train, didn't see the woman, let three more go by, and felt lost and disconnected when there was no sight of her. The same thing happened the next morning. The following day was a

PETE HAMILL

Friday; he told his boss he would be late, and went uptown and waited in front of the Art Students League. Dozens of young women entered the building, and a few young men, but he didn't see the woman with the aura. At twenty past nine, he started back to the subway. And saw her hurrying around the corner, head bent into the winter wind.

"Miss?"

She looked up, blinking. "Yes?"

"I, uh, well, I wondered if, uh, well, if you'd like to have a cup of coffee with me sometime."

She shook her head, an amused smile curling her mouth.

"Are you a lunatic or something?"

"No, no, I swear. I just…You were on the subway the other day, and you were reading that book *And Quiet Flows the Don,* and I…it's hard to explain. Maybe I am a lunatic. I'd just like to have coffee with you, that's all."

That evening, they sat in a booth in a coffee shop on Broadway. She told him her name was Daria Stark, and her parents were from Russia, and she lived in Coney Island. Hugo told her about his life, his job, his time in the navy; he talked in great torrents about life and death and love. She listened to him in an enigmatic way, offering little comment, laughing out loud at some of his more extravagant flights, her amber eyes turning glassy when he fumbled for the Meaning of It All. Then it was time for her to go. Not home. To meet friends. In the Village.

"Can I go with you?"

"I don't think that's a good idea," she said, and then, as if to ease the blow, added, "but—"

He rushed into the opening. Coffee again? She shrugged. Why not? Monday? Okay. Here? Sure. All the way home to Brooklyn, Hugo felt like singing. Daria Stark, he thought; my Russian. He went to the library, borrowed *And Quiet Flows the Don,* and spent the weekend in the Soviet Union, in heroic encounters with Whites and Reds, Cossacks and Separatists. He felt the aura of Daria Stark on every page. He heard her whisper the words to him: "Blinding and irresistible shines the feather grass along the steppe...." He identified with the protagonist, Gregory Melekhov, as he groped from one incomplete collision with history to another; Daria would make him complete. They would forge a union based on intelligence, art, generosity, the heroic ideal....

She didn't show up on Monday. She wasn't at the Art Students League, either. She wasn't there that week or the following week or even after that. He looked for her in the subway, he called everyone named Stark in the Brooklyn phone book, he walked along Surf and Neptune Avenues, looking for her; he wandered the Village, haunted art galleries and museums, never seeing art, simply looking at faces. He never found Daria Stark.

Weeks passed, and then months, and finally years. Hugo left the advertising agency, went to work for a magazine, moved from Brooklyn to Manhattan. He dated other women, of course, and even entered into a few serious affairs. But each time he began to make that mysterious leap into total commitment, he would pass a coffee shop or come out of Carnegie Hall and look left to the Art Students

League or hear a fragment of conversation about Russian novels or see a woman with a portfolio, and Daria Stark would force her way again into his consciousness, filling it completely with her enigmatic smile and her dark presence. He couldn't ever explain this to the wounded and baffled women in his life; he couldn't make clear the extraordinary moment of connection on the D train long ago; he couldn't describe the…aura.

After a while, he stopped going out with women altogether. He became a Village character; his beard grew out, a rich brown at first, and then scratched with gray. His eyes, weakened by endless copywriting, were soon masked by thick glasses. He was a steady, controlled drinker, but every once in a while, on clear days in winter, he would sometimes drink too much. I met him on one such day in the Lion's Head. His voice was choked, slurred, guttural. "She had the aura," he said, trying to tell me the story. "Her name was Daria Stark and she had the aura…."

At such times, he would get drunk for a few weeks, and lose his job, and then suddenly stop at the edge of the abyss, and go for a haircut, have his suit pressed, move to another magazine, and resume the routine of his life. He was often embarrassed after such binges, as if uncertain about how much he had revealed of himself while drunk. But most of the time he was just another one of those quiet wounded men who live out their lives in bars.

Then one humid summer afternoon, Hugo was sitting on a bench in Union Square Park. He tried to read a paper, but the day was too hot. He watched the junkies and winos for a while, and the pair of cops who moved through them like pedestrians feeding pigeons. Then he dozed, dreamy with summer exhaustion, and then was snapped awake by the backfiring of a truck.

He looked up at a thick-bodied, white-haired woman walking across the park, stepping tenderly, as if her feet hurt. Her head was down. She went to the curb at Fourth Avenue, waited for the light to change, and then hurried across the street to get on a bus. And then Hugo knew that it was Daria Stark. This lumpy middle-aged woman. It was her. And suddenly he was up, rushing to the corner, seeing the bus wheeze into the distance, heading uptown for Grand Central. He jumped into traffic, and a cab stopped with a squeal of brakes, and a cop turned to face him from the opposite corner, and a truck pulled around him, and Hugo began to run. Uptown. Calling her name. Through traffic. And never saw the taxi running the red light on 20th Street.

When I went to see him at Bellevue, his voice was an injured croak. His left leg was broken, his pelvis smashed, his skull fractured; there were tubes in his arms.

"I saw her," he whispered. And started to cry. "She's old. Like me...."

The pelvis healed, and the leg, and the skull, but Hugo didn't. He left Bellevue, but he couldn't learn again how to live in the world. He gazed out windows; he avoided the bars, and the company of men. He couldn't walk and didn't eat. The cops found him one afternoon, standing alone on a subway platform in Brooklyn, watching D trains arrive and depart. Someone reported him as a possible degenerate. The cops were gentle and took him to a hospital. His condition was simple; he was inconsolable. He likes it where he is now.

"There's trees," he said one day. "And feather grass, blinding and irresistible, like the steppes…"

Good-bye

MITCHELL SAT IN THE corner of the old couch, fingering the worn armrest, looking out past the metal window gate at the gray winter sky. He heard his wife, Sybil, stacking the dishes beside the sink, and soon she came to join him, sitting heavily in her favorite armchair. They were separated by the round mahogany table they'd bought the day they moved in, back in 1946. There was a lamp on the table, and a bottle of wine, and two glasses, and a dish with some pills.

"It'll be dark soon," she said.

"Yes, it will," Mitchell said. "But tonight we don't have to worry anymore. Ever."

"We'll be safe, won't we, Mitch?"

"Yes," he said, pouring the wine into the glasses. "We'll be safe."

PETE HAMILL

He always loved this time of the New York day, when the sun faded and the light turned a warm gray, softening the hard edges of the world. It reminded him of the old Warner Bros. movies they'd seen together before the war; the blacks were really black in those movies, the grays all silvery. They'd held hands in the dark, in the Sanders, in the RKO Prospect, in Loew's Metropolitan, in the RKO Albee. Held hands, with the future spread out before them. Safe. In Europe, darkness had fallen; Hitler was killing Jews, but he and Sybil were together in the safe darkness of movie theaters. Back then. It would be a long time before fear entered his heart to stay.

"You mailed the letters?" Mitchell said.

"Yes, dear," she said. "They should have them Monday."

Mitchell sipped the wine. "You think they'll get them at the same time? I mean, one goes to Florida and one to California. I wouldn't want one of the kids to get one before the other."

"They go on airplanes, dear. They'll be there the same day."

She was quiet for a long time, then sipped her wine, and gazed at the crowded bookcase beside the window. It even held textbooks she'd used at Columbia Teachers College, before the war, when Mitchell was at CCNY. It held everything else she'd ever cared for: Chekhov and Turgenev, Tolstoy and Gogol, all of Dickens, all of Stevenson. They'd come through life together, she and those books; they were her treasures. Now the girl would have them; the boy never did care for reading.

52

"Do you think they'll be upset?" Sybil said.

"Of course," Mitchell said. "But the girl will come. She's always been responsible."

"He was, too," she said. "But he always had these other things to live for. His job, his children, the two wives."

"The first wife was the better one," Mitchell said.

"How would you know, dear? You never met the second wife."

"True," he said. "But I liked the first one. She had... what's the word? Spirit?"

Sybil smiled. "Well, she was certainly wild."

Mitchell was quiet then, remembering the children when they were small, running around this apartment like puppies. That was after the war. He was teaching at Brooklyn Tech then, Sybil at Julia Richmond. He remembered the girl, learning how to read when she was three, explaining the comics to her older brother, then reading books to him. The books about the elephant. Babar. Yes. Babar. They were around here somewhere, those books. Still here.

"You don't have to do it," she said abruptly.

"No, my mind is made up," he said.

"You're sure?"

"I don't want to go back to the hospital," he said. "I don't want to be alone. I don't want to be afraid."

"All right."

"Sybil?"

"Yes."

"Come and sit beside me."

She got up slowly, exhaling hard, and sat beside him. The

gray was deeper now. There were no lights on in the apartment. She sat beside him, and he put his arm around her.

"Tell me about the old places," he said.

"I don't want to."

"Please," he said. "Then we'll have them forever."

She snuggled against him, her eyes unfocused. And she began to name the places of their life together.

"Sea Gate," she said. "Kiamesha Lake. Luna Park."

"Luna Park..."

"The dances at Prospect Hall. Union Square on a Saturday afternoon, and Fulton Street at Christmastime. Joe's on Myrtle Avenue..."

"We had dinner there the first night we ever slept together. I had four dollars in my pocket, and you had two, and we left a dime tip."

She smiled. "And the skating rink at Rockefeller Center. And the old Madison Square Garden. Remember how you took me to see CCNY play basketball there? And we walked through Times Square and looked at the giant waterfall, the Bond sign, and the big one for Camels, with the man blowing smoke rings, and everybody looked so glamorous, and we went to Lindy's and waited for a long time, and saw Milton Berle sitting in a booth."

"Yes," he said. "I remember that."

"We bought the *News* and *Mirror,* they were two cents each, and we took the subway home to Brooklyn, and you read me Pushkin that night in bed."

"Yes, I remember."

"And then in the summer, we both had two months off,

and the kids went to camp that time, and we went to Penn Station, the old Penn Station, and we took a Pullman to Florida, the two of us sleeping in the train, and it made clackety-clack sounds all through the night, and soon we could smell the oranges. We couldn't see them, but it was morning, and the train was still moving, and we could smell oranges everywhere, a million of them, a billion, the air full of oranges, and the heat was damp and wet when we walked to the dining car, and we still couldn't see the orange trees, but we were in Florida. We knew it. The oranges told us."

"I remember."

"And one New Year's Eve we went to the Waldorf," she said. "You'd saved all year to surprise me, and Guy Lombardo was there, and we saw Mayor O'Dwyer in the lobby, with that beautiful wife of his. You kissed me at midnight. And we stayed that night in the Waldorf, and you made love to me, and we looked out the window in the morning, and New York was the most beautiful place we'd ever seen."

"Yes."

"That summer we went to Lewisohn Stadium and heard Beethoven under the stars. We walked all the way downtown that night, through the streets, through Harlem, into the park, and the Tavern on the Green was still open, and we had cake and coffee and the waiter gave us a look and you laughed and left a dime tip, just for old times' sake."

"We could walk everywhere...."

"We walked around the Battery on a Sunday morning,

and you bought some flowers from a flower seller and laid them on the steps of the Custom House, because Melville once worked there. And we took three round trips on the Staten Island Ferry...."

"We were very tired, we were very merry...."

"The poem was terrible, but it seemed to fit."

"Yes. It seemed to fit...."

She was quiet then. They sat very still. Mitchell picked up the bottle of wine and filled their glasses again. Then he looked into her face.

"We can't go to any of those places anymore," he said.

She shook her head, her eyes brimming.

He kissed her on the mouth, and then he reached for the pills.

Changing of the Guard

SANNO SAT FOR A long time in the Eldorado with Ralphie Boy, both staring at the lights of the restaurant across the street. They were parked on a pump, the lights out, the engine running so the wipers could peel back the rain. Sanno rubbed his eyes, wishing he could go home to Brooklyn, get in bed with Marie, watch Johnny Carson. I'm sixty-two years old, he thought; I should be on a bench somewhere in Florida, not sitting here in the rain.

"I don't like it," Ralphie Boy said.

"Neither do I," Sanno said wearily. "But what the hell."

"Anyway, Junior's in there," Ralphie Boy said. "And Sidge. And Tony Dee. The guy tries anything, they destroy him."

"He won't try anything," Sanno said. "He's too smart."

"He's a freaking maniac," Ralphie Boy said. "All them Cubans are maniacs."

"He's Colombian, Ralph," Sanno said. "That's a different country from Cuba."

"Cuba. Colombia. They're all maniacs. Women, children, girls. They hit anybody. They don't care. Look at them nuns was killed down in Nicaragua."

"It was El Salvador, Ralph."

"You know what I mean. They're all freakin' nuts."

Sanno glanced at his watch. "I better go in."

"I'll be right here."

Sanno got out and hurried through the rain to the restaurant. There was a bar to the right and then an entryway into a large room with booths along the wall to the left, tables filling the room, a trio playing tepidly at the far end. Sanno gave his hat and coat to the hatcheck girl and turned to the maître d'.

"Carlos," Sanno said, and the maître d' nodded and led him through the crowded room to the booths. The Colombian was sitting alone. He was tanned, clean-shaven, and as he rose slightly in the booth and extended his hand, Sanno thought: a banker. Sanno shook the man's hand and sat facing him. A Rolex gleamed on his left wrist.

"Good to meet you," Carlos said, in slightly accented English. "I hear about you a long time."

"I heard about you, too."

Carlos laughed. "Hey, don't believe everything you hear, okay?" He waved to a waiter. "Drink?"

"Scotch would help. Ice. Soda."

Carlos ordered in Spanish. Sanno turned to look at the trio, which was playing "We'll Be Together Again." He saw Junior eating alone at a small table. Sidge was at the bar, facing the mirror. He couldn't see Tony Dee.

"The other one's down in the john," Carlos said, smiling. "He should be back soon."

Sanno stared blankly at the younger man. One waiter brought the Scotch and soda and placed it before Sanno on a plate. A second waiter brought Carlos a fresh cup of coffee.

"What do you want?" Sanno said.

"Everything."

Sanno felt the whiskey burn its way through him and then settle and grow warm.

"You really are crazy," Sanno said. "Like they said."

"You asked a question, you got an answer."

"You better study a little more English, pal," Sanno said. "Like that word 'everything.' I don't think you know what it means."

"It means the jukeboxes. It means the loan-sharking in the produce market. It means the line to Montreal. And, oh, yeah, it means the union, too. I like that part mos' of all. I like the union. I like everything." He sipped the coffee. "One of my favorite words."

Sanno laughed and sipped some more whiskey and looked around. Junior was gone. Tony Dee was at the bar with Sidge.

"You seen too many movies, Carlos," he said. "This is the real world. This ain't *The Godfather*. This ain't *Scarface*."

"You saw *Scarface*? What'd you think?"

"Too violent. But I liked the girl, Al Pacino's sister."

"Beautiful."

"She's Italian," Sanno said. "Like Pacino."

"Don't put me on."

"You could look it up," Sanno said.

"I like the movie," Carlos said.

"It ain't a documentary, Carlos," Sanno said. "It ain't even a training film."

"Yeah, but it gotta point, man. I think you know what it is."

"No. What is it, Carlos?"

"It's our turn now."

"That's the point? What are you, a critic, too?"

"No, but I read history. First the Irish had it. Then the Jews had it. Then you people had it. Now we're gonna have it."

"What's 'it,' Carlos?"

"Everything," he said, and laughed.

A waiter came over with two plates of marinated shrimp, placed them in front of the two men, bowed, and went away.

"Suppose I tell you to get lost," Sanno said.

"Mistake."

"I'm thinking just sitting here's a mistake."

Carlos tested one of the shrimps, then chewed it in a distracted way. He gazed out at the trio, which was now playing "Yesterday."

"Don't worry," Carlos said. "We'll take care of business.

And we make you a deal. You get a percentage the rest of your life. You move down t' Florida someplace, you get a condo, you go to the track every day, you get a tan. You need girls, we get you some girls. You need a driver, we get you a driver. You be like a consultant. The percentage goes anywhere you want it. A bank here, a bank down there. Switzerland. The Caymans. Don't matter to us." He sighed. "It's easy. You just get outta the way, and tell the right people it's ours."

"Suppose I tell the right people to blow your head off?"

Now he could see Junior, at the end of the bar, acting as if he didn't know Sidge or Tony Dee. Carlos took a pack of Benson & Hedges from his inside coat pocket. Nothing moved in his face, and his eyes were cold and unblinking.

"Look, I'm tryin' to make this easy," Carlos said. "We could come in, fight you for it. What happens? Lots of dead people. And we win that. Know why? We know you, and you don't know us. You don't know where we live. You don't know nothin'. But you know we're here. You're not dumb, Sanno. You wouldn't've lasted this long. But why have a mess? Why have a war?"

"Maybe I'd just like to see you with a hole in your head."

Carlos smiled, and began to recite addresses. In New Jersey, in Brooklyn, in Lido Beach, in the North Bronx. Even in Huntington Beach, California. And Sanno knew who lived in all those places: his wife, his two daughters and his son, each of his grandchildren.

"Now, if anything happens to me, something bad happens to the people that live in those houses," Carlos said, smiling thinly. "Not just you. Not just the three dummies at the bar, and the other dummies you got workin' for you. Everybody. Wives, children, babies: don't matter. War is war, right? Anyway, they all been livin' off what you made, so they're part of it. We got one rule: hurt us, we hurt you back worse. Know what I mean?"

He was serious. Sanno was certain of that. He struggled to contain the old instincts, the street rage, the urge to strike and hurt. But he showed nothing. He took another sip of Scotch, then glanced at his watch. He saw Marie, watching television. Then covered with blood.

"I gotta run," Sanno said.

"Stay and eat."

"Not with you, pal."

Carlos speared another shrimp, and said: "So?"

"I'll get back to you," Sanno said, and started easing out of the booth. Carlos touched his forearm, and Sanno paused.

"The girl, Al Pacino's sister," Carlos said. "She's really Italian?"

"You could look it up," Sanno said, getting out of the booth, nodding at Junior at the bar, going for his hat and coat, thinking: Yeah, it's their turn. He looked out at the cold winter rain and saw palm trees and white sand and could hear the long slow roar of the sea.

Footsteps

Nydia glanced at the ceiling. "There," she said. "Did you hear it?"

Ira blinked, his hands flat on the round oak table. She was cleaning away the dishes.

"No," he said. "I didn't hear anything, honey." He forced a smile. "You sure you're not getting paranoid?"

"I know what I *heard*, Ira. It was someone *walking*. Someone on the roof. I heard it."

"Well, I didn't hear a thing," he said, abruptly rising and taking some of the other dishes to the sink. The room filled with the aroma of brewing coffee. He looked out the window at the darkness of the Brooklyn night.

"I heard it last night," she said, rinsing dishes and placing them in the dishwasher. "When you were over at Fred's...I heard it last week, too. Footsteps. Someone walking. And now again, just now. There's someone up there, Ira."

He whirled, a savage curl in his voice. "Well, what do you want me to *do* about it? Go up there and start *shooting*? If you're so freaked, call the super! Call the cops! But stop whining!"

Her face crumpled. She turned off the faucet and hurried into the bedroom and closed the door behind her. He held the edge of the sink and breathed out heavily. Brooklyn. What a mistake....He glanced around the loft, her stacked paintings, the new one on the easel, the cluttered table where she kept her paints. His own desk was piled with textbooks, yellow pads, red pens, the armory of a schoolteacher. It looked almost peaceful. And this loft, this space, was what they had wanted, what they had searched for through those grinding, humiliating months, wanting to live together in some civilized way. They had looked everywhere and at everything, at cramped one-bedroom places in SoHo, they'd trampled roaches on the West Side, badgered doormen on the East Side, and then had given up on Manhattan and crossed the river. They'd given up quickly on Brooklyn Heights, too, and Park Slope, and then they found the Factory.

"It was closed for a few years," the real estate man said, "and then someone bought it and decided to make it into co-ops. That didn't work out too well. So it's a rental now...."

The block-square building was a rambling nineteenth-century redbrick pile. It had one of those names invented by real estate developers, of course, but Ira soon discovered that the old-timers in the neighborhood still called it the Factory. And they talked about it in a sour, bitter way. Once, it had been a reason for the existence of the neighborhood, almost seven hundred jobs filling its floors, the workers living in the now-ruined streets around it, eating, drinking, growing old in the stores and bars along the avenue.

Then had come the big strike, the men picketing through a brutal winter, management treating them with iron indifference, and finally there was a fire. Dozens of strikers rushed into the fire before the engines arrived, trying to save the machines that had given them jobs and life for generations. Some of them died. And then the Factory itself died, the owners packing up the remains and leaving for Taiwan or Alabama, and when the Factory died, so did the neighborhood.

"You know what it meant when you people started moving in?" one old man said to Ira. "It meant jobs would never come back. Never. They were gone forever...."

Still, the price was right, and there was space for Ira's books and Nydia's paints, and the subway was only three blocks away. Brooklyn. It would be all right. It was the best they could do. What a mistake, Ira thought, moving across the loft to the bedroom door with a cup of fresh coffee as a signal of truce. He knocked.

"Can I come in?" he asked.

He heard no answer and opened the door. She was lying facedown on the large brass bed. The picture of her father outside their old house in San Antonio was tipped over. "Here's your coffee, honey...."

65

She turned to him.

"Thanks, Ira. Thanks. But I'm just too tired. I took a pill, and…"

"Okay, I have some papers to grade."

She just didn't know how to live in cities, he thought, never mind the Factory. That was the problem. There were sirens at night, bottles breaking, shards of arguments, a hundred radios blending into jumble and din. In the summer, he bought an air conditioner, and sealed the windows, but that didn't work. The sounds of the Brooklyn streets still came at her like an assault.

"I'll never live in a quiet place again," she said to him one Sunday morning. "I just know it…."

And he knew then that people from cities and people from the West had grown up in different corners of the universe. On that Sunday morning, Ira from the West Bronx was washed by a sense of peace; the trembling weekday urgency was mercifully gone, the streets as bare of tumult as paintings by Hopper. Subways were almost quiet. And yet Nydia, of the San Antonio suburbs, heard sounds that his New York childhood had edited away forever. That day, he doubted for the first time his vision of the rest of their lives.

Now thinner and tauter than when they moved to the Factory, her body poised like an exclamation point, she was hearing strangers on the roof. Ridiculous. He sighed and sat at his desk to begin the melancholy task of correcting essays.

Then he heard the footsteps.

Right above him. Someone walking slowly and deliberately. He sat very still, holding his breath. The footsteps described a small circle. And then stopped. Directly over his desk…His skin pebbled with fear.

He picked up the telephone and dialed 911, and waited, and then tried to explain to a female voice that someone was walking on the roof of his building, and the woman said, "Yes?" As if saying, this is not news. And then Ira felt foolish, and hung up the phone.

The footsteps moved again. Another small circle.

"Goddamn it," he muttered, and got up, and went to the door, taking a ski jacket off a peg, thinking: It's probably some dumb kids, fooling around on the roof, smoking dope or something. But it can't go on. I've got to tell them. He went into the hall. A flight of stairs led to a door that opened out onto the roof. As he hurried up the stairs, adrenaline rushed through him, fueled by anger. Kids. It must be kids. But whoever the hell it is, they shouldn't be prowling around the roof of the Factory at night. He turned the lock and pushed open the heavy metal door.

The roof was a black tar-paper field, from which jutted strange figures: chimneys, and cowled metal objects, and deep shadows cast by the smothered lights of the street. There was no moon. The wind made a whining sound. He stood for a moment, forcing his eyes to adjust to the darkness, but the far shadows were deep, blank, impenetrable.

"Hey," he said loudly. "Who's out there?"

The wind lifted his words and tossed them into the night. He tried to locate himself on the roof in relation to the apartment, to locate the spot on the roof that was above his desk. That was the street. That was the avenue. It should be…He walked out, and circled and knew where he was. Then the wind moaned, and he wanted to run. It was as if some gigantic figure loomed behind him, and he felt his scalp riffle, as if something were scurrying between skin and skull. But he couldn't turn to look. He waited, glanced at the light from the street, warm and inviting. Suddenly there was a loud slam, metallic and final. The door.

He grabbed for the handle, twisted it, yanked at it, then pounded against its painted metal skin. But the door was firmly, solidly locked. For the moment, at least, he was trapped in the black terrain of the roof. He cursed now, blunt obscenities retrieved from his youth, the words like impotent weapons hurled at the wind and the darkness and his own dread. And then, far across the rooftop, he saw something move.

A man. In a T-shirt on this cold night. There were tattoos on his arms, and a bandanna around his brow, his skin a sickly white. "Who are you?" Ira asked hoarsely, across the distance. But there was no answer. Then he saw another figure, smaller, with Hispanic features, and then another, a heavy-bellied white man, and then a muscular black man, all of them emerging from the darkness.

He tried to speak, but the words wouldn't come, and he backed away, backed away, seeking light and escape, and still they came, more of them now, possessors of the roof and the Factory. He thought he heard the word "strike" once, then again, whispering at him in the darkness, "strike," and then, at the lip of the roof, one final time, "strike," before he plunged into the light.

A Poet Long Ago

THERE WAS A DOUBLE-PARKED panel truck on 52nd Street near Ninth Avenue, and a sanitation truck trying to squeeze by, and a line of backed-up cars from Jersey, their drivers leaning on the horns in the cold, anxious morning. Then one of the sanitation men came around from the front to see whether the squeeze was possible. He was very calm. He gave soothing signals to the people in the cars and then estimated the room the truck needed to pass through. I knew him. Sonny Rosselli.

"Hey, Sonny!"

He turned and I waved and he came to my car and peered at my face, as if trying to remember. I told him who I was and got out of the car. He embraced me and then the Jersey drivers were crazed again, and I told Sonny I'd pull around the corner after he got the truck through the morning slalom.

Sonny Rosselli. Thirty years ago, he'd been Sonny Rosselli the poet.

"Hey, listen, I'd love to talk to ya," he said. "But I can't leave the truck. I'm off at half past eleven. Can I meet ya someplace?"

"The coffee shop next to the Music Hall," I said. "Eleven thirty."

All morning I thought about Sonny Rosselli. I had met him in the seventh grade, when he moved to our Brooklyn neighborhood from the Bronx. He was a good stickball player, a strong, curly-haired son of Sicilian immigrants, with a beautiful sister and two older brothers. He was lousy in math, but he could write like an angel.

"I love the way these words sound," he'd say. "*Shore,* I mean. 'Shore' sounds like a *shore,* know what I mean? Like the ocean's comin' right up there and making that sound. Shooore." He liked "meadow," too, and "dusk," and "dark." And soon he began to string these words together and make poetry. I don't remember any of the poems, and perhaps they weren't any good; I remember that Sonny's major ambition was to have a poem published in Nick Kenny's column in the *Daily Mirror.*

"Look at *this,*" he'd say, showing me Nick Kenny. "Listen to what these guys do wit' *words.*"

We had a nice Xaverian brother named Rembert in the seventh grade, and he must have realized that Sonny Rosselli was special; he gave Sonny a rhyming dictionary and thesaurus, and gave him passing grades in math as long as Sonny kept making poems. He explained to Sonny that there were people called poets; that was their job; they wrote poems. And Sonny started saying that maybe when he grew up he could be a poet.

"Imagine," he'd say. "You write poems all day and they pay you for it!"

That spring, the miracle happened. Sonny Rosselli sent a poem to Nick Kenny and Nick Kenny published it. It was about love, of course. And Brother Rembert had to fight back tears as he held up the *Mirror* for all of us to see and then read us that poem. We were all rough kids from the wrong side of Brooklyn, but one of us, at least, had made it. Sonny Rosselli was a celebrity. A poet. An honest-to-God published poet.

His great moment didn't last. The other boys teased him brutally, making swishing gestures at him, talking with pursed lips as they read off the verses. Sonny was confused; why wouldn't they want to hear something beautiful? He fought three separate schoolyard fights on one afternoon, hurting his hands. He won all three, but he left the last one in tears.

"They're so *dumb*," he said later. "They're so *stupid*, know what I mean?"

He didn't show his poems to everybody now; he took them to Brother Rembert, and a few of the other kids; but he didn't get up to recite in class. He didn't talk about becoming a poet, either. In that neighborhood in those days, you could say you wanted to be a cop or an ironworker, a fireman or dock worker; you never said you wanted to be a poet. Then one Friday, Nick Kenny published another poem. Sonny Rosselli was embarrassed. Even afraid.

"I hope my father don't see the paper," he said. "Or my brothers."

That Monday, he didn't come to school. I went around to his house in the afternoon and his mother said he wasn't feeling well. I looked past her and saw Sonny. His face was swollen, and there was a bandage over his left brow. I didn't find out for three more days that when he came home that Friday night, his father had beaten the poetry out of him forever.

"He says poetry's for fags," Sonny explained later. "Maybe he's right."

We went to different high schools, and then I went into the navy and he joined the army and we lost track of each other. And now, on this late morning years later, we were sitting in a booth in a midtown coffee shop, eating scrambled eggs. He told me about his life: a nice wife, three grown-up kids, a house in Queens Village that was almost paid off. His brother Frankie lived in California. His sister married a cop and was a grandmother already. His parents were still alive, living in Bensonhurst.

"Do you ever write poetry any more?" I asked.

"Nah."

"You sorry you didn't follow it up?" I asked.

"Sometimes."

He looked out past the booths to the street. Traffic was

jammed. Three Rockettes from the Music Hall hurried in and took a booth together.

"Maybe I was born ten years later, it would've been different," Sonny said. "Maybe I could've gotten into rock and roll. I *know* I could write as good as them guys." He laughed. "But who knows? It's a long time ago now. And, hey, it's not the most important thing in the world. I'm *alive,* right? My brother Charlie got killed in Korea. I'm still here."

The Rockettes finished their coffees and left. Sonny ordered another cup. The waitress took our plates away.

"The truth?" he said quickly. "I never forgave my father. I tried. I used to say to myself he don't *know* any better. He's from the *old* country, all he knows is *work*. Work is what you do wit' your *back,* your *hands*. Everything else is stealin'. He meant right. But if he ever said to me, 'Sonny, this is beautiful, this poem,' I would've lived another life.

"I mean, I don't mind my life. I love my family. I do honest work. But if he'd've been wit' me, maybe I could've taken the rest of it. The crap from the neighborhood, I mean. I was a kid. I didn't want to be different. I used to think, jeez, I got this *thing,* like a *gift*. And how come God give me this thing? But maybe I didn't deserve it. Maybe that was why I gave it up so easy. Get what I mean?"

He played with the coffee, and then asked me a lot of questions about my life, and I talked about accidents and luck, kids and a marriage, disappointments and mistakes. We finished our coffees and paid and went out into the cold morning.

"It's gonna snow soon," he said. "I can feel it in my bones."

"Yeah."

"I love a snowstorm," he said. "I love how quiet it gets. I love the way everything stops. I love the way all the dirt and the garbage gets covered up, and we got this great big beautiful white city all around us. I always used to take the kids for walks in the snow. Show them how the trees looked and the way the wind makes these sculptures, know what I mean?"

"Yeah, I do."

We walked toward Seventh Avenue, where the sanitation truck was waiting. He had made a life of cleaning up the mess left behind by humans, and I wanted to thank him, but didn't know how.

"You know this guy Yeats?" he asked. "The greatest, isn't he? *I will arise and go now, and go to Innisfree* ... I used to read him to the kids when they were little. I'd turn off the TV and then I'd read Yeats. I'd make them repeat the lines. I'd try ta explain what the guy was *gettin'* at, even when I didn't understand myself. I'd say, it's like a *song*. It's like *music*. Like some beautiful *music*. And you know something? They loved it." He laughed. "They loved me standin' there and readin' that Yeats. Oh, wow, did they love that."

I realized suddenly that his eyes were brimming with tears. "I gotta go," he said quickly. "Someone'll say I'm, you know, malingering." He hurried away, and climbed up on the truck, waved, and was gone with a rumble and a clanking of gears. A cold wind blew in from the river. The sky was the color of steel. It felt like snow, all right. I walked quickly to the west through the crowds, thinking of Sonny Rosselli and his lost gift, his poet's lovely heart, and the astonishing gifts he gave his children. It began at last to snow and the city huddled in the great white silence.

The Car

CAVANAUGH BOUGHT THE CAR at a city auction on Atlantic Avenue. It was a pale-blue two-door 1979 Chevy with only 21,000 miles on it, and the $800 price was a bargain. After finishing the paperwork and paying cash, he drove the Chevy to a car wash, had it cleaned inside and out, and then went home to Bay Ridge. That night, after dinner, he stood up and faced his wife, Marie, and his daughter, Kelly, and with a grand flourish handed the younger woman the car key.

"Oh, Daddy," Kelly said. "I don't be*lieve* it."

"With an A average at Hunter," he said, "you deserve it. Besides, I don't like that you have to use the subway. All I ask is you drive safe, you use the safety belt. No drinking, you know. No speeding."

"Daddy, I'm twenty years old," she said, trying to smother her irritation. "I'm not a kid."

"I know, I know," he said. "But you never know what happens you get some numskull in the car. Come on, take a look...."

The three of them pulled on coats and went outside and down the block. The car was parked in front of a grocery store, and it gleamed in the light.

"I love it!" Kelly said. "I want to drive it, right *now*."

"It's late," Cavanaugh said. "Tomorrow's Saturday. Take it out tomorrow. A nice long drive. Out on the Belt. Jones Beach, someplace like that."

"He's right, sweetheart," her mother said. And that settled it. They went home, and Kelly called her boyfriend, Mike, and made a date for the morning. She said, "You're gonna love it, Mike." He said, "I'm sure I will."

The next day Kelly and Mike took turns driving the car. They went to Coney Island for hot dogs; they strolled in the bright cold sunshine on the winter beach at Riis Park; they drove into Nassau County, stopped for coffee at a Howard Johnson's, drove back. Before dinner, they sat in the car and necked. They agreed to meet later that night and go to a movie. Kelly said she wished a drive-in was open. "I've never been to one," she said. "I just see them in movies."

"We'll go every weekend next summer," Mike said.

That night, driving home from Manhattan, where they'd seen *Terms of Endearment* and Kelly had spent three full minutes crying in the lobby, they first noticed the smell.

"What's that smell, anyway?" she said, opening the window. "It's like Starrett City in here." She checked the emergency brake; it wasn't engaged. "Wow…"

"That smell isn't rubber," Mike said. He was driving now. "It smells, I don't know, *disgusting*."

The smell was loamy, decaying, rotting. They opened both windows and let the cold winter air blow around them. Mike turned off the heater. The smell remained.

"It's like maybe an animal is caught in the engine or something," he said. "Maybe a rat or something."

"Well, pull over and let's look."

They stopped on Fourth Avenue and Mike got out and opened the hood. He peered into the engine, tried to look under the chassis, saw nothing. He opened the trunk. It was empty.

"I don't know what the hell it is," he said. "Tomorrow, when it's light, we'll go over it with a fine-tooth comb."

The next day, the smell was gone, but Kelly and Mike examined the car in a gas station run by one of Cavanaugh's friends. There were no traces of dead animals, no forgotten fruit or plant that might have rotted or decayed. The engine was clean, the chassis in good shape. On the floor of the trunk there was a faint outline of a stain, but it gave off no odor. Kelly wet her fingers from the station's water fountain and rubbed them in the stain. There was no smell.

"Jeez," Mike said, "maybe it was *me*."

Kelly laughed. "Get out the Right Guard."

"I guess I better."

Kelly reported all of this to Cavanaugh, who smiled and dismissed the problem with a small wave of his hand.

"Maybe it was one of those inversions you read about," he said. "You know, from the stuff they're always burning in Jersey and it floats over here and gives us diseases? Otherwise, how does it drive?"

"Like a dream," Kelly said. "A real dream, Daddy."

That night, as Kelly and Mike drove from Brooklyn to a party in Manhattan, the smell returned.

"Oh, God," Kelly said. "What'll we do?"

"I don't know."

"We've gotta do *something*, Mike!"

"Hey, don't get mad at me, Kelly. Okay? I didn't make the thing smell. And it's *your* car!"

"But what if the smell *sticks* to us?" she said, her voice rising as Mike drove the Chevy across the Brooklyn Bridge. "What if it gets into us? And we sit at dinner tonight with these people, and we *stink*?"

"Just say we're from Brooklyn," Mike said, smiling.

"It's not funny!"

He slammed the dashboard with an open palm. "Stop! Okay? No more! I don't want to hear about it! If you're worried, we'll park and grab a cab, take the subway. Okay? But stop talking about it!"

They drove in silence to the party, and Kelly remembered a year when she was small and her father had taken then to Florida, and one night they drove on a road through a swamp, and the swamp smelled like this, too: rotting, dense, fetid, full of slimy things that died in the dark. Somehow...corrupt.

"I'm sorry," she said, as they parked on an industrial

street in SoHo. The party was in a loft down the block. "I just...It's such a nice car. I wanted it to be perfect."

"Look, Kelly, let's forget it, okay? I don't want to discuss it."

She got out and slammed the door hard. "You are a real ass...."

"Hey, why don't you go to this party on your own? Okay? They're *your* friends and it's *your* car, and maybe without me around you won't have to worry about the *stink*!"

She leaned on the fender and started to cry. Mike put his arm around her. "I'm sorry, baby. I really am. I am. Let's just...We've gotta get rid of this car."

But Kelly Cavanaugh didn't get rid of the car. The next day she had it scrubbed again, steamed, cleaned. She had the mat removed from the trunk, replaced with a new one; there was some kind of stain on the metal beneath the mat, as if a chemical had burned its way into its surface; but nothing that should create an odor. Driving away, the car smelled fresh and clean.

And then at night, the fetid breath of the swamp once more engulfed her.

She went to her father and told him. He laughed, she protested, then he promised to see what he could do about getting rid of the odor.

"It's not a matter of cleaning, Daddy," she said. "There's something else wrong with the car. It's like it's, I don't know...cursed."

Cavanaugh blinked. "I'll check it out."

The next day he called the city auto pound, trying to learn the history of the car, and got nowhere. He called a cop friend, gave him all the relevant numbers, said nothing about the smell, told a few jokes about firemen, laughed, hung up, and went about his work. Late in the afternoon, the cop called back. He had the history.

"The weird thing is this," the cop said. "The car was found out at Kennedy Airport in the fall. No plates, no ID marks. Probably stolen somewheres, out of state. Dropped off here. But here's the thing: there was a guy in the trunk. With three bullets in the head. A doper, they figure. He'd been there maybe a week, so I guess he was a little ripe."

Cavanaugh thanked him and hurried home. He was watching the news when Kelly arrived from school. He turned down the sound.

"We'll sell the car tomorrow, honey," he said. "And get a new one."

She looked at him and smiled. He turned back to the news.

"I mean, what do you need with a car that smells, right? We'll get another one." He hadn't smoked for four years, but he patted his shirt pocket, looking for cigarettes. "So how was school?" he said. "How's everything going?"

Just the Facts, Ma'am

FACTS McCARTHY KNEW EVERYTHING. He'd meet you in the street and ask which continent was the largest, and you'd hesitate, and he'd say triumphantly: "Asia! It's seventeen million, one hundred and twenty-nine thousand square miles, twenty-nine point seven percent of the world's land. You could look it up." You'd light a cigarette and he'd tell you that the geographical center of the United States was near Castle Rock, South Dakota, and Gaborone was the capital of Botswana, and 116,708 Americans died in World War I.

"Who led the American League in home runs in 1911?" he asked one night in Farrell's Bar in Brooklyn. "Don't even try to answer. It was Franklin 'Home Run' Baker. But here's the beauty part; how many did he hit?"

"Er...uh...thirty?"

"Eleven!" Facts McCarthy shouted. "He led the whole league with *eleven* home runs! Can you imagine? Look it up!"

Information was a kind of sickness for Facts, and the infection began in the sixth grade. That was when he discovered he could memorize entire chapters of geography books, most of the Latin Mass, great swatches of the Baltimore Catechism. In the Catholic school that Facts and I attended, such prodigies of memory were always rewarded, and Facts became an A student. As an A student, he was a kind of star, acknowledged to be superior, his memory overwhelming certain weaknesses in the essay form. Nobody had a happier childhood.

But later, when Facts left school and ventured into the real world, he swiftly discovered that his talent was not so universally acknowledged. The world did not, after all, usually give out grades; the world was more of an essay than a multiple-choice exercise, and Facts did not do well in the face of the world's chilly indifference. Eventually he made his accommodation. He worked in the post office, and, in his spare time, devoted himself anew to the acquiring of information.

"Who ran with Tom Dewey on the 1944 Republican ticket?" he'd ask. "John W. Bricker! One of the all-time greats!"

The information would come in a great flow. The name of Richard Nixon's wife is really Thelma; she picked up "Pat" from her father. The most common name in the

United States is Smith, which belongs to 2,382,509 people, followed by Johnson. The birthstone for August is peridot. Savonarola was burned at the stake in Florence in 1498, the same year that Leonardo da Vinci finished *The Last Supper* in Milan. Babe Ruth was given the most bases on balls in major league history, 2,056 over twenty-two seasons, and the planet Jupiter has sixteen moons. Facts was almost always right, although a lot of bars had to buy almanacs and the *Guinness Book of Records* just to be certain. But as he moved from his twenties to his thirties and then into his forties, the mass of information became denser and more impacted. Running into Facts McCarthy was like running into a black hole.

Naturally, he lived alone.

"Women just don't understand an intellectual like me," Facts said modestly one winter night. "Women are emotional, intuitive, know what I mean? They don't understand facts. They never let facts get in the way of their opinions. I mean, they're nice to *look* at. But, hey, I'm not *missing* anything."

This could be dismissed as a carryover into adult life of his weakness in the essay form. But it was more than that. The truth was that no woman would have him. In a bar it was easy to put up with a man who said hello by asking you the name of the largest glacier in the world. You can always leave a bar. But it isn't so easy to leave a marriage.

And there was the added impediment of the Facts McCarthy Memorial Library. In the four-room flat that

Facts kept after his mother died, every surface was covered with sources of information: all editions of every almanac, three different sets of the *Encyclopedia Britannica* (marked with yellow markers), an almost complete set of *National Geographic,* complete runs of *Facts on File* and *Current Biography,* sports, science, business and political yearbooks, and almost eight thousand other books, not one of which was a novel.

"Being me," said Facts McCarthy, "is a full-time occupation."

And then Mercedes Rodriguez moved into the flat downstairs with her widowed mother. Mercedes was a twenty-two-year-old blonde from the Dominican Republic, and when Facts saw her that first day, unloading a Chevy filled with household goods, he thought he had never seen anyone more beautiful. When he should have been studying the 1963 *Information Please Almanac,* he found himself watching her walk up the block to the grocery store. He mooned over her. He sighed a lot. In the bars he was even silent. And then he decided it was time to act. He had to talk to her, and one day, in the vestibule, they found themselves facing each other.

"Hi," Facts said, with his great gift for small talk. "Do you know how many books there are in the Enoch Pratt Free Library in Baltimore?"

"What?"

"In 1978, there were two million, three hundred and seventy-five thousand, seven hundred and twenty-one. You could look it up."

"What'd you say?" Mercedes asked, and laughed out loud.

This was obviously love at first sight. Two days later, Facts was sitting with her in Loew's State in Times Square, blitzing her with information about past Academy Award winners. Later he took her to Coney Island, and he rolled on, and Mercedes listened, nodding, offering no resistance. On the weekend, with her mother as chaperone, and Facts as a tour guide, she visited his apartment. The mother sighed a lot, saying, *"Ay, bendito,"* fanning herself with an *Editor & Publisher International Year Book*. Facts left them in the former living room and went to the former kitchen to make coffee.

"¿Cómo se dice 'loco' en inglés?" the mother asked.

"Crazy," Mercedes said.

"Ah, sí," the mother said. *"Crazy. Es Crazy. Este Irlandes es crazy."*

Yes, Mercedes said, the Irishman was crazy, but wasn't he crazy like her father? Didn't Papi sit in the house in Santo Domingo cutting articles out of newspapers, piling them up in closets, asking everybody questions about everything under the sun? Didn't Papi know about baseball and ice-making machines and Indian gods and the Gulf Stream? Yes, her mother said, and he died young.

Facts came back from the kitchen with three cups of coffee.

"It's an interesting place, the Dominican Republic," he said. "Known by the Indians as Quisqueya, eighteen thousand, eight hundred and sixty-one square miles, population, about five million, four hundred and fifty thousand in 1980." He sipped his coffee. Mercedes looked at him with glassy eyes. "The main rivers are the Yaque del Norte, the Haina, the Ozama, and the Yaque del Sur." The mother squinted at him, impressed by the names of familiar places. "You got bauxite there, nickel, silver, and gold, and the average life expectancy is sixty-one years...."

"Oh, Facts," Mercedes sighed.

They didn't see Facts around the bar much anymore, and there were rumors that he was memorizing the entire written work of Joseph Stalin. Someone saw him once, walking in the park with a pretty girl, but nobody could believe it. And then one day, the invitations came by mail, in English and Spanish, and we learned that Facts McCarthy was getting married to Mercedes Rodriguez. This was stunning news.

"Yeah, it's absolutely true," Facts said on the phone. "We're tying the el knotto."

He was not willing to surrender the library, but neither was Mercedes; they brought in a contractor who cut a hole in McCarthy's floor into the Rodriguez apartment and connected them with a spiral staircase, giving the mother her own room and Facts a duplex. We all went to the wedding, and then Facts disappeared into the Brooklyn winter, his studies, and his marriage. I didn't see him again until the spring. Then I came out of the subway one afternoon and saw him walking alongside the park with Mercedes. She was pregnant and obviously happy.

"*Ola,*" Mercedes said, smiling broadly. "*Dígame,* what's

the longest suspension bridge in the world? You never guess. The Humber! In Hull, England, four thousand, six hundred and twenty-six feet long."

"You could look it up," Facts said proudly.

"You could."

6/6/44

DRUM AND KEEGAN, OLD now, steel-haired, their skins freck-led, shirts too tight, sat together in the warm June sunshine on a bench across from the playground. Prospect Park smelled of new-mown grass. There was no breeze. Keegan smoked a cigarette and glanced at the newspaper on his knee. Drum watched young mothers pushing children on swings.

"I don't even give a hill a beans what's in the paper," Keegan was saying. "I carry it around because you gotta have sumpthin' to do. Or sit on. Old guy sits on a park bench nowadays, they think you're a degenerate."

"I know what you mean."

"But lookit this stuff." He tapped the newspaper. "Nicaragua. El Salvador. We're mining harbors in a country we ain't at war with, Harry. We pay all these el creepos—the contras—to fight for us. These people kill nuns, Harry. I don't get it anymore, Harry."

Drum smiled. "It's no concern of ours anymore, Charlie."

"Yeah? Well, we didn't pull crap like this when I was a kid, when you was a kid."

Drum leaned forward, his elbows on his knees. "That woman in the dungarees. With the yellow blouse. Remind you of Helen, doesn't she?"

Keegan looked at Drum. "I thought you weren't gonna talk about her anymore."

"I'm not talkin' about her. I'm just sayin', that woman looks like her. A statement of fact. Look at me. You see a tear? You see me upset?"

"No, but I don't want to, neither. Every time you talk about Helen, you get weepy."

"I was married to her for thirty-two years, Charlie."

Keegan opened the newspaper. "Hey, lookit this! Forty years! The anniversary. Forty years since D-day. Can you believe it?"

"Yeah."

"Jeez, I forgot, Harry. You was there, right?"

Drum shrugged and stood up. "Let's take a walk."

They loaded us on the LCVs in the dark, thirteen miles out, the waves rising and falling, bazookas and TNT piled on the deck, and all of us with full field packs, knowing everything came to this moment, this night, this day in the English Channel; all the training, the convoy across the Atlantic, the boredom and pubs and women of England. I wrote Helen 121 letters from England alone, crazy letters, mad nutty kid letters, the words just pouring out of me, nothing about the war, nothing about Nazis or democracy or freedom or any of that; just me crazy for her, crazy to be with her, crazy to come back alive, crazy to have kids with her, a house with her, crazy to live a life. With her. And in the LCV, jammed in with Smitty and Ralph and Cappy and Max, that's all I thought about. If I could think about Helen, her face, her hair, the way she laughed, the smell of her in the park in summer, then I wouldn't have to think about what was on the other side of the Channel. I dozed and thought about her. I squatted there, and thought about her, I even thought of her as we rose and fell and moved through the waves, and the big guns pounded the shore.

They came over a rise and looked down at the broad green sward of the meadow. The parks department had erected metal fences for ballplayers, and Drum hated them. Drum wanted the world to stay the same for all of his life.

"I see those fences," he said, "I want to blow them up."

"They put you in the can for that," Keegan said, laughing in his wheezy way. "And I'm too old to come visit you."

"But do you blame me?"

"Everything's changed, Harry. You can stand here and pray for a week, you ain't gonna see a trolley car, you ain't gonna go to Ebbets Field, you ain't gonna go to Luna Park."

"I know."

I never forgot the noise. The guns of the Texas *and the engines of the assault craft, and planes bombing, and guys yelling with megaphones from one boat to another. The sky went from black to gray. Miller, the farm kid from South Carolina, got up and lurched to the side of the LCV and vomited over the side, and the wind blew it all around, and then another guy was puking, and then dozens of them, and next to me Max was stiff against the steel bulkhead, his teeth chattering, and all of us were wondering who would live and who would die. The boat rose on the crest of a wave and I could see LCVs everywhere, and right ahead of us was Omaha Beach.*

They strolled down to the marsh that used to be the Swan Lake. Keegan dropped the newspaper in a trash can. There were ugly chunks of dirty concrete where the boathouse used to be.

"There was a waterfall over there," Drum said. "Remember? And paddleboats shaped like swans, and a guy selling Cracker Jacks, and everybody walking across the park to the ball games."

"Yeah, and up there, past the waterfall, there was a stream. Cleanest water I ever seen."

"Devil's Cave was next to the stream."

"On the left," Keegan said. "I used to hide there when it rained."

He looked at Drum, who was staring out at the dead lake. "It was nice, sitting there in the rain."

"It was."

And then it was day and we were a thousand yards from shore and the coxswain's eyes were panicky and the lieutenant unsure of where he was, looking at this map, which was soaking wet, and peering out over the top and moving his mouth without making words. I could see the beach, two tanks with smoke pouring out of them, the wind blowing the smoke flat, and a church steeple and then the high dull thump of explosives got sharper, splitting the air. And then I saw tracers coming from the cliffs and rows of bundles on the beach. There were huge poles rising from the water with contact mines hanging from them like pie plates, and huge logs cantilevered out of the sand, and Belgian gates, these huge steel-frame doors leading to nowhere, and we were getting closer, and bullets were caroming off the steel bulkheads, and we were closer, and then I saw the bundles on the beach again, and they weren't bundles, they were men, the men of the first wave, and the second wave, and the third; and two tanks were burning, and there was no artillery, and we were closer, and the coxswain was screaming at the lieutenant, and then there was a grinding sound, and the engines idled, and then the ramp was lowered, and waves pouring into the LCV, and we were moving into the water. It was over our heads. I saw Cappy go under and Ralph thrashing in the water and then Miller's head exploded and there was blood and bone and tissue all over us and then Robert shoved him out ahead of us into the water and then it was my turn and I said, Helen. I said, Helen. I said, Helen, Helen, Helen.

They left the park at Eleventh Avenue.

"Come on over later, eat something, Harry," Keegan said. "I don't like it that you're living alone. You're what? Sixty? That's a young guy nowadays, Harry. You should—"

"I'll see you tomorrow, Charlie."

I lay behind two bodies while the machine guns hammered. I could see two battleships and a couple of cruisers, and someone was screaming off to the left, and mortars exploded in the sand, and there was blood on my face and hands and my carbine and none of it was mine. The noise was ferocious, shells screaming in from the Texas, *metal and rocks breaking and splintering, rifle fire and machine guns hammering and mortars and my face in the sand, and then I turned and saw two cans racing in near the shore, unloading their five-inchers, and a whumping sound, and more screaming, and one of the guys I was huddled behind was whimpering. And then someone shouted that we better get up or we'd die on the damned beach, and I waited, and then got up, and started to run, and then I was down and I could see planes overhead and my leg burning and when I tried to move I couldn't and I looked at the sky again and thought, that's it, it's over, I won, that's my war, I thought. That's it, Helen. I thought, it's June 6, 1944, 6/6/44, and I just got my ticket home.*

The Trial of Red Dano

EVERY NIGHT, IN HIS room at the Hotel Lotus, Red Dano would try desperately to sleep. He would lie in the dark on the sagging bed, logy with beer, listening to the murmur of the street. He would shift position, lying first on his left, then on his right. But sleep wouldn't come.

There was no television in the room, but pictures moved constantly through his brain. He saw the cell at Dannemora. The yard at Green Haven. He saw a thousand faces, a hundred scenes, the debris of meals, and iron corridors: the jumbled, detailed scrapbook of nine years in prison. Sometimes other pictures forced themselves onto Dano's private screen, and then he would get up and walk to the window and part the slats of the venetian blinds and stare into the street to verify that he was truly there.

"Corinne," he sometimes said aloud, as if uttering the name would grant him forgiveness, and forgiveness would grant him sleep. "I'm sorry, Corinne. I'm very, very, sorry, Corinne."

But there was nobody present to forgive him, and he walked around the room, his damp bare feet making a peeling sound on the linoleum, a million miles from Brooklyn. And then, long after midnight, when the Spanish restaurant was closed downstairs, and the street wheeze of the crosstown bus came less often, and even the hookers and junkies had retired for the night, Dano would sleep.

Working through the day, exhausted from the sleepless nights, he loaded and unloaded trucks for Sherman and Dunlop, and felt old among the hard young kids beside him. He told them nothing about himself, but they seemed to know, without being very interested. "Bet you didn't work this hard in the can," the one named Ralph said one morning, as they loaded canned peaches. Dano grunted his agreement, and Ralph then turned his attention to the troubles of the Yankees. The young man's indifference was to Dano at least one small consolation: after eleven weeks on the outside, he was finding a small place in the city he'd lost for nine long years.

"I hear you killed someone," Ralph said when they stopped one Friday evening for beer after a Hunts Point run. "That true?"

"Yeah."

"I hear you killed your girlfriend."

"True."

"Amazing. I never met anyone killed anyone. Except guys who were in the army."

"It's nothing to be proud of, kid."

"Ah, well, some of them deserve it."

"She didn't."

Later that night, Dano went to a movie. Burt Reynolds. Fat sheriffs. Car crashes. Then he stopped in the Oasis, a bar near the hotel. The news was on TV: marines killed in Lebanon, a big shot quits a subway job, a woman jumps off a building. None of it mattered to him, and he nursed a beer in silence. A few stools away, a toothless old drunk mirthlessly repeated a line from a song: "Pack up yer troubles in yer ol' kit bag an' smile, smile...." The drunk stopped, sipped his beer, began again, while the bartender shook his head and watched the ball game. Dano glanced at himself in the mirror: the red hair now gray, face lean and white and pasty; thinking, I'm old. She would be twenty-three forever. Corinne. But I'm walking around with her inside of me still, and I'm old.

A pudgy, dark-haired woman came in the open door, her hair ruffled by the huge fan, and the bartender looked up.

"No trouble, Mary," he said in a kind of warning.

"What do you mean? I'm sober. I never been in trouble when I'm sober."

"No. But then you get drunk, Mary. Then you throw things. Ashtrays..."

"Shut up, Harry," the woman said. "Who ast you?"

"Pack up yer troubles in yer ol' kit bag an'..."

Dano wondered if he'd ever be able to sleep with a

woman again. On his third night out of prison, he'd tried, with a kid from West Street, but it hadn't worked. Maybe that's how I'll pay, he thought. I'll just live in a little prison of my own, forever. He glanced past the singing drunk at the pudgy woman, wedged now on a stool, a whiskey in her small, thick-fingered hand. Thirty, maybe. A shiny black dress. Dark stockings, high-heeled maroon shoes. Her face was almost pretty, with liquid brown eyes, a short nose, hair piled in curls, a dirty laugh. Come with me, Dano thought. But he said nothing. Come, we'll have dinner somewhere and tell each other lies and then go to my room and you can help me sleep. But he did nothing. He glanced at her, then picked up his change and walked into the night.

He had his key in his pocket and walked through the bright, cramped lobby without stopping at the front desk. He felt very tired as the elevator groaned to the fourth floor. He walked down the corridor to room 411, stopped, un-locked the door, and reached for the light switch.

There were three of them waiting for him in the room. One was at the window, his foot up on the radiator. Another was in the chair and the third was sitting on the bed. They didn't move. Dano knew the one at the window, the lean gray man holding the gun.

"Hello, Charlie," Dano said.

Charlie gestured with the gun in an offhand way. "Close the door, Red."

"You put on a little weight, Charlie," Dano said, closing the door behind him. The one on the bed came over and patted him down, shrugged, looked at Charlie, went back to the bed. "Ten pounds?"

"Ten years, ten pounds," Charlie said. "Not too bad."

"You still in Brooklyn?"

"Same street, same house, Red. Except my mother ain't there. She died, Red."

"I'm sorry to hear that."

"She never got over Corinne, Red."

"I understand."

"You better, Red. You broke her heart with what you did to my sister."

"And I paid for it, Charlie."

"Not enough."

Charlie took a pack of cigarettes from his shirt pocket, lit one with a cheap lighter, reached out, and offered the pack to Dano. He held the gun casually at his side. Dano took a cigarette from the pack, fighting to control the shaking of his hand.

"Ma used to wake up in the middle of the night, Red. Shouting Corinne's name. We'd go to her and she'd be shaking and crying and all and cursin' you, cursin' you for ever livin', for comin' into Corinne's life, into our lives, cursin' your fancy talk and your big-shot smile. Ma never forgot you, Red."

Dano leaned in for a light without looking at Charlie's eyes. Charlie raised the gun and snapped the lighter into flame.

"She used to go quiet, Ma did, like for days, Red, never

sayin' anything. For weeks, even. When they sent you up, I think she went a little crazy. Fifteen years for her daughter's life? You can imagine what she was thinkin', knowin' you'd be out in nine, ten with good behavior an' all. It drove her crazy, Red. First Corinne, and then her."

The one in the chair shifted, glanced at his watch. "Let's get it on, Charlie," he said. "It's late."

"Let him finish his cigarette."

Dano took a deep drag on the cigarette. A tune started moving in his head: "Pack up your troubles in your…" He wondered about the full, ripe body of Mary, sitting on her stool a block away, getting ready to throw ashtrays. And his body felt limp, the muscle like liquid, the bone grinding into sand. He took another drag, the cigarette burning down to his fingers now.

"What do you want with me, Charlie?" he asked.

"We're gonna take a little trip over to Brooklyn, Red. Maybe down Gerritsen Beach. Somewhere. You'll find out."

"And then what are you going to do?"

"Kill you, Red. I got no choice."

"No," Dano said. "I guess you don't."

Leaving Paradise

When Gillis opened his eyes, the window shade had rolled up on itself and the furnished room was sluiced with hard, white, merciless light. He didn't move. His tongue felt thick and furry, and there was something ridged and padded over his right eye. His right hand lay flat beside the pillow, and he saw the raw, pink-skinned knuckles, and then he closed his eyes again, remembering Saturday night at the Paradise.

No, no, he thought, that didn't happen. But it had happened, all right, and as he returned, feeling a coarse gas moving between his brain and his skull and a dull pain throbbing in his shoulder and something sharp stabbing his ribs, Gillis saw fragments of the night before, like scenes from a movie with the reels mixed up.

He saw the big pitchers of beer on the bare plastic-topped

table in the booth along the wall of the huge saloon. He saw Curly and Vito laughing, and bowls of pretzels, and heard the jukebox pounding. The Stones: "Brown Sugar." The dance floor full, and Vito talking about the girl from Coney Island and the things she could do, and Curly egging him on. The lights were dim, red, rose-colored, blood-colored, and the dance floor throbbed, and more people came in, guys and chicks, and a few old dudes, guys at least thirty, cruising around the edges of the hall, looking at the young women. Another tune:

I'll never be your
beast of burden...

Then as he turned again in bed, he saw the great blinking neon sign, bright against the Brooklyn sky: THE PARADISE. And being hurt. And voices. No. That was later. No, first there was the girl in the pink sweater. Or was that last week at the Paradise? He sat up in the narrow bed in the hot bright morning room and touched the ridge over his eye. A bandage. And remembered a dark-skinned doctor in the emergency room, leaning over him, his eyes large and tired, peering at him. No, that was later, too. That was all later.

He was in the Paradise, he and Vito watching Curly dance with a green-eyed Puerto Rican girl, putting on all his baddest moves, chopping space out of the crowd, while more and more people came in, and the waitress brought more beer, and then Gillis glanced back at the door and he saw her. It was Cathy.

"Hey, there's that chick from the dry cleaner," Vito said, his voice loud above the music. "The one you like, man. That Cathy."

She was wearing tight white jeans and a black turtleneck and high-heeled red shoes, and she was with a small, compact, red-haired guy in a sport jacket. They were walking to the corner where the Quiñones crowd hung out. Gillis hated that crowd. All of them went to college, and when he talked to them, Gillis felt slow and stupid. Quiñones was a tall Puerto Rican who wore blue blazers and gray socks, and always looked as if he knew something that nobody else knew. Gillis watched him embrace the short red-haired guy, and shake hands formally with Cathy.

"Maybe she's gonna leave the dry cleaner store," Vito said. "Maybe she's gonna go to college."

"Shut up, Vito, will you please?" Gillis said, and drank his beer. That's when the girl with the pink sweater came in. Right there. Short, with a big pink hairdo, and chewing gum. Came right over and grabbed his hand and took him out on the floor. Rod Stewart singing "Passion." The girl in the pink sweater chewing gum like it was her job. And Gillis saw Cathy dancing with the red-haired guy. She was staring right into the guy's eyes. And the guy was dancing in a tight, bundled-up way, every move precise. Gillis felt big and clumsy.

"That's it," he said to the girl in the pink sweater.

"Whaddya mean? I'm just warmin' up!"

He walked away and she grabbed his arm and he pushed her and she tottered and fell. He heard her cursing, but

Gillis kept walking to the booth. Curly was there, and the green-eyed Puerto Rican girl was dancing with Quiñones now, and Curly was dripping with sweat. Gillis lifted the pitcher in both hands and took a long swallow. Then the girl in the pink sweater stood over him.

"You do that again, you big faggot, and I'll kick your knees off."

"Get outta here while you can walk," Gillis said, and the girl stalked off, and he sat there staring at the wet tabletop. Curly was laughing. He remembered that. Curly was laughing. And when he looked through the crowd, he saw Curly again, and he was laughing, and Quiñones was laughing, and the red-haired guy was laughing, too. Everybody was laughing.

"Who is that guy, anyway?" he said. "The red-haired jerk."

And Curly said the guy's name was Carder, or Carlton or something. Part of that college crowd. From Staten Island or someplace. Gillis remembered him vaguely now. In a sports car. A foreign job. Coming to the gas station. Alone. Always alone. Paid with a credit card, too. Now he's with Cathy.

"I thought *you* was goin' with her, Gillis boy," Curly said.

"Hey, I just took her out a coupla times," Gillis said, sipping from a glass now. "She's nothin'. She don't mean a *thing* to me. Not a *thing*."

"I don't know, Gillis boy. You sure got a funny look on your face."

He remembered that, and drinking, and Vito dancing,

and then Curly with the green-eyed Puerto Rican chick again, and more drinking, and the music pounding. And then he was pushing his way across the dance floor to the corner where the Quiñones crowd was standing, and he saw Cathy beside the red-haired guy, Carder, or Carlton, or whatever his name was. There was panic in her eyes. Her hand went to her throat.

"Let's dance," he said.

"Gillie, I'm with—"

"I said, let's *dance,*" he said, grabbing her wrist. You took what you wanted in this world. No other way. *"Now!"*

And then he felt a sharp pain in his right arm, and the red-haired guy was in front of him, looking up in a cool way. He was smiling.

"That's bad manners, man," the red-haired guy said, in a way that made Gillis afraid. "I think you ought to apologize. To Cathy. And to me."

And Gillis did what he had done so many times before; knowing what he would do, from beginning to end.

"Let's go outside," Gillis said. "We'll settle this there."

The red-haired guy was still smiling. "I don't want a fight, pal," he said. "I want an apology."

And Cathy said: "Oh, Gillis, stop, don't ruin everything."

"Outside," Gillis said.

The red-haired guy shrugged, turned to Cathy, and sighed: "Wait here." Quiñones was there now, trying to calm things down. Gillis remembered that; trying to settle it. But the red-haired guy was walking out the door past the bouncer, peeling off his coat, and then Gillis was behind him, and so were Curly and Vito and Quiñones, and then he and the red-haired guy faced each other in the parking lot.

Gillis loaded up on the right hand, the right hand that had dropped so many other people in parking lots and outside bars and in school yards and on beaches. He came in a rush, and threw the right hand, and felt terrible pain in his belly, and then a swirl of chopping motions, and he looked up and saw the Paradise sign, and Curly's astonished face. Then he was up, and then down again, his face in the gravel, something wet on his face and hands; blood. He got up one final time and hit the smaller man, but the smaller man was still smiling and then there was more pain, and a high, bright light, and broken pieces of speech, and a scream, and he was in the gravel again, and he stayed there, afraid. I can get up, he thought. But I won't.

"Stop," he said in a hoarse whisper. "Please stop."

And now he was in the furnished room, with the morning light as cruel as truth, thinking: Everything is different now. I dogged it, and they all know it. The little guy made me quit. I'll never walk down the avenue the same way. I'll never walk into the Paradise the same way or hang around the gas station the same way. Everything is different. And I hurt. I hurt.

Lullaby of Birdland

ONE MORNING THAT SPRING, Dwight Roberts first saw the horn man. Dwight and his mother were going down the stairs of the house on Gates Avenue, he to school and she to work, and the horn man was coming up. He was a large man, with hooded eyes that made him look Asian, tan skin, a wrinkled blue suit, and dirty black-and-white shoes. He had a cheap canvas suitcase in one hand and the horn, in a scuffed black case, in the other. He was wheezing.

"'Scuse me," he said in an exhausted voice. "Where's 4D at?"

"Keep climbin'," said Dwight's mother. "It's in the back, right over us." She paused. "You lookin' for Jimmy?"

"He moved," the horn man said. "Went south."

The man paused, as if gathering strength, and resumed the climb.

That evening they were having dinner, Dwight and his mother and his two little sisters, and first they heard the man walking, his tread heavy on their ceiling, and then the sound of water running. And then, suddenly, abruptly, they heard music. The windows were open to the warm spring air, and first there was a series of incredibly quick notes, up and down the scale, glistening, running, and then a shift into a beautiful, clear, lyrical song—a complaint, a sigh, a lament. Dwight Roberts had never heard anything like it before in his life.

"Just what I thought," Dwight's mother said. "A musician. Now, you stay away from him, Dwight, boy, you hear? You stay away from that horn man."

"But why, Momma?" Dwight asked.

"Cuz he be playin' the devil's music."

The horn man finished after twenty minutes, and in a while, they heard him thumping down the stairs into the night. The next day was Saturday, and in the spring morning, Dwight was reading a comic book on the stoop when a taxicab pulled up and the horn man got out. He looked up at the building and said to Dwight: "Need an elevator here. This ain't human, man."

And hurried up the stoop.

On Sunday mornings, Dwight and his mother and sisters always dressed for church. This was the most important day of Dwight's mother's life, the day she prayed for everybody: her mother, and President Truman, and the children, and Joe Louis, and Clark Gable, and even Dwight's father, who'd gone out for a bottle of milk one night during the war and had never come back. On Sundays, starch cut Dwight's neck; his sisters smelled like soap; his mother wore her blue hat with the white veil. Today was Sunday, and Dwight's neck hurt.

When they came out onto the stoop on Gates Avenue, the biggest car in the world pulled up to the curb. It was all shiny and black. A man with a cap was driving. The door opened and the horn man got out, and waved good-bye to a white woman. A white woman. The horn man looked bleary and surprised. He put the horn down.

"Where the hell I'm at?" he asked as the limousine pulled away.

"Brooklyn," Dwight's mother said sharply. "Outside the house you're stayin' at." A pause. "On Sunday. The Lord's Day."

"Well, abide by me, Momma," the horn man said, smiling a big, wonderful smile. "And hey! Lay a little prayer on me, would ya, Momma? Like a good Baptist."

"I don't even know your name," Dwight's mother said icily. The horn man lofted the scuffed black case.

"Charlie Chan," he said, bowing formally at the waist, and then hurrying up the stoop. Dwight had never seen his mother look the way she looked at that moment.

The horn man did not go out that night, or the night after that, and, at dinner, Dwight wondered out loud if the man was all right. Dwight's mother said he was probably worn out from sinning. Then Dwight said it would be Christian to bring the man some soup, and Dwight's mother was trapped. The boy brought the bowl of soup upstairs, with a plate over the top to keep it from spilling. Then he heard the horn: the door to the roof was open and Dwight followed the sound. The man was standing on the roof in a gray bathrobe and street shoes, his eyes closed, playing his glistening horn for the trees and the backyards and the birds of Brooklyn.

Dwight waited there, mysteriously chilled by the music, until the horn man finished. Then the man opened his eyes and looked at the boy and smiled. "What you got there, man? Oh, hey, chicken noodle! That for me? Chickendamnnoodle! The best! Damn!"

He laid the horn against a chimney and took the bowl in both hands and drank greedily. Dwight offered him a spoon; he ignored it, and shoved the final noodle into his mouth with his fingers. Then he saw Dwight looking at the horn. "Go ahead, man. Give it a try."

Dwight lifted the horn, feeling the chill enter him again, and blew into it. Nothing happened. The man showed him how to hold it, where to put his fingers, how to breathe, and that evening on the roof on Gates Avenue, it began. He hummed a tune in bed. Over and over. A tune he learned from Charlie Chan. At the end of the week, the eleven-year-old boy could play "London Bridge" on this thing called an alto saxophone. He went up to the roof every day. The horn man was his teacher. The boy added "Mary Had a Little Lamb." They met each evening on the roof, and played together for an hour, the boy bringing soup, the man full of music. After their session, the man went to work, way over in New York. Dwight's mother began to include the man in her prayers. And Dwight told everybody he was going to be a musician just like Charlie Chan. Everyone except his mother.

One afternoon, after playing stickball with his friends, he hurried to the family apartment. The kitchen window was open to the summer. His mother was beside it, listening to the music of the horn man drifting down from the roof. She was very still, her face lost in melancholy. Then she heard Dwight and turned.

"Jus' takin' a break, son," she said with a chuckle. "Need something to eat?"

"No, Momma. I gotta go back. Just, you know—"

He darted into the bathroom, closed the door. When he returned, he took a deep breath.

"Momma, I wanna tell you something," he said. "I want to be a musician. Just like Charlie Chan."

"No, no, no," Dwight's mother protested. "You're gonna be a lawyer! A doctor! No musicians! Just look at that man. *He* plays. He plays *real* good. Sometimes, he plays…beautiful. And where's he livin'? Right here with *us*! I don't want you endin' up where you started, Dwight Roberts!"

But Dwight persisted. He took a summer job at a grocery store a few blocks away, saving money for his own Selmer. He found a radio station that played jazz. He learned sixteen bars of "April in Paris." One evening, he even told Charlie Chan he wanted to be a musician.

"Now, hold on, man," Charlie Chan said. "You know what you're saying? You know what it *means,* man? It means you gonna go to *school,* gotta learn to *read,* gotta learn harmony and composition. Not just play. You gotta *create,* man. You gotta know *everything.* Louis Armstrong, Stravinsky, Mahler, Bessie Smith, *everything,* man. You gotta see if you got it *here,*" he said, tapping his heart, "even more than up *here,*" he added, tapping his head. "You gotta have the other thing, too. You gotta have…I dunno, man. It's mysterious. It ain't got a name. Max got it. Dizzy got it. I got it. It don't have a name. But you gotta *have* it, man. You gotta have it." He looked sad. "It ain't easy, man."

The next day, while he was working at the grocery store, Dwight Roberts heard the sound of the fire engines. They were screaming up Gates Avenue. Dwight went out to look, and saw in the distance that smoke was pouring from his own house. He ran all the way. The street was a wilderness of hoses, engines, a pumper, three police cars. Kids were clambering on the apparatus or watching from across the street. Then he saw his mother against the fence, shaking and sobbing. The horn man was beside her, his arm on her shoulder.

"You be quiet now," he was saying to her in a crooning, singsong voice. "You jus' be calm, you jus' be quiet…."

And Dwight ran over and heard the story, about the fire in the kitchen, and his sisters screaming, and the wall of flame, and how the horn man was suddenly coming through the rooms, a blanket over him, grabbing kids, shoving his mother into the hall, the great large man knocking over furniture, shouting for them to get low, and then banging on all the doors on the way to the street. The apartment was ruined. But they were alive. And now the horn man was asking about the subway, his clothes gone, his horn in the rubble. He kissed Dwight's mother, hugged Dwight, and started walking. Dwight shouted after him: "Where you goin', Charlie Chan?"

"I'll be around," the horn man said, and walked out of the neighborhood, and out of Dwight's life. Dwight turned to his mother, who was sobbing and praying, waiting for a chance to inspect the ruins. She glanced at the corner where Charlie Chan had disappeared.

"He was just like a bird," she said. "Come here in the spring, and then flown away. Just like a bird."

The Boarder

MISS FLANAGAN WAS FORTY-ONE when Mr. Macias came knocking at her door. He had a newspaper under his arm and a tentative look in his eyes. Did she have a room to rent? The words stumbled, then broke; his English was not good. But she understood. Yes, she had a room to rent.

"Well," he said. "I can see it, please?"

She looked down at him; he was a small man with a neat mustache, a cheap brown suit wrinkling at elbow and knee, black-and-white shoes. On the stoop beside him there was a battered suitcase. His eyes convinced her to let him into the hall; they were filled with rejection, and on that subject Miss Flanagan was an expert.

"Yes, of course."

The room was at the back of the parlor floor, directly off

the stoop. When her parents were alive, they'd used it for a bedroom; her mother liked the view of the garden, the fireplace in winter, the parquet floors, the elegant molding that was popular when the old craftsmen built the brownstones in this part of Brooklyn. But Miss Flanagan could never sleep there; she felt as if she were usurping part of her own past. It was all right for strangers; it simply wasn't for her. When she opened the oak door, with its solid-brass fittings, and showed the room to Mr. Macias, he issued an involuntary little breath of surprise.

"Oh," he said. "Is so beautiful."

"Yes," Miss Flanagan said. "It is beautiful."

He ran a hand over the polished wood mantelpiece. He gazed through the windows at the garden, white with winter, the tree as precise as calligraphy. He turned to her, and his mouth trembled, and rejection washed through his eyes.

"How much it is?" he said.

She thought: a Hispanic man, the neighbors will be alarmed, I don't know him, I don't know where he came from, I don't know what he might have done in his past. And then: to hell with it. He has sad eyes.

"Thirty dollars a week," she said.

The sum must have been enormous to him. He inhaled, placed a hand in his pocket, took out some bills, and handed three tens to Miss Flanagan. He gazed again around the large, bright room and said: "I can move in now?"

And so it began. Every morning at nine, Mr. Macias left for work; every evening he arrived back at precisely seven; every Friday morning, the envelope with thirty dollars in cash was in her mailbox. Gradually, he bought himself new shoes, another suit, and a guitar. And the guitar changed everything. Miss Flanagan would lie alone at night in her bed on the third floor, trying to read or watch television, tired from the day's work at the hospital, and she would hear Mr. Macias playing softly and singing in his own language.

She didn't understand the words, but she knew their meaning. They were full of heartbreak, loss, exile; and she remembered her father when she was a little girl, when the uncles would come over for dinner, and the house would be loud with laughter and argument, and then, as night arrived, the mood would change, and her father would stand at the kitchen table and sing the old ballads of a lost home across a sea, of heartbreak, of exile.

She met him in the hall one Saturday morning and said: "Oh, Mr. Macias, you sing so beautifully."

"Oh, sank you, sank you," he said, and his eyes sparkled, and he smiled for the first time since coming to the room on the parlor floor. Miss Flanagan thought he had the most wonderful smile. "I'd love to hear you sing more," she said. "And maybe you could teach me the words?"

"Oh, yes, okay. And maybe you teach me English better?"

Spring came and then the summer. She began to cook for Mr. Macias, to anticipate his arrivals, to sit with him at the kitchen table after dinner, and show him the meaning of the words in the newspapers, and give him books, and correct his pronunciation; and then he would sing the songs of Mexico. She loved a song called "La Cama de Piedra," about a man who lies on a bed of stone, awaiting execution; she was moved by a song called "¿Dónde Estás?" and its line that said "Yo, sin tu amor, yo soy nada," which meant "I, without your love, I am nothing." He explained where Guadalajara was, Jalisco, and where the revolutionary heroes fought the battles mentioned in some of the songs, and he smiled his wonderful smile and she thought, Yo, sin tu amor, yo soy nada.

One night he took her to Roseland, and Miss Flanagan, who had considered herself too plain for most men, who was heavier than the fashion, whose clumsiness was a family joke when her parents were alive, Miss Flanagan began to dance. Mr. Macias showed her the simplest steps, in the shadows along the wall, and then led her into the crowd while a Latin band played a bolero. She was almost a foot taller than Mr. Macias, but he guided her firmly, and calmed her trembling, and held her closer than a man had held her in almost twenty years. That night, she moved to the room on the parlor floor.

There was no talk of marriage. That idea had died in her long ago; she would be what they used to call an old maid, she was certain of that. Certainly she could never propose such a thing to Mr. Macias. If she did, he might panic, flee; he might even have some buried secret, some wife in the old country, someone in his life whose existence Miss Flanagan didn't want to know about. If Mr. Macias did not raise the question, then neither would Miss Flanagan. She would just enjoy this time for as long as it might last, this sudden, rich, and lovely interlude, this delayed portion of her youth, this gift.

Of course, it was technically a sin. She knew that. And yet Miss Flanagan believed in a merciful God: how could something so sweet, so tender, so human, be an offense against a just and merciful God? When her mother died, and her father lay sick and old for so many years, she had surrendered all hope of union with a man. She had sacrificed, denied herself, endured the long penance of loneliness. Did that mean she would go to her grave on the cama de piedra? Yes, she thought, I am a sinner, and I am now reduced to going to confession in different churches; but I am here, alive, on this earth, and I want Mr. Macias. Yo, sin tu amor, yo soy nada.

Then one morning, as she left for the hospital, she saw two men sitting in a blue Plymouth parked beside a fire hydrant. They seemed to be watching her, and Miss Flanagan was suddenly alarmed. She walked to the corner to take the bus, and looked back, and saw the blue Plymouth pull away. She stepped into a telephone booth and called her own number. Mr. Macias answered.

"There were two men in a car watching the house," she said. "Do you think they were looking for you?"

He hesitated. "Why? Why would they look for me?"

"I—I don't know," she said. "I just thought—"

"Don't worry. Please don't worry."

But all day at the hospital, she worried. And when she came home that night, and started to cook a meal, and realized swiftly that Mr. Macias was late, panic rushed through her. Suppose he never came back? Suppose he was afraid, scared of the police, an illegal alien who would be arrested and shipped home to Mexico? She tried to imagine the house with Mr. Macias gone, and she began to weep.

Then she heard the key turning in the gate beneath the stoop and the double doors opening, and when Mr. Macias entered, smiling, holding a large bunch of roses, she ran to him and wrapped her arms around him and held him to her generous breasts and thumping heart and wept some more.

A week later, at seven o'clock on a Friday morning, the doorbell rang. It was as she knew it would be. She pulled on a robe and walked along the parlor floor. Through the cut-glass inner doors, she could see the two men from the Plymouth. One was tall and blond, the other shorter, balding, smoking a cigarette. They each wore raincoats and bored expressions. She opened the door.

"Good morning," the blond one said. He reached into his back pocket and took out his wallet and showed her a plastic card that bore his picture.

"We're here to pick up a man named Macias," the shorter one said, flipping his cigarette into the street.

"Can I help you?" she said, and smiled. "I'm Mrs. Macias."

The Men in Black Raincoats

IT WAS CLOSE TO midnight on a Friday evening at Rattigan's Bar and Grill. There were no ball games on the television, old movies only made the clientele feel more ancient, and the jukebox was still broken from the afternoon of Red Butera's daughter's wedding. So it was time for Brendan Malachy McCone to take center stage. He motioned for a fresh beer, put his right foot on the brass rail, breathed in deeply, and started to sing.

> *Oh, the Garden of Eden has vanished, they say,*
> *But I know the lie of it still,*
> *Just turn to the left at the Bridge of Finea,*
> *And meet me halfway to Cootehill...*

The song was very Irish, sly and funny, the choruses full of the names of long-forgotten places, and the regulars loved Brendan for his quick, jaunty singing of it. They loved the roguish glitter in his eyes, his energy, his good-natured boasting. He was, after all, a man in his fifties now, and yet here he was, still singing the bold songs of his youth. And on this night, as on so many nights, they joined him in the verses.

The baby's a man now,
He's toil-worn and tough,
Still, whispers come over the sea
Come back, Paddy Reilly, to Ballyjamesduff
Come home, Paddy Reilly, to me.

Outside, rain had begun to fall, a cold Brooklyn rain, driven by the wind off the harbor, and it made the noises and the singing and the laughter seem even better. Sardines and crackers joined the glasses on the bar while George, the bartender, filled the empties. And Brendan shifted from jauntiness to sorrow.

If you ever go across the sea to Ireland,
Then maybe at the closing of your day...

The mood of the regulars hushed now, as Brendan gave them the song as if it were a hymn. The bar was charged with the feeling they all had for Brendan, knowing that he had been an IRA man long ago, that he had left Ireland a step ahead of the British police, who wanted him for the killing of a British soldier in the Border Campaign. This was their Brendan: the Transit Authority clerk who had once stood in the doorways of Belfast, with the cloth cap pulled tight on his brow, the pistol deep in the pockets of his trench coat, ready to kill or to die for Ireland.

He was singing now about how the strangers came to Ireland, the bloody Brits, and tried to force their ways upon the Irish, his voice was a healthy baritone, a wealth of passion overwhelming a poverty of skill, and it touched all of them, making the younger ones imagine the streets of modern Belfast, where their cousins were still fighting, reminding the older ones of peat fires, black, creamy stout, buttermilk in the morning. The song was about a vanished time, before rock and roll and women's liberation, before they took Latin out of the Mass, before the blacks and the Puerto Ricans had begun to move in and the children of the Irish had begun to move out. The neighborhood was changing, all right. But Brendan Malachy McCone was still with them, still in the neighborhood.

A little after midnight two strangers came in, dressed in black raincoats. They were wet with rain. They ordered whiskey. Brendan kept singing. Nobody noticed that his voice faltered on the last lines of "Galway Bay," as he took the applause, glanced at the strangers, and again shifted the mood.

Oh, Mister Patrick McGinty,
An Irishman of note...

The strangers drank in silence.

*   *   *

At closing time the rain was still pelting down. Brendan stood in the open doorway of the bar with Charlie the Pole and Scotch Eddie, while George the bartender counted the receipts. Everyone else had gone home.

"We'll have to make a run for it," Charlie said.

"Dammit," Scotch Eddie said.

"Yiz might as well run, cause yiz'll drown anyway," George said. He was finished counting and looked small and tired.

"I'll see ya, gents," Charlie said, and rushed into the rain, running lumpily down the darkened slope of 11th Street to his home. Eddie followed, cutting sharply to his left. But Brendan did not move. He had seen the strangers in the black raincoats, glanced at them in the mirror for a while as he moved through the songs, saw them leave an hour later. And now he was afraid.

He looked up and down the avenue. The street lamp scalloped a halo of light on the corner. Beyond the light there was nothing but the luminous darkness and the rain.

"Well, I've got to lock it up, Brendan."

"Right, George. Good night."

"God bless."

Brendan hurried up the street, head down, lashed by the rain, eyes searching the interiors of parked cars. He saw nothing. The cars were locked. He looked up at the apartments and there were no lights anywhere and he knew the lights would be out at home, too, where Sarah and the kids would all be sleeping. Even the firehouse was dimly lit, its great red door closed, the firemen stretched out on their bunks in the upstairs loft.

Despite the drink and the rain, Brendan's mouth was dry. Once he thought he saw something move in the darkness of an areaway and his stomach lifted and fell. But again it was nothing. Shadows. Imagination. Get hold of yourself, Brendan.

He crossed the avenue. A half block to go. A ways off he saw the twin red taillights of a city bus, groaning slowly toward Flatbush Avenue. Hurry. Another half block and he could enter the yard, hurry up the stairs, unlock the door, close it behind him, undress quickly in the darkened kitchen, dry off the rain with a warm rough towel, brush the beer off his teeth, and fall into the great deep warmth of bed with Sarah. And he would be safe again for another night. Hurry. Get the key out. Don't get caught naked on the stairs.

He turned into his yard, stepped over a spreading puddle at the base of the stoop, and hurried up the eight worn sandstone steps. He had the key out in the vestibule and quickly opened the inside door.

They were waiting for him in the hall.

The one in the front seat on the right was clearly the boss. The driver was only a chauffeur and did his work in proper silence. The strangers in the raincoats sat on either side of Brendan in the backseat and said nothing as the car moved through the wet darkness down off the Slope, into the Puerto Rican neighborhood near Williamsburg. They all clearly deferred to the one in the right front seat. All wore gloves. Except the boss.

"I'm telling you, mister, this has to be some kind of mistake," Brendan said.

"Shut up," said the boss without turning. His skin was pink in the passing lights of street lamps and his dark hair curled over the edge of his collar. The accent was not New York. Not Belfast. Maybe Boston. Maybe somewhere else. Not New York.

"I don't owe anybody money," Brendan said, choking back the dry panic. "I'm not into the bloody loan sharks. I'm telling you this is — "

The boss said, "Is your name Brendan Malachy McCone?"

"Well, uh, yes, but — "

"Then we've made no mistake."

Williamsburg was behind them now and they were following the route of the Brooklyn–Queens Expressway while avoiding its brightly lit ramp. Brendan sat back. From that angle, he could see more of the man in the right front seat: the velvet collar of his coat, the high, protruding cheekbones, the longish nose, the pinkie ring glittering on his left hand when he lit a cigarette with a thin gold lighter. He could not see the man's eyes but he was certain he had never seen the man before tonight.

"Where are you taking me?"

The boss said calmly, "I told you to shut up. Shut up."

Brendan took a deep breath, and then let it out slowly.

He looked to the men on either side of him, smiling his most innocent smile, as if hoping they would think well of him, believe in his innocence, intervene with the boss, plead his case. He wanted to tell them about his kids, explain that he had done nothing bad. Not for thirty years.

The men looked away from him, their nostrils seeming to quiver, as if he had already begun to stink of death. Brendan tried to remember the words of the Act of Contrition.

The men beside him stared out past the little rivers of rain on the windows, as if he were not even in the car. They watched the city turn into country, Queens into Nassau County, all the sleeping suburbs transformed into the darker, emptier reaches of Suffolk County, as the driver pushed on, driving farther away, out on Long Island, to the country of forests and frozen summer beaches. Far from Brooklyn. Far from the Friday nights at Rattigan's. Far from his children. Far from Sarah.

Until they pulled off the expressway at Southampton, moved down back roads for another fifteen minutes, and came to a marshy cove. A few summer houses were sealed for the winter. Rain spattered the still water of the cove. Patches of dirty snow clung to the shoreline, resisting the steady cold rain.

"This is fine," the boss said.

The driver pulled over, turned off the car lights, pulled under some trees, and turned off the engine. They all sat in the dark.

The boss said, "Did you ever hear of a man named Peter Devlin?"

Oh, my God, Brendan thought.

"Well?"

"Vaguely. The name sounds familiar."

"Just familiar?"

"Well, there was a Devlin where I came from. There were a lot of Devlins in the North. It's hard to remember. It was a long time ago."

"Yeah, it was. It was a long time ago."

"Aye."

"And you don't remember him more than just vaguely? I mean, you *were* best man at his wedding."

Brendan's lips moved, but no words came out.

"What else do you vaguely remember, McCone?"

There was a long pause. Then: "He died."

"No, not *died*. He was killed, wasn't he?"

"Aye."

"Who killed him, McCone?"

"He died for Ireland."

"Who *killed* him, McCone?"

"The Special Branch. The British Special Branch."

The boss took out his cigarettes and lit one with the gold lighter. He took a long drag. Brendan saw the muscles working tensely in his jaw. The rain drummed on the roof of the car.

"Tell me some more about him," the boss said.

"They buried him with full military honors. They draped his coffin with the Tricolour and sang 'The Soldiers' Song' over his grave. The whole town wore the Easter Lily. The B-Specials made a lot of arrests."

"You saw all this?"

"I was told."

"But you weren't there?"

"No, but—"

"What happened to his wife?"

"Katey?"

"Some people called her Katey," the boss said.

"She died, too, soon after...the flu, was it?"

"Well, in the family, there was another version. That she died of a broken heart."

The boss stared straight ahead, watching the rain trickle down the windshield. He tapped an ash into the ashtray, took another deep drag, and said, "What did they pay you to set him up, Brendan?"

He called me Brendan. He's softening. Even a gunman can understand it was all long ago.

"What do you mean?"

"Don't play games, Brendan. Everyone in the North knew you set him up. The British told them."

"It was a long time ago, mister. There were a lot of lies told. You can't believe every..."

The boss wasn't really listening. He took out his pack of cigarettes, flipped one higher than the others, gripped its filter in his teeth, and lit it with the butt of the other. Then he tamped out the first cigarette in the ashtray. He looked out past the rain to the darkness of the cove.

"Shoot him," he said.

The man on Brendan's left opened the door a foot.

"Oh, sweet sufferin' Jesus, mister," Brendan said. "I've

got five kids. They're all at home. One of them is making her First Communion. Please. For the love of God. If Dublin Command has told you to get me, just tell them you couldn't find me. Tell them I'm dead. I can get you a piece of paper from one of the politicians. Sayin' I'm dead. Yes. That's a way. And I'll just vanish. just disappear. Please. I'm an old man now, I won't live much bloody longer. But the weans. The weans, mister. And it was all thirty years ago. Christ knows I've paid for it. Please. Please."

The tears were blurring his vision now. He could hear the hard spatter of the rain through the open car door. He felt the man on his right move slightly and remove something from inside his coat.

The boss said, "You left out a few things, Brendan."

"I can send all my earnings to the lads. God knows they can use it in the North now. I've sent money already, I have, to the Provisionals. I never stopped being for them. For a united Ireland. Never stopped. I can have the weans work for the cause. I'll get a second job. My Sarah can go out and work, too. Please, mister. Jesus, mister..."

"Katey Devlin didn't die of the flu," the boss said. "And she didn't die of a broken heart. Did she, Brendan?"

"I don't—"

"Katey Devlin killed herself. Didn't she?"

Brendan felt his stomach turn over.

The boss said, very quietly, "She loved Peter Devlin more than life itself. She didn't want him to die."

"But neither does Sarah want *me* to die. She's got the weans, the feedin' of them, and the clothin' of them, and the schoolin' of them, to think of. Good God, man, have ye no mercy? I was a boy then. My own people were starvin'. We had no land, we were renters, we were city people, not farmers, and the war was on, and…They told me they would only arrest him. Intern him for the duration and let him out when the fightin' stopped, and they told me the IRA would take care of Katey while he was inside. Please, mister, I've got five kids. Peter Devlin only had *two*."

"I know," said the man in the right front seat. "I was one of them."

For the first time he turned completely around. His eyes were a cold blue under the shock of curly dark hair, Katey's eyes in Peter's face. He stared at Brendan for a moment. He took another drag on the cigarette and let the smoke drift from his nose, creating lazy trails of gray in the crowded car.

"Shoot him," he said.

The man on his left touched Brendan's hand and opened the door wide.

The Radio Doctor

EVERY NIGHT FOR TWO months, Tommy Mungo tried to get through to Dr. Verity Ambler. On the radio each night, she gave strength and advice to all the other callers: tearful young wives, husbands who thought they were gay, lonely widows, men whose women had run off, pregnant teenagers, parents who hated their children and children who hated their parents. He would listen to her alone in his bedroom, wearing a headset so his mother wouldn't waken, listening to her cool, perfect voice, her strong words, her certainties. He was sure that somehow she could help him. She would give him some words and those words would change his life. So each night he dialed the station, and each night there was a busy signal, and this deepened Tommy Mungo's sense of failure and despair.

Then, amazingly, suddenly, without explanation, one night he got through. A man picked up the phone and asked Tommy his name and his problem, and Tommy Mungo told him, and the man said he would put him on hold, and when Dr. Ambler picked up, he should be certain that his radio was turned off. Tommy Mungo lay there with his heart pounding for another twenty minutes. And then suddenly he heard her voice.

"Yes, Tommy, this is Dr. Verity Ambler. What can I do for you?"

"Well, I uh, you see, I'm twenty-eight years old," Tommy said. "And I feel like I failed at everything."

"Yes, Tommy..."

"For example, I can't seem to finish anything. I never finished high school. And then I went to night school, to get a GED, you know? But I couldn't finish that, either. I got a job in a sheet-metal shop. Like an apprentice, you know? You're an apprentice for two years, then you move up the ladder, and eventually you become a journeyman and make good money. But I couldn't stick with it, I couldn't finish. My mother says—"

"Do you live at home, Tommy?"

"Yes, yes, I do."

"And you're twenty-eight years old?"

Tommy's stomach knotted. He could feel Dr. Ambler staring at him with cold eyes, across the miles from her studio in Manhattan to his apartment in Brooklyn.

"Yes," he admitted. "Yes, I live at home."

"How does your mother feel about that, Tommy?"

"Well, she doesn't say much."

"And your father?"

"My father...passed away."

Her voice was suddenly accusatory. "You sounded *hesitant,* Tommy. What was *that* about?"

"Well...the truth is, he didn't pass away, actually. That's just something I tell people since I was fifteen. Actually, he just left. He took off somewhere; I don't know where."

"I see," Dr. Ambler said. "And how did your mother feel about *that?*"

"She felt bad, of course," Tommy said quietly. "But she always says to me, 'Thank God you're still here.' And—"

"Ah," Dr. Ambler said, drawing the word out. "Don't you see, Tommy? That's the real problem, okay? And you can't finish anything. What does it suggest to you, Tommy?"

"I don't know."

Her voice was reasonable, soft. "Well, what do you think is the first thing you must finish?"

"I'm not sure. That's why I—"

"You must finish your *adolescence,* Tommy!" She was scolding now. "You have to move out of that house and go out on your own and become a mature adult, okay? Don't worry about your mother. She'll be fine. In fact, I think your mother's being terribly unfair to you, Tommy, by refusing to let you grow up, okay? You're not a surrogate for your father. You're not a safeguard against your mother's loneliness. You have to be your own person. You have to be your own best friend. You have to become a mature, 'together' person. Finish your adolescence and you'll be able to finish other things in your life, okay? Thank you, Tommy...."

There was a click and she was gone, and Tommy felt suddenly abandoned, the unspoken words choking in his throat. He switched on the radio, and Dr. Verity Ambler was saying she would be back after "these messages" and the news. Tommy Mungo punched the pillow and said out loud: "You didn't let me finish...."

I wanted to tell you about the crash on the Belt Parkway, he thought. And how my mother was crippled, her spine smashed, while nothing at all happened to my father. I wanted to tell you how he stayed with her for three years after that, until one night I saw him alone on the stoop, crying his eyes out. All of that was before he left. And then when she was alone, I promised her I wouldn't let them stick her in some home or some hospital, wouldn't leave her to charity. You didn't let me tell you that, Dr. Ambler.

The radio doctor was talking now to a woman whose fifteen-year-old daughter was still wetting her bed, and Tommy Mungo dialed the station again, got a busy signal, tried again, got another busy signal. I could write her a letter, he thought, and put in all the things she never gave me time to say. But no: she must get thousands of letters; she could never read them all, or answer them. No. He glanced at the clock beside his bed. Ten minutes to two. She'd be on air until three. He got up and started to dress. He had to speak to her; it could be months before he got through to her again. He'd have to go to the radio station and see her.

*   *   *

All the way to Manhattan, driving the beat-up Pontiac across the Brooklyn Bridge and through the empty streets, he listened to Dr. Verity Ambler. He wasn't angry at her; he was certain it must be his own fault, something in his voice, something in his manner. She was so logical with the others. She told a man whose wife was playing around that he must become "creatively selfish," give his wife an ultimatum—tell her to stop fooling around—or leave. A man whose wife was an alcoholic was told to forget about her being cured; alcoholism can be treated, she told him, but not cured. "And you are obviously a terrific person," she said, "so I think you should get into yourself more, okay?"

Now he was in midtown Manhattan, a block from the station. She would be finished in twenty minutes. He parked across the street, listening to the radio show, and smoked a cigarette. At five minutes to three, he locked the car door and walked to the station entrance. Beyond the locked double door, there was a long empty corridor leading to a bank of elevators. A security guard sat in a chair beside the elevators, reading a newspaper. Tommy Mungo waited. A taxi pulled up and double-parked, the off-duty sign burning.

Then a large man and a smallish woman stepped out of the elevator. The security man smiled and stood up, had them sign a book, and started walking with them along the corridor to the entrance. It was her. Dr. Verity Ambler. He had seen her picture once in a newspaper and another time on *The Regis Philbin Show*. But she seemed smaller than he imagined she would be, walking along in a fur coat and slacks, with the large man in front of her and the guard behind her. As the guard unlocked the doors, they all looked at Tommy Mungo.

"Okay, back up," the large man said.

"But I've got to talk to Dr. Ambler," Tommy said. "I was on the show tonight, talking to her, and I never finished explaining—"

"Back it up!"

The woman's eyes seemed wide and alarmed, as the large man stepped between her and Tommy Mungo.

"I never got to tell you!" Tommy shouted. "I can't leave my mother! She's not like you think. But I need help, I need advice, you have to help me!"

He tried to get around the large man, but the man placed a huge hand on Tommy's chest and pushed him backward.

"Jack!" Dr. Ambler said. "Don't do that, Jack! He might sue me or something!"

"Please," Tommy Mungo said. "Let me explain. I got through tonight! After months! After being on hold for hours and hours and hours, *I got through!* And then I never got to explain to you. I—"

"Come on," the woman said, taking the large man by the arm and leading him to the waiting taxi. She slammed the door behind them, and the taxi pulled away. Tommy Mungo stood there for a long time, wishing that somewhere in the city there was a person he could call.

The Challenge

Shank was sitting on the windowsill, staring down at Algren Street, when Maria came in. She was big now; the baby would come soon. A month at most. Maybe sooner. He walked from the small living room into the smaller kitchen to greet her. Her face was troubled as she placed the grocery bag on the kitchen table and removed her coat.

"He's down there," she said. "At the corner."

"So what?"

"This time he said something to me."

Shank tensed, took her hand.

"He did?"

She pulled away from him, opened the refrigerator door, put milk and oranges on the metal shelf. "He said, 'Hello, honey. I'm Rojo. Gonna get your ol' man.' Just like that. With those eyes of his."

"He's crazy," Shank said.

"I know," Maria said. "That's why we gotta move, baby. Now. Tonight. Tomorrow. We gotta move, before the baby. We gotta get out of here, all the way out of the neighborhood."

"I can't do that," Shank said. "You know I can't."

Her voice rose. "Why not? Why not just get outta here?"

"'Cause I'm the president of the Dragons!" he said. "No punk Marielito makes *me* move!"

"Yeah, but you're twenty-one years old! You're married! You gotta baby coming! You can't go on like this, baby. Bein' what you was when you was sixteen! You got…responsibility!"

The word entered Shank like a blade. It was one of those grown-up words, like "opportunity" or "retirement," that could chill his heart. He had no way to argue with her; she was right. But she didn't understand a lot of things. She didn't understand what it meant to be a Dragon, how much of his life was tied up with the Dragons, how hard it would be for him to just go away. He was president; he had been a junior before that, and a Tiny Tim, in the days when he used a knife as an equalizer against men older and tougher and meaner than he was. That's how he got the name Shank. Back then. Four Dragons had died in street rumbles since he became president at seventeen; more than twenty had ended up in hospitals. Shot or knifed, battered with tire irons or chains or bats. Three had died of overdoses, early on, which was why Shank had led the war against heroin, kicking out users, crippling dealers. Guy wanted to smoke a bone here and there, okay. A little blow now and then, okay. But no smack. Smack kills. Smack was death. All those wars had brought them together, closer than a family. And Maria would never understand any of that.

"My girlfrien' Carmen, remember her?" Maria said. "She told me about this place, four rooms, steam heat, in Sout' Brooklyn. Two eighty a month. And it gotta yard, Shank. We could go see it tonight. We could have all this stuff packed by morning. My brother Ralphie, he could get a U-Haul and—"

"Stop," he said. "I ain't goin' nowhere."

She shook her head and walked past him into the living room. She turned on the TV set and then sat back in the worn green armchair and watched a game show. Shank leaned on the refrigerator, thinking about this new kid, Rojo, this wild Cuban with crazy eyes and tattooed fingers and spiky red hair. Three weeks after Rojo had moved into the neighborhood with his mother, he'd stabbed a kid in the school yard on Farrell Avenue. A week later, he opened a wino's belly on Lonigan Street. A smack dealer on Shulman Place was found with his neck sliced, and everybody said Rojo musta did it. He came over to Pepe's one evening and said that he wanted to join the Dragons, and Pepe said, Yeah, maybe that could be worked out. And then Rojo said: "I want to be the president." And Pepe laughed, and then found a blade at his neck, and Rojo saying: "Don't laugh at me, man. I want the whole club."

Shank told Maria about that, trying to laugh when he

told her. But she didn't laugh. She started this business about moving, about getting away. But where could he go? He worked in this neighborhood, at Jaime's Flat Fix. He came from this neighborhood and knew everybody, and they knew him. He couldn't go to some strange new place where he wasn't known. That would be like being fourteen again. This was his place, his turf, and the Dragons were his family.

"I'm going out," he said, stepping out of the kitchen.

"Don't," she said, starting to rise. "Don't go near him. Please don't."

"I'll be back," he said, and going down the stairs, he thought: I should have a piece. I should stop at Benny's and borrow his piece. That Walther P38. Put it in a newspaper. Go down and find this Rojo and just blow him away. But what if the cops land on me? What if I end up in the can? What happens to Maria? What happens to the baby? No: I gotta talk to the dude. I gotta work it out.

Shank came out onto Algren Street. Mrs. Velasquez nodded hello, and Old Man Farley smiled. Shank saw Little Willy John sitting on the stoop across the street, and walked over to him.

"Take a walk," Shank said.

"What's up?" Little Willie John said.

"Rojo."

They picked up Face and Sammy Davis and Willowbrook, and told Zeppelin to take his car around the block and wait across the street from Chuckie's Bar. Somebody went to get

Benny, and with Shank in the lead, they walked toward Farrell Avenue.

Rojo was standing alone in front of Chuckie's Bar. The afternoon sun made his hair look even more red. He was wearing shades and a sleeveless lavender T-shirt. His hands were in the back pockets of his jeans. He didn't move when he saw Shank coming around the corner, with the others behind him. He just smiled.

"Wait here," Shank said to the others. "I'll talk to the dude."

He walked slowly over to Rojo, standing six feet away from him, out of range of the blade. He knew the blade must be in one of Rojo's back pockets. One of his hands was on it. Rojo smiled.

"I hear you been talkin' about me," Shank said.

"Yeah? How you hear that?"

"From my wife."

"Yeah? Which one is your wife?"

"You know, man. Don't play dumb."

"The pretty one, she having a baby? That one?"

He smiled again. Shank fought down the urge to close with him and break his face apart.

"Yeah, that's the one. She says you're gonna get me, man. Other people say you still want to run the Dragons. So I figure I better talk to you. I better hear it from you myself."

Rojo looked left and right, moving forward almost imperceptibly, the smile on his face.

"Yeah, you heard right. I want it. I want what you got. You can give it to me. Or I can take it."

141

"It don't work that way, man. The Dragons, you get elected president." He turned and saw the others at the corner, all watching him. "You can join—then, who knows? The guys in the crew like you, and I decide to pack it in, maybe you end up president. But you don't get the gig with a blade."

"I become president," Rojo said, "I get your wife, too? She's pretty, man. I dig her. I—"

Shank slammed into him, crashing him against the window, reaching desperately for his hands. He locked a hand on Rojo's left wrist. The knife was in the other hand. And then Rojo was whirling, squirming, a high-pitched animal whine coming from inside him, and Shank heard shouts and a scream, all the while smashing at Rojo, tumbling, using every move he'd ever learned. And then he heard the shots. Pap-pap, two of them, pap-pap-pap, three more. And Rojo stopped moving. Shank rolled off him and started to get up, and couldn't, and then saw the blood, all over his hands and his stomach. And his wife's forlorn face. And Little Willie John, crying, and whispering:

"It's okay, it's okay, brother, it's okay. You gonna live, man, you gonna live. It's okay."

"Yeah," Shank said, a high ringing in his ears, the world turning white, faces bleaching out, and heard Maria saying: "Goddamn you, baby, goddamn all of you."

A Hero of the War

Billy Fitzgerald idolized his father and nobody in the neighborhood could blame him. Paulie Fitzgerald was, after all, a hero of the war. In the bars, in the veterans' clubs, they all knew the story well: how Paulie had gone to Korea in that first brutal winter of the war, when the ground froze to iron, and how his outfit was cut off in the night and the flanks were overrun, and how Paulie fought off the Communists all by himself, killing eleven of them, until help arrived in the morning. Billy knew the story as well as anyone, although his father was a modest man and didn't talk about it much, except when he was drinking.

"Let's just say it was terrible," his father would say. "War is hell, kid. War is hell."

But there were medals and ribbons in the top drawer of

143

the bureau in his parents' bedroom and, in their way, they were enough. Sometimes when nobody was home, when Billy was a boy, he would take them out and examine them. The Bronze Star. The Distinguished Service Medal. The Purple Heart. They thrilled Billy and, handling them, he would imagine his father, young and tough, with a machine gun in his hands, marching across barren hills, and then fighting hard through fear and blood to save his buddies. Sometimes, Billy would wear the medals, pinning them to his chest, as his father did on Memorial Day, when he marched with the other veterans. In some important way, the medals made Billy feel directly connected to that larger, braver world that seemed to exist only in movies.

"I don't talk about it," his father said one night, after coming in late from Rattigan's Bar and Grill, across the street. "But I must have fired three hundred rounds. Cohen got it, and Lloyd, and Charlie Ramirez, and I kept shootin' and the Commies kept comin' and I thought the night would never end."

In 1971, when Billy was eighteen, he felt it was his duty to volunteer for the army. His mother cried and protested, and his younger brothers told him not to do it, but Billy insisted that as the oldest son he had no choice. In his time, his father had done his duty; now it was Billy's turn.

At night in basic training, he was tormented by fear, afraid that in a crisis he would never be as brave or as tough as his father. He would falter. He would cry. He would break and run. But in the end, none of that happened. Billy was assigned to Germany, not Vietnam, and his father remained secure as the only hero in the family.

"You're better off," his father said. "That goddamned war's just not worth fightin'."

This was on a night in Rattigan's, as Paulie stood with friends at the bar, while a ball game droned away on TV. His son was in uniform, leaving in the morning.

"What outfit were you with anyway, Dad?" the son said.

"First Cav," he said. "But it doesn't matter anymore. That was long ago and far away."

Then there was basketball excitement on TV, the others shouted, the conversation shifted. In the morning, Billy left for Germany. He came back almost two years later with a German wife, tall and blond and placid, and announced that they were moving straight to California. He took a job at McDonnell Douglas in Long Beach, went to night school on the GI Bill, learned drafting. Once a year, he came back to New York with his wife, and then with his kids, and each time his father was fatter. Chins multiplied; blue veins blossomed on his nose; his belly made him look as if he'd swallowed a safe. Billy had to explain to his children that under the layers of flesh there was a man who had once been young and tough and a hero.

"Always remember that about your grandfather," he said. "He was really something once."

One afternoon at McDonnell Douglas, the foreman called him to a phone. It was Billy's wife. She told him in her precise English that his mother had just called with terrible news. His father was dead. Just like that. A heart attack. Billy began to sob, and the foreman put his arm on Billy's shoulder and told him he'd better go home.

"He was only fifty-something years old." Billy protested. "I loved him. He wasn't just my father. He was a hero in Korea. A real-life hero."

"Then bury him like he was a hero," the foreman said. "He deserves it."

All the way across the country, with his wife beside him in the plane, and the two boys in the row in front of them, Billy kept thinking about one thing: Arlington. He must bury his father in Arlington. There would be a flag on the coffin and a bugler playing taps and Paulie Fitzgerald would join the endless rows of white crosses that marked the presence of men who had fought and sometimes died for their country. Some of them might even have been with him that terrible night in Korea.

"It's the right thing to do," he told his mother, who just wanted her husband buried in St. John's cemetery, close to home. "He'd want it that way, Mom."

The undertaker told Billy what he had to do to get Paulie buried at Arlington. There was a number to call in Washington and he'd need discharge papers and his father's service number and the name of the outfit in which he served. For a full day, Billy rummaged through his father's papers and drawers, but could find nothing. Nothing, that is, except the ribbons and medals.

Finally, he called the number in Washington again, got a young clerk who called him sir, explained his problem, gave his father's name and years of service and the part about the First Cavalry. The clerk said he would call back, and Billy returned to the business of the wake, the loss and grief of his mother and brothers, the sad admiration of his father's friends. On the morning of the third day, the clerk called from Washington.

"I'm sorry, sir," the clerk said. "Our records show that nobody by that name served with the First Cav during the Korean conflict, sir."

Billy insisted that there must be some mistake, and repeated his father's name. He was told that a man by that name from Brooklyn, New York, had served in 1951 and 1952 on Guam, not in Korea. He gave Billy an address in Brooklyn; Billy's heart split and flew away and then reassembled itself. The clerk had given his father's old address, the house he'd shown him so many times on trips to the old neighborhood. Quietly, Billy thanked the young clerk and hung up.

"The poor man," Billy said to himself. And then he slowly rose and went out to walk alone through the chilly afternoon. Everywhere he walked, he saw his father. He was throwing a football in Prospect Park in the fall, or hitting grounders to kids at Park Circle in the spring. He was standing outside Rattigan's on a summer afternoon, talking with the other men, quiet and proud. He was marching with the veterans in the parade along the park side of the street, the medals like patches of color on his chest.

And in a grove deep in the park, Billy began to cry again. To cry for his father and the lifelong trap of the lie. He

PETE HAMILL

had no idea how the lie had started, and now, of course, it was too late to find out. But he cried for his father's silence, his isolation, his inability ever to be plain Paulie Fitzgerald. And when he stopped crying, Billy thought that it had been a tough, hard life for his father, after he had shouldered the role, assumed it, and played it out for a lifetime, living every hour of his day with the knowledge that, at any moment, he could be found out. And in that moment, deep in the empty park, Billy Fitzgerald loved his father more than ever.

The next day, there was a Funeral Mass for Paulie Fitzgerald. The coffin was draped with an American flag and there was an honor guard from the American Legion. The organist played "America the Beautiful," and Billy's mother was comforted by her son's decision to take the body to St. John's after all. At the end of the Requiem Mass, Billy Fitzgerald, the bearer now and forever of his father's terrible secret, placed his hands on the shoulders of his sons.

"Remember," he said to them as the Mass ended. "Your grandfather was a hero of the war. A real American hero. Remember that. Don't ever forget it."

The Final Score

THE LITTLE GRAY-HAIRED MAN walked into Rattigan's a few minutes before closing time and went straight to the bar. He was wearing a navy peacoat and faded jeans, and bounced when he walked. He was carrying a Pan Am flight bag. Jabbo Collins knew him right away.

"Harry Willis," Jabbo whispered, reaching across the bar with both hands to grip the little man's shoulders. "I don't believe it."

"I've been lookin' for ya for weeks," Harry Willis said. "You ain't easy to find, Jabbo. Nobody in the old neighborhood knew where you was. Except Father Conners. He knew."

"He knows everything," Jabbo said, and smiled. He glanced at his customers: Fitzie was asleep, with his head on his forearms, and Old Margaret was humming the words to "Mona Lisa." Jabbo whispered: "When did you get out?"

"Three weeks ago," Harry said, laughing in that high-pitched way that always sounded to Jabbo like the sound of a bird. Jabbo shook his head, ran a hand through his thinning hair, and began to close for the night. He put a shot glass and a bottle of Dewar's in front of Harry Willis, wiped off the bar, woke up Fitzie and led him to the door, then waited while Old Margaret threw down her nightcap, gathered her coat, purse, and dignity, and walked into the night. Jabbo locked the door and turned to embrace Harry Willis.

"Eight years," Jabbo said, his old swimmer's body swelling with a deep breath as he stepped back. "I thought three years was bad. But eight…I don't know how the hell you didn't go crazy, Harry."

"Maybe I did," Harry said, and threw down a shot. Jabbo turned off all the lights except the night-light over the register; he stashed the night's receipts under the floorboards; he removed his apron and poured himself a shot and a beer. All through this, Harry was talking. He talked about the people they knew when they were young, and the good times they all had. He talked most about the summers, when Jabbo was the greatest swimmer in the history of Coney Island, and of the Sunset Park pool and Red Hook, too. Jabbo laughed at that, and talked about the women they once knew, remembering all their names and who they married, and which ones were divorced, and the few that were already dead. And Harry talked about the first job he and Jabbo pulled, at the Aladdin Carpet Company one Saturday night, carrying away four rugs, selling them for the price of a couple of pairs of pegged pants.

"Dumb kids," Jabbo said.

"I don't know," Harry said. "We did time. That's as dumb as you can get."

There was a long, silent moment. Then Harry said: "Let me ask you something, Jabbo. Would you—"

"Forget it, Harry. Don't even ask. I'm through with alla that. I been clean for five years and I'm gonna die that way, Harry. I don't make much more here, but it's mine. I'm single. I got only my own mouth to feed. I got a nice little apartment. I'm never goin' back to the can."

"You never let me ask the question."

Jabbo sighed and said: "You don't have to, Harry. I know you. I see what's in your face, Harry. It's a scheme, Harry. And schemes are trouble, Harry, and I don't want trouble anymore."

Harry took a pack of Pall Malls from his pocket and lit one with a book match. He inhaled, sipped the whiskey. Then he said, "You remember the last job?"

"Yours, Harry?" Jabbo said. "Or mine?"

"The one I did."

"I never got to talk to you about it, Harry. Remember? You pulled the job and they grabbed you the next day."

"Yeah," Harry said. "But they never got the swag. Remember that part? Remember how the papers said it was worth fifty grand? I mean, fifty thousand dollars' worth of jewelry. Remember that part?"

Jabbo squinted and reached for Harry's Pall Malls.

"Well," Harry said. "I know where the stuff is."

Jabbo said, "You're kidding me."

"You got a car?"

"I do," Jabbo said. "A piece of junk, but it runs."

"Let's go for a ride."

They drove through the empty Brooklyn streets, heading down off the Slope toward the waterfront. Harry gave directions and talked all the way. He talked about the old days, and the fun they had in the Cube Steak on 9th Street, and the night Jabbo flattened Danny Mac in Bickford's and the night Cacciatore the Cop and his partner, Bill Whalen, locked them up for burglarizing the RKO Prospect. Harry talked about Ocean Tide, too, out at the end of Coney Island, and how terrible he felt because he couldn't swim, and how proud he was of Jabbo the day he raced Vinnie McAleer out past the third barrel, and thought Jabbo wouldn't stop swimming until he reached Europe.

"That was all a long time ago," Jabbo said. And then he slowed the car and looked ahead at the Columbia Street dock.

"It's out there," Harry said.

"In the bay?"

"In a metal box, nailed to a piling under the pier."

Jabbo laughed and stopped the car. "You're out of your mind, Harry," he said. "It couldn't be there after eight years. The tide woulda ripped it away. Kids woulda found it."

"I think it's there," Harry said. "Charlie Barrett put it there for me. Remember him? Big guy, good swimmer. Got killed in a stickup right after. Down in Florida. He told me an atom bomb might take it away, nothin' else."

"If he knew where it was, he'd'a taken it himself, Harry," Jabbo said.

"I put him on the Greyhound that night, Jabbo. He got killed in Lauderdale two days later. When'd he have time?"

Jabbo thought about this, and then stepped out of the car. Harry did, too, carrying the flight bag. They could smell the sea, and hear the ding-dinging of buoys, and see the skyline to the right and the lights of Staten Island and Jersey beyond. They walked to the end of the pier. The water was black and glossy. There was no moon.

"I've been seeing Mary Larkin," Harry said, counting pilings at the end of the pier. "She'd divorced, you know. Kids grown up. We get this score, Jabbo, me and her are gonna go south. Orlando, St. Pete. I'll have a grubstake, maybe buy a car, a 7-Eleven, something like that. Hell, fifty grand then must be worth three hundred *G*s today." He stopped at the seventh piling. "This is the one."

"And?"

"All you gotta do is go down and get it."

Jabbo shook his head, smiling thinly, as he looked down at the swirling black water, fifteen feet below the pier.

"I'm forty-nine years old, Harry," he said. "I'm not what I was. How do I get back up? And what do I use to pry the box off the piling? Presuming the box is even *there*... It's nuts, Harry. Let's go get eggs."

Harry opened the flight bag and removed a coil of heavy rope, a claw hammer, a face mask.

"I'll give you half," he said.

Jabbo looked at the rope and tools, walked to the edge of the pier, gazed off at the black harbor. Then he started unbuttoning his coat. "What the hell," he said. He tied one end of the rope around a piling. Five minutes later, barefoot, masked, the hammer in hand, Jabbo stood at the edge of the pier. "See ya," he said, and went over.

Harry stared at the roiled water, held his breath as if in sympathy, then saw Jabbo's head come up, gasping for breath. Jabbo gulped, his legs shimmering and pale in the blackness, then bent over and dived again. When he came up again for air, he was fifteen feet away from the pier. A tide was running. He bent and dove, and this time was under a long time. Harry banged his hands together, tense and cold. There was no sign of Jabbo. Impossible. He couldn't be under this long.

And then he saw him, maybe forty feet out, shouting something Harry couldn't understand, just his head bobbing in the water, receding, going out. The tide was ripping along now. And then above Jabbo's head, he saw the box. Jabbo waved it once. Then he was gone.

"Jabbo!" Harry shouted. And then screamed: "Jabbo!" He heard nothing but the dinging of the buoys and the tide slapping against the pilings, and the distant moaning of a foghorn. And he thought: I've got to get out of here. I've got to go to the palm trees and the sun. He looked one last time at the harbor, which was as flat and black and final as death, and then he began to run.

Gone

WHETHER HE WAS AWAKE or asleep, the New York craziness never left Hirsch alone. Sometimes he tried to tell his wife, Margaret, about his dreams—the dark roaring tunnels, the gleaming yellow eyes of the leopard perched in the back-yard tree, the baby with the metal tongue who never stopped screaming. She would always cut him off. "Hirsch," she would say. "Calm down. You're letting it get to you, Hirsch. You're sounding paranoid, Hirsch."

"Yes," Hirsch would say. "But I do have enemies."

Waking, a mask of calm pasted to his face, Hirsch would leave for the advertising agency promptly each morning at nine. He no longer took the subway from Brooklyn Heights. Junkies waited in the doorways near the station, he thought, and the subway was itself a brutal morning

155

assault, an iron purgatory jammed with knife artists, hammer swingers, lobotomized crazies. They, too, inhabited his dreams, spraying paint down his throat, ramming switchblades into his heart, slicing him with smiles on their faces. Them. He was afraid of Them. Blacks and whites, people speaking mysterious languages, young men with eyes full of ancient evil: *Them.* Now Hirsch drove a car. A dark blue Oldsmobile. In a car, he wouldn't have to deal with Them.

Except that on this rainy Brooklyn morning, the car was gone.

"They've stolen the car," he said, coming back up the stoop of the brownstone, his eyes wild: "They took the car!"

Margaret calmed Hirsch and called the police. Then she arranged for a car service to pick him up and take him across the bridge to work. Hirsch waited inside the vestibule for the car, seeing killers and marauders walking down his street. They don't work, he thought; they patrol. They come around like rats, seeking weakness and vulnerability, and then they strike. I should have a gun. I should be able to shoot all of them.

There were two policemen in the reception room of the advertising agency when Hirsch arrived with his coffee and danish. Someone had broken into the office during the night and stolen two IBM Selectrics. The cops looked weary as they made notes in spiral pads.

"They wrecked the Xerox machine, too," said Ruthie, the receptionist. "Just poured rubber cement into it and ruined it. Can you imagine?"

"Yes," Hirsch said. "I can imagine."

Hirsch went into his office and sat at his desk. One of his desk drawers was open. Suddenly, Hirsch was afraid, as if one of the intruders might still be watching, examining his courage from a distance. They had been here, a gang of Them, invaders from the darkness, and they had rummaged through this small part of the world that was his. Hirsch hurried out to tell the cops. They were gone.

"You mean they didn't take fingerprints or anything?" Hirsch asked. Ruthie laughed. "Come on, Mr. Hirsch. They don't do stuff like that anymore." She powdered her nose. "They just fill out the forms for the insurance company."

That was typical. The craziness was now general. Thievery, robbery, violence; knives, guns, blood, and pain. They were as natural now as breathing. He examined his desk. Nothing had been taken except a cheap old onyx-handled letter opener his wife had bought for him during their honeymoon in Acapulco in 1958. Of course. If they could, they would steal only the small things that you loved. Hirsch was very still for a long time, and then worked through the morning in a gray fog, trying to infuse his copy with images of joy and romance. His wife called to say that all the forms had been filled out about the stolen car. Hirsch ate lunch at his desk, then napped on his couch.

Again, he saw the leopard in the garden, its eyes the color of typhoid. The baby with the metal tongue screamed in a higher pitch. He saw gray horses leaping from a pier and a woman in a white dress on the deck of a boat receding into a dark sea. He awoke with chills.

157

The afternoon was a blur. He went home at four, another car service picking him up at the curb, outside his office. When he got to Brooklyn Heights, he froze.

The blue Oldsmobile was parked across the street from his house.

Hirsch paid the car service and felt his heart twitching. He went over to his car, walking around it as if it were booby-trapped. No dents. No graffiti. But there was an envelope stuck to the steering wheel. Scrawled on the outside were the words: "To the Owner."

Cautiously, Hirsch unlocked the door and opened the envelope. It contained two theater tickets to *Dreamgirls* and a typed note.

To the owner of this car:

Please forgive me. Last night I was desperate. My mother was rushed to the hospital in New Jersey. She was dying. I tried to get a taxi to take me to Jersey, but none would take me. That's New York. It was too late for the bus. So I helped myself to your car. I know this is a crime. But I was desperate. I also know that I must have caused you great inconvenience and anger. To make this up to you, I've bought these tickets for you. I hope you enjoy the show. It's the only way I can think of to make this up to you.

The note was not signed. But Hirsch was suddenly flooded with a feeling of redemption and hope. His car was back! One of Them had explained himself. One of Them even had offered reparations. Hirsch rushed up the stairs to tell his wife, and she laughed, and told him it just proved that New York was not as crazy as Hirsch thought it was, and said that they really should celebrate. The tickets were for that night. They should use them.

"Why not, Hirsch?" Margaret asked. "We can drive the car to Manhattan, so it shouldn't get stolen again."

Hirsch immediately agreed. He made a reservation at Frankie & Johnnie's for after the theater, took a hot bath, dressed in his best suit. He thought his wife looked beautiful. He wished the kids, grown up and moved away, could see her like this. And at 7:15 they went off to the theater. Margaret enjoyed the show more than Hirsch did; he simply didn't identify with the problems of show-business people. But still, it was a Broadway show, a night in New York.

With an act of will, he ignored the crazies, the autograph nuts, the shopping-bag ladies, the junkies and knifers and walking wounded of Times Square. The lamb chops at the restaurant were delicious. They drove home in near silence, Hirsch saying that such nights were what made him love New York in the years when he and Margaret were young.

"Now, if you find a parking spot, "Margaret said, "it will be a perfect night."

"Maybe our benefactor, the thief, will hold one for us," Hirsch said, and they both laughed.

They cruised the streets of Brooklyn Heights for twenty minutes, and finally found a spot. They strolled home hand in hand, and Hirsch went up the stoop with his key out. He opened the door and right away knew that something was wrong. The framed lithograph of the Brooklyn Bridge was gone. He motioned for Margaret to wait, and stepped inside to the right, where the living room was. Everything was gone. Paintings, photographs, chairs, couch, lamps, tables. The kitchen, too, had been emptied. He went back to the staircase and looked upstairs into the darkness, but he didn't move.

"They took everything," he whispered, backing up, fear rising in a wide band across his back. "They've been here. They've got it all."

And now he wanted to run. Margaret took his arm, her face ashen, as they stared into the violated, plundered house.

"There's a leopard in the yard." Hirsch said. "It's in the tree." His eyes were wide with horror. "It has yellow eyes."

Then, in the quiet street, with a slight breeze combing the trees, and a half-moon crossing the city, Hirsch held onto the railing, threw back his head, and began to scream.

You Say Tomato, and…

DURING THE LONG DECADE after his mother died, Bondanella lived in a furnished room in Park Slope. The room was cozy and warm, with a small refrigerator and an electric stove, a clothes closet and a large chair. The bed was a bit hard, but Bondanella didn't mind; he was used to it now, as he had become accustomed to the bathroom in the hall. He had his sink, his TV set, the plastic hamper for his dirty clothes, and didn't care too much about the small pleasures. He had eliminated passion from his life as if it were a bad habit, and was frequently puzzled when he observed the tumultuous fortunes of the people he saw on TV. They lived dangerous lives, and Bondanella lived in safety.

Part of his sense of safety came from his insistence on routine, the only souvenir of his three years in the United

States Navy. Routine pleased him: it eliminated choice, it gave his life structure. And so each day he rose precisely at seven, did precisely ten minutes of exercise, spent precisely five minutes in the shower, and took precisely twelve minutes to dress. He walked six blocks to the Purity Diner, and always ordered scrambled eggs and bacon, rye toast, coffee, and orange juice. The subway sometimes gave him problems, because it refused to follow Bondanella's own careful schedule. But most mornings he was at his desk in the brokerage house on Broad Street at precisely ten minutes to nine. He took precisely an hour for lunch, and left the office at exactly 5:15.

There were, of course, no women in his life. Somehow all that had passed him by, although Bondanella had no real regrets. He saw marriage as a huge invasion of privacy, a disruption of safety. So in the evenings, Bondanella arrived alone at precisely seven at Snooky's Pub, ordered the hamburger platter, and was home in bed, watching TV, by nine o'clock. On Saturday nights, he was a cautious adventurer. He went to Chinatown once a month; he tried other neighborhood restaurants; he ventured to downtown movie houses. He was always alone.

Then, one Saturday morning, he saw the tomato.

He was bringing his shirts to the laundry when he saw it, lying with other tomatoes on a stand in front of the Korean fruit and vegetable store. The tomato stood out from the others because it was still brushed with green. An ordinary young tomato. But when Bondanella lifted it, he felt youth, warmth, firmness, and he knew he had to have it.

The Korean gave him fifty-one cents change from a dollar and slipped the lone tomato into a bag, and Bondanella went out, heading to the laundry, and was astonished to find himself whistling some old tune, with jumbled words, something about an umbrella. A tune he hadn't thought about in thirty years. He fought down a sudden urge to forget about the laundry and go directly home. But that urge was frightening; it was a clear threat against routine, and as he dropped off the shirts, Bondanella discovered that his hands were sweating.

"You're a beautiful tomato," he said out loud as he closed the door to his room behind him. But it took him a while to open the paper bag, to reach in and lift out the tomato, and then heft it in the palm of his hand. He took it over to the windowsill and placed it directly in the center. The sun was streaming in, emphasizing the highlights on the tomato's glossy skin. Bondanella trembled.

That evening, he went to see *Return of the Jedi,* sitting alone in the orchestra, baffled by the abrupt shifts in the story, unable to make sense of the dialogue. He went to Lombardi's on Spring Street after the movie, and casually ordered rigatoni. But when the plate came, and he saw the luxurious sauce, his mind filled with an image of the tomato, home in Brooklyn, alone on the windowsill. He poked at the pasta, but had trouble eating it; the waiter was upset, afraid that the food had displeased a customer.

"It's not the food," Bondanella explained. "It's me. I, er, don't feel too good…."

He went home, wondering what his mother would say if

she knew that he'd paid for food he hadn't eaten. Poor Ma. She led a hard life. But as he reached the house in Park Slope and hurried up the stoop, he was feeling better. He whistled the same half-remembered tune about a fella with an umbrella. And then, safe in the furnished room, he approached the tomato. He couldn't see the color clearly in the artificial light, but he thrilled to its firmness and youth. When he tried to sleep, he tossed about, filled with odd anxieties....

On Sunday morning, the tomato seemed larger. And redder.

"You...you're growing!" Bondanella said in an amazed voice. He swallowed hard, reached out, and lifted the tomato from its sunny perch. *She's growing up,* he thought. *She's changing....* The room was very hot now, and Bondanella felt tiny beads of perspiration on the tomato's skin. *Do tomatoes sweat? Or is it me?*

"You're the most beautiful thing I ever saw," he said. He filled a bowl with cold water and placed her in it, the water intensifying her pale greens and deeper reds. The bowl was kind of her room. Then he heard the landlady's heavy footsteps in the hall, and a sudden sharp knock on the door. He opened the door about a foot and stared at her powdery face, the mole on her chin, her rheumy, colorless eyes.

"Do you have someone in here, Mr. Bondanella?" she asked in her throaty voice. "If you do, I want the room."

He opened the door wider. "Of course not, Mrs. Reilly. I was just, you know, humming a tune, I guess. Or maybe talking to myself...."

She glanced past him, her colorless eyes prepared to prosecute at the first sign of sin. "Well, have a nice day, Mr. Bondanella," she murmured in a disappointed voice, and went out through the hall doors to the stoop. Bondanella's heart pounded. That night, he took the tomato to bed. He placed her in a small bowl so he wouldn't roll over and crush her, and he slept solidly, a man content and complete.

Now there was a new element to his routine. In the evenings, he hurried home, picking up food at the deli or the Chinese take-out place. He would gaze at the tomato while he ate, enchanted by her plumpness, her size, her quiet beauty. By Wednesday, the streaks of green were gone; she had survived adolescence. He entered her gently in cool, clear water, drying her with a soft cloth. And she inhabited his dreams. Once, he came home in a dream and the tomato was sitting in a chair, with sewing beside her. In another dream, she wore a veil, mysterious and sensual, peering at him from a corner of the room. And there was a time when she grew to fill the entire room, from wall to wall, keeping Bondanella in and Mrs. Reilly out.

"You're so beautiful," he said one night that first week. "You're so perfect. I wish you could speak…."

And then he knew that somehow he was sure to lose her. She was, after all, mortal. And knowing that, Bondanella became angry. He cursed fate, the universe, nature, God. He had lived a long solitude, and suddenly, absurdly, the solitude had been broken, and he knew that the union would be only an interlude. And knowing that, Bondanella held the tomato to him and rubbed her smooth skin against his cheek and began to cry.

*　　*　　*

The next day, he called in sick for the first time in nine years. There was so little time left. He took her to Coney Island, showed her the beach, took her on the Cyclone and the merry-go-round. He whispered to her in the wax museum. He explained to her about the clam sandwiches at Nathan's. They went home for a nap, and that night he took her to Yankee Stadium, trying to make clear to her the elegance of the game. The next day it was the Statue of Liberty, and Washington Square Park and the Empire State Building. She was very brave, and Bondanella had never been more charming, more full of life.

When she began to fade, he put her back in the bowl and laced the cool water with vitamins and herbs. He talked about winter trips to the country, about getting tickets in the spring for *La Cage aux Folles*. But nothing reversed; youth was gone; she shriveled into inevitable old age. Bondanella found himself talking to her without actually looking at her. He wanted to remember her the way she was.

He buried her on a starry Saturday night in Prospect Park. He found a thicket on the hill beside the Quaker cemetery, dug quickly and furtively with a soup spoon, and laid her gently in the dark, moist earth. He made a triad of smooth stones to mark the spot, and then said a short prayer. It was over. At the end, he looked up at the sky, at the infinity of stars, let out one aching cry of loneliness and loss, and then walked in silence down the hill and back into the safe routine of his life.

'S Wonderful

ALMOST EVERYBODY LOVED WONDERFUL Kelly. He had a wonderful wife and three wonderful kids and lived in a wonderful house on Fuller Place, two blocks from Holy Infant Church. They thought he was wonderful at the church, too; he was an usher at two Masses every Sunday, he helped coach the eighth-grade softball team in the spring and the football team in the fall. In the summer, he always volunteered to take the poorest kids to Coney Island or the Sunset Pool. He had a good job in one of the neighborhood banks. He didn't smoke. He didn't drink. Just a wonderful guy.

"You're so lucky, Carol," the women would say to Kelly's pretty young wife. "You've got a wonderful guy. Not like some of the bums we married."

Carol Kelly would smile in a shy way and keep walking

up the avenue to the meat market or the hardware store, trailing her wonderful children. There were, of course, some neighborhood dissenters. Most of them could be found on a Saturday afternoon in winter, peering through the steam-fogged windows of Rattigan's Bar and Grill, while Wonderful Kelly strode along the avenue. Dinny Collins, the bus driver, was one of them.

"Lookit this guy," Dinny said one afternoon. "Walking along, bouncing on the balls of his feet, breathing in that clean winter air, his skin all pink and healthy. Lookit the hair. The guy's forty but his hair's black and he looks twenty-five. It makes you sick."

"Come on, Dinny. Everybody says he's a wonderful guy."

"Oh, yeah? What'd he ever do for you that's so wonderful? I'll tell you. He did for you exactly what he did for me. Nothing. So how wonderful can Mr. Wonderful be? Could he make me fifteen years old again? Can he get me a raise? Can he pick me a winner at Belmont? What is this 'wonderful' crap, anyway?"

"The wives like him."

"They would," said Dinny Collins, who lived alone, a knockout victim in the marriage tournament. "They'll like him even more when he goes to heaven."

That summer, Wonderful Kelly extended his good works into the saloons. He said he was shocked by the high rate of neighborhood drunkenness, especially among married men. And he convinced the church to host a meeting of Alcoholics Anonymous in a large basement room on Tuesday nights. Then he started touring the bars, talking to each drunk in his quietly wonderful way about the evils of John Barleycorn, as he called it. Dinny Collins, of course, ignored him. What did Wonderful Kelly know about drinking? He'd never even been a drunk. But Wonderful did recruit some of the men, and when the existence of the AA meeting became known, a number of the wives issued ultimatums to their husbands: join AA or sleep in the subway.

After several weeks, a few former drunks could be seen nursing club sodas at the bars, even in Rattigan's. They told stories about the meetings, how everybody got up to describe what alcohol had done to them, the wreckage it had caused, the chaos it had fueled. Coffee and tea and doughnuts were served, and priests were available for those who wanted to make general confessions, cleaning their slates of decades of mortal and venial sins. Kelly was, of course, delighted.

"I feel like a million bucks," Charlie Deane said one night. "I'll never touch this stuff again." He was sitting on his usual stool at the bar. His pants were pressed, his hair neatly trimmed, his face closely shaved. "The wife even talks to me now. First time in three years."

Dinny Collins scoffed. "Wait'll you hear what she's been saying. You'll want to get stewed another three years."

A few of the converts did fall off the wagon; but many stayed dry. Kelly's stock in the neighborhood rose even higher. The monsignor of the church wrote a note to the archbishop, telling him how wonderful this fellow Kelly was; the archbishop wrote the bishop, and the bishop wrote to the president of Kelly's bank. Within the month, Kelly

PETE HAMILL

had been named manager of the neighborhood branch.
Everybody thought this was wonderful. Wives streamed
into the branch to congratulate Kelly, and dozens moved
their small accounts to Kelly's bank. The first sign of Kelly's
wider prosperity was a new car. A small trophy, to be sure,
but too much for Dinny Collins.

"Well, he got himself an early Christmas present," Dinny
said one Saturday afternoon that winter, watching Kelly
drive by, his wife and kids in the car. "What's next?"

At the AA meetings, Kelly gradually displayed other
changes. His hair was more carefully cut; he had two new
suits, wonderfully tailored, and had replaced his old Thom
McAn brogans with some wonderfully polished English
shoes. He was a banker now; a watch fob appeared in his
vest; a smile was permanently pasted to his face. Since he
could help with loans, everybody was polite to him; some
even fawned. The ability to grant a loan, or forgive a bounced
check, was, of course, a form of power. Wonderful Kelly used
that power judiciously, urging his supplicants to give up the
sauce, to go back to church, to be kinder to their wives.

Then one Friday evening in the spring, Carol Kelly appeared in the door of Rattigan's. The bar was almost empty.
Dinny Collins was playing a game on the shuffleboard machine with JoJo Mullarkey, who used to get drunk and eat
glasses before joining AA. Dinny looked at the woman,
who had never been in Rattigan's before, and nodded. Her
hair was blowsy, her light spring coat open, her eyes scared.

"Uh, er, uh, excuse me, but, uh…have you seen my husband?" she said.

"You mean Wonderful Kelly?" Dinny Collins said. "No, ma'am, I can't say as I have. He doesn't come in that often, and when he does, it's bad for business."

"I see..."

"You try up the church?" JoJo Mullarkey said. "I mean, that's where he is lots of the time."

"Yes, I...well, thank you, gents."

Dinny came closer. "Is there anything wrong?"

"No, no, nothing's wrong. I er, uh—"

And she hurried into the night. An hour later, Father Donnelly came in, also looking for Wonderful Kelly. They learned that Wonderful had gone out for lunch that day and had never come back. By midnight, two detectives from the 72nd Precinct had been in, and there had been two more calls from Carol. But nobody had seen Wonderful Kelly.

They didn't see him that weekend, and he didn't come to work that Monday. And when the cops descended upon the bank, and the big shots came over from the main office in Manhattan, and the examiners were finally called in, they all knew why. There was $276,000 missing from the bank, along with Wonderful Kelly.

This news appeared on page 1 of the *Brooklyn Eagle,* and its first effect was to destroy the AA meeting that night. Many of the men felt they would rather be honest drunks than disciples of an embezzler. Others felt that Wonderful Kelly had absconded with more than money; he had embezzled their emotions, too. Rattigan's was packed that night, loud with the sounds of men falling off wagons. Dinny Collins sat in righteous splendor at the bar.

"Hitler didn't drink," he said. "Stalin didn't drink. And neither did Wonderful Kelly. You don't have to be a genius to see the moral of this story, do you?"

When the details emerged, so did the neighborhood's anger. Kelly had worked out a system of faking the paperwork on loans. People from the neighborhood would sit at his desk and sign for a $3,000 loan, and when they were gone, Kelly would change the paperwork and make it $5,000. The bank said it would not hold the customers to the phony figures, of course; but many people felt that Wonderful Kelly had used them for his own gain. There was no pity for him, and very little for his wife and children. After a week, the wife stopped coming to church; the children were teased terribly in school, and there was talk that they were all going to move. And there wasn't a word from Wonderful Kelly. He seemed to have vanished from the earth.

Then one snowy Saturday morning the following February, Dinny Collins walked into Rattigan's with a *Daily News*. He held it up for all to see. "Will you look at this?" he said. And they all gazed at a picture of Wonderful Kelly on page 4, his hair longer, his hands cuffed in front of him, and a bosomy, handcuffed blonde beside him. The story was out of Tampa, Florida, under a headline that read: EXEC, STRIPPER NABBED IN BANK THEFT. The men standing grimly behind Kelly were FBI agents.

"He ran off with a *stripper*?" JoJo Mullarkey said.

"He sure did," Dinny Collins said. "I think it's the most wonderful thing he ever did."

The Warrior's Son

MOST MEN IN THAT neighborhood thought Soldier Dunne had been born in a most fortunate year: 1937. This accident of birth made him too young for Korea and too old for Vietnam, a stroke of luck that would have overjoyed the young men who had to fight those wars. But Dunne did not consider himself lucky; in fact, he was furious at his fate. More than any man in that neighborhood, he thought that a real man's greatest glory was war. In 1955, when a perforated eardrum kept him out of the peacetime army, his anger soared into rage.

"This country is soft as mush!" he shouted one night at the bar in Rattigan's. "We shoulda done what MacArthur wanted, just keep on goin' into Red China! We should be fightin' them right now!" He slammed the bar for emphasis. "Then they wouldn't keep me out of it! Not for a damn pinhole in an eardrum!"

But the bureaucratic decision was final; Dunne was doomed to remain a civilian all his life. And so he tried to make up for his loss in other ways. He bought most of his clothes in army-navy stores, appearing in smartly cut khakis in the neighborhood bars, his jump boots gleaming, his posture erect, his hair chopped short in a crew cut. He read military history, lecturing late at night about great battles "we" fought, and—during Vietnam—how victory could be won. When he was in his mid-twenties, the men of that neighborhood began to call him Soldier, and, grim-faced, squinty-eyed, shoulders squared, Dunne wore the ironic title as a badge of honor.

Along the way, Soldier Dunne married a quiet, pretty neighborhood girl named Marge Rivington, went to work at the gas company, and fathered two daughters and a son, each of whom was required to call him sir. He ran his home with the discipline of a company commander. Food was "chow," the kitchen was "the mess," the bathroom "the latrine." On the walls of the living room he hung framed photographs of Douglas MacArthur, Omar Bradley, and Mark Clark; a huge American flag billowed on a pole outside his window every day of the week; he mourned the death of John Wayne, traveled once a year to Arlington to salute the fallen heroes of the republic, and when asked his favorite song would always reply: "You gotta stand when they play it."

Naturally, his first daughter ran away and married an

ironworker when she was seventeen. The second lasted until her eighteenth birthday; she took $216 she had saved, flew off to Orlando, became a tour guide at Disney World, and married an animal trainer. Soldier Dunne's attention then fell most heavily upon his son, Jack. His attention, and his alarm. For Jack was not the son that Soldier had hoped for.

"He's a nice kid," he said a few times, when pressed by other members of the Saturday night infantry. "Takes after his mother, know what I mean? Reads a lot. Smart, that kid. Smart."

But the truth was that at home they barely spoke. Jack had refused when he was thirteen to call his father sir, a small mutiny that Soldier punished by confining the boy to quarters. Confinement was ended through the tearful intercession of Soldier's wife, Marge, whom Dunne started calling the judge advocate general. The boy said nothing. He never called his father sir again.

Worse, the young man resisted the military impulse. He thought parades were boring. He wouldn't play with guns. He laughed at John Wayne movies. He read his books, listened to rock and roll, kept the door to his room closed. When Soldier offered to take the boy on his annual pilgrimage to Arlington, the boy turned him down; he was going with his friends to see the Rolling Stones. Then one evening, in the young man's seventeenth year, Soldier Dunne came to his son's room. He was carrying a thick manila envelope. Jack was listening to music on a Walkman. He looked up at his father, but he didn't move.

"Hey!" Soldier shouted. "You think I'm standing here for my health?"

Jack removed the headset and sat up. "What is it, Dad? The Russians invade or something?"

"Don't be a wise guy," the father said. "I want to talk to you."

"Shoot."

"Look," the father said. "You're almost eighteen. You gotta start thinking about the rest of your life."

"Yeah."

"And I think I know what you gotta do. Nex' June, when you graduate, go right in the army. They're giving great deals now to high school graduates. You can pick a career. Electronics. Computers. All kinds of things. The money's great. It'll be the bes' thing ever happened to you, believe me."

He opened the manila envelope and took out a batch of brochures; the army, navy, and marines were all represented.

"Where's the air force?" the young man said, smiling.

"Ah, hell, that's not for you," he said. "That's not like the real service. But if you want, why don't you..."

"Forget it, Dad," Jack said. "I'm not going in the service."

The father stood very erect. "Why not?"

"I don't want to."

"You're a man, ain't you?" the father said, his voice rising. "A real man serves his country if he has the chance. I didn't have the chance. They turned me down. But you got nothin' wrong with you. They won't turn you down. They..."

"I'm going to college, Dad."

"College?"

The word fell between them like a sword. Soldier Dunne turned abruptly on his heel and walked out of the room and out of the house. At the bar across the street, he drank a beer in silence. College. Not even West Point, or Annapolis. Just college. It wasn't as if he had already served his country and was going on the GI Bill. He was just going to college. That's why the country was going to seed; these kids were soft; they had no discipline; they didn't know what it was like to fight, to bleed, to die for your country. No wonder the Russians were pushing us around everywhere. They had infantry, planes, bombs, tanks, trained killers, spies; we had college boys!

"You all right, Soldier?" said Loftus, the bartender. "You look like yer gonna cry."

"It's a sad day for this country," Soldier said.

"What happened?" Loftus said. "I miss the news?"

"My kid's going to college."

Loftus laughed out loud. "That's great. Soldier. Why're you sayin' it's sad?"

Soldier snapped to attention and said: "You'd never understand."

He walked out of the bar and marched through the dark streets of the neighborhood for hours, until his legs grew heavy and his hands cold and he headed home. As he crossed the avenue, he saw a figure standing in the vestibule of his building. He tensed, ready for combat. But when he came closer, he saw that the shadowy figure was only his wife. Good old Marge. Waiting up for me. He smiled and opened the outer door.

She stepped forward and slapped him hard across the face.

"You dumb son of a bitch," she said.

Soldier stepped back, a hand to his stinging face, and said: "What is this? What's going on? What's this about?"

"Your son's upstairs bawling his eyes out," she said. "That's what this is about!" Then, her face furious, she slapped him again. "I took your crap for a long time, Mr. Dunne. All this soldier-boy gobbledygook, all this yes-sir-no-sir baloney. Well, you drove the girls out with it. But you're not gonna do it to Jack. I'm not gonna let you, Mr. Dunne."

"What do you mean?"

"I mean I want you out of the house," she said in a cold voice. "Tonight. Pack your bags and go. Get a room at the Y. Sleep on the subway. I don't care. But get the hell out."

Soldier backed up against the wall, stunned, riddled with words that came at him like bullets. He tried to speak, but nothing came out of his mouth. His legs were gone, his head ringing. He slid down the wall to a squatting position. His post had been overrun.

"I'm sorry," he whispered. She looked down at him, as if prepared to shoot the wounded.

"Save it for the boy," she said, doing an about-face and hurrying up the stairs. Soldier squatted there for a long time, listening to the wind blow down the avenue. After a while, he thought: Maybe he'll at least join the ROTC. And then slowly, he rose to his feet and started up the stairs, hoping the enemy would accept his unconditional surrender.

The Second Summer

THE HADDAMS WERE SYRIANS and they ran a small grocery store on the corner of Eddie Leonard's block. It was not unusual to be a Syrian in that neighborhood in Brooklyn; there were Syrians at Holy Virgin School, and Syrians running other shops. Most of them were Catholics, and many of them had moved to the neighborhood after the war, when Little Syria in Lower Manhattan had been cleared to make way for the Brooklyn–Battery Tunnel. But some, like the Haddams, had come directly from Syria.

To Eddie Leonard and his friends, Syria was itself a mysterious place; they knew that if you went to Ireland and Italy and kept going east, you'd find it. But it was not clearly defined on the old roll-down prewar maps. It was like Lithuania, where Eddie Waivada came from. A lost country. Atlantis.

Eddie Leonard always felt this mystery when he went into the Haddams' dark, cramped store. The father was a gray, bony man, with desolate eyes; he spoke in his own language to his small, gray wife, and sometimes in another language, which Eddie Leonard later realized was French. Mr. Haddam's weariness infected his older daughter, a thin, pale young woman named Victoria. She had a large nose, large hands and feet, and seemed always to be chewing the inside of her mouth.

Dotty Haddam was her opposite, and when Eddie Leonard was fourteen, she started making him feel strange. She was two years younger and a foot shorter than Victoria, with clean straight features, hard white teeth, small hands, and the blackest hair Eddie Leonard had even seen. She rode a bicycle everywhere, pedaling furiously on a shiny blue Schwinn, and as a result, she had legs like a man's legs: hard and defined, with a ball of muscle at the calf. Those legs added to Eddie Leonard's uneasiness when she waited on him diffidently in the store. She was a year behind him at Holy Virgin School, but she seemed much older.

Through the winter of his first year in high school, Eddie Leonard didn't see much of Dotty Haddam. He was trying to translate Caesar's *Gallic Wars* into English and deal with the baffling abstractions of algebra. From time to time, he saw her moving through the snow, bundled up against the cold, head down, legs encased in boots. He saw her in the back of the store, watching a small black-and-white television set, or studying for school. But he didn't truly see her again until spring, when the stirring of the earth in the park and the broadcast of the Dodger games from Florida combined to tell him that the winter was over. Suddenly Dotty Haddam was back on her bicycle, taller now, her breasts fuller, her black hair longer. She smiled at him when he came into the store, and then he met her at a party in Betty Kayata's house, and asked her to go to a movie, and she said yes, and after that they were inseparable.

Across the thick, ripe summer, he explained Latin to her; warned her about algebra; taught her some Irish songs. She told him she wanted to be a poet, although her father objected; she showed him her poems, shyly at first, then with greater confidence. She had discovered Keats and Byron, and made him read them out loud to her in Prospect Park. She showed him where Syria was, too, pointing to maps that showed Damascus and Beirut. She had a postcard from her cousin Frankie, who lived in Beirut; it showed a lovely city on green hills, spread in a semicircle, facing the sea. Eddie Leonard pointed out that the map called the place Lebanon. She said it was really all Syria. Her father said so. The French had decided the borders, but it was all really Syria, although her father said that Damascus was an ugly city.

That summer, the war broke out in Korea, but they didn't talk about the war; it was in a remote place; it had nothing to do with them. But they were aware that the world was changing around them. People were locking doors that had never before been locked. A boy from 17th Street was found dead in the park, and for the first time Eddie Leonard heard the word "overdose." The word "they" began to appear in the common narrative of the neighborhood. "I hear they stuck up Barney Quigley's last night." Or: "They stabbed a kid outside the Y this afternoon." Or: "They robbed the Greek's." Another new word was "heroin."

Late in August, after a Saturday night movie, Eddie Leonard and Dotty Haddam climbed the hill above the Swan Lake in Prospect Park, and when they came down, they were no longer virgins. The rest of the summer was a blur; joy, fear, and amazement were combined with a sense of intimate conspiracy and, of course, the heart-stopping knowledge of sin. Moving among the others, on the beach at Coney or at the dances in the park, they felt special, certain of their shared love and damnation, guarding their dark secret.

But as the nights became chilly, Eddie Leonard started to dread the coming of winter. In that neighborhood in those years, no young people had cars or apartments or the price of a hotel room. They had the park and the beach. Nothing else. Eddie began to talk to Dotty Haddam about running away to Florida, about how amazing it must be to sleep between sheets in a bed, and wake up together in the morning. She resisted, retreated into silence, or told him that such ideas were foolish. They were too young. They would end up in jail.

And then one night, such talk became academic. Eddie Leonard and Dotty Haddam went to their hill. They murmured, kissed, collapsed on the grass. And then from the shadows, screaming in his language and flailing at them both with a broom handle, came Mr. Haddam. His eyes were wide with anger, and when he tried to strike his daughter with the broom handle, Eddie Leonard stepped in and knocked him down. That was the end of it. Two days later, Dotty Haddam was taken from the neighborhood to live with an aunt in New Jersey. Eddie Leonard never went into the store again.

He heard from her while he was in the army in Germany. The letter was brief, almost businesslike, and it told him that she was marrying a Syrian guy whose family came from Beirut. But she thought of Eddie often and would always remember him. When he looked at the date, he realized she was already married, and he crumpled the letter, threw it in a corner, and went into Wiesbaden to get drunk.

Then, one hot afternoon in the summer of 1969, he ran into her on 57th Street. She called his name, and for a moment he stood looking blankly at this short, heavyset woman, until she said: "Eddie, it's me. Dorothy…" He embraced her and they went into a coffee shop next to Carnegie Hall, and told each other how their lives had turned out. Eddie was a lawyer now, divorced, with two sons, living alone on the East Side; Dotty had three daughters, one of them a junior in high school. Her mother was dead, her father had gone home to Beirut with her sister. Dotty's husband ran a large grocery store in Washington Heights and they lived in New Jersey. She said all of this in a cool way, as if reciting a résumé. Then Eddie asked her if she loved her husband.

She smiled, and glanced into the crowded street.

"Love is for children," she said. And then looked at him frankly and added: "Maybe you get one good summer. If you're lucky."

They went to his apartment and made love, in a sad, grieving way, for the first time together in bed. And when they were finished, she began to cry uncontrollably, saying that they must never ever do this again. It was wrong. She was married. She had children. It was a sin. She'd never done this before, and would never do it again. She was back the following Thursday afternoon, dressed more elegantly, more carefully made up; and the Thursday after that; and every Thursday that summer. She lost weight. She wrote poems for him again. He gave her, with a laugh, a copy of Caesar's *Gallic Wars*. And they lived again the tangled emotions of that old summer. It ended again in the fall.

"He knows," she said that final Thursday. "He doesn't know who it is, but he knows. And he'll find us. I don't want that. For me, or you, or my daughters. Or for him. I hope you understand that."

And that was that. Until five years later. Sitting over coffee one morning with the *Daily News,* he saw her picture, her face contorted in anger and protest. She was standing outside a grocery store, a cop beside her. The story explained that her husband had been shot dead in a holdup. Two nights later, Eddie Leonard went to the wake. The room was packed with wailing mourners, and Eddie Leonard found Dotty in the front row of folding chairs. She was all in black, her face covered with a veil. He uttered the conventional words of sorrow and asked her about her plans.

"I'm taking him home," she said, staring through the veil at the coffin. "To Beirut. And all of us are going with him. It's finished here. Killers everywhere. Junkies. Murderers. We'll sell the store and the house. And just go away. Away from killers. Away. Away." She paused. "Goddamn New York."

A week later, she sailed for Beirut. The following year, the civil war began, and in the evenings, watching the terrible films on the news, Eddie Leonard would remember summer evenings in the placid hills of Brooklyn, when he and Dotty Haddam were young. He never heard from her again.

The Sunset Pool

THAT SUMMER, GERRY GROGAN was the greatest dancer among the neighborhood girls who shared our summer evenings. She was not conventionally beautiful: her nose was too violently sharp, her chin prominent, her legs too short. But none of that mattered. Geraldine Grogan was smart, bawdy, and fierce with energy. When she danced her intricately executed Lindys or hard-driving mambos, you couldn't look at another girl.

On those summer evenings, we assembled early at the foot of the two giant stone columns that guarded the entrance to Prospect Park. Someone long ago had dubbed those columns "the totem poles" or "the totes," and "the totes" were our clubhouse. One Friday night in August, the usual crowd had assembled to drink some Rheingold, listen to a portable radio, and discuss the destinations of the night. This was not always simple: we made decisions as some loose collective; a casual suggestion was made, debated, rejected, or embraced. Should we go to the Caton Inn or Diron's? Moriarty's or "over New York"? And, most important, what about Saturday? Coney Island? Or somewhere else?

Duke was there that night, along with Vito and Betty Gahan and Jackie Mack and the others. Gerry Grogan was with her boyfriend, a tall, red-headed Swede named Harry Hansen, from Bay Ridge. She'd met him dancing somewhere, and they were an unusual couple: she was vivacious, a talker, a beer drinker; he was tall, quiet, even morose, a ginger ale drinker among the barbarians. Vito nicknamed them the Mutt and Jeff Bandit Team, because the newspapers in those days were full of such partnerships, and we all forgave Hansen his dour silences because Gerry Grogan was so full of life.

"Let's go out Sunset tomorrow," Duke said. "I ain't been out there all summer."

"Sunset Pool?" Vito said. "You know, I almost forgot the place was there."

Duke said, "I like that sixteen-foot diving board. The girls' bathing suits come off when they hit the water."

Betty Gahan said, "You're disgusting, Duke."

"What was disgusting? The water? What?"

Gerry Grogan giggled, and Hansen gave her a look. Someone said the pool at Red Hook was better, and someone else said they'd rather be at Ocean Tide in Coney and eat sandwiches at Mary's. But the argument over Sunset Pool and Red Hook went on for a while.

"They both stink," Gerry Grogan said. "You gotta go in that locker room and take off all your clothes and—"

"I'll go with you, Gerry," Duke said.

"And then they have that key on that gray elastic band, with who knows what kind of diseases in it, and there's too many people and all those jerks from down the Hill, they're always throwing you in the water. Nah…"

Betty Gahan said, "He just wants to watch bathing suits come off, the slob."

"I just want to see some new faces," Duke said. "Every week it's the same old faces."

"You could get polio at Sunset Park, Duke," Gerry Grogan said. "It spreads in the water. Even Roosevelt got it swimming."

"In Sunset Pool?" Duke shouted.

Gerry punched Duke on the arm, and he backed away, laughing, and she said, "Duke, you get it in swimming pools. From all the degenerates like you that go there and swim."

Then Hansen said, "You worry too much, Gerry. You always think something's going to go wrong."

She looked at him and laughed. "It usually does."

Then Betty Gahan said, "Well, let's talk about it down at the Caton."

That's how we decided to go to the Caton Inn. There were about fifteen of us, crowded together in the cigarette smoke at the far end of the horseshoe bar. We started a dollar pool. Everybody drank beer, except Harry Hansen. On TV, Joe Miceli was boxing a muscle-bound black guy while Don Dunphy sold Gillette Blue Blades. Tony Bennett was singing "I Won't Cry Anymore" on the jukebox, and the place was filling up. That summer I was in love with a girl who didn't love me back, so I was alone, and this made Gerry Grogan uneasy. She thought every girl should have a guy, and vice versa. She also thought that everybody should get married as soon as possible, and she was determined to be the first one in our crowd to do so. And Harry Hansen was the man. I asked her if he was going swimming with us the next day.

"I hate that Sunset Pool," she said, and I agreed. "But that horny pervert Duke has everybody hot to go."

"So go to Ocean Tide with Harry."

She turned and watched Harry make his way through the crowd to the men's room. "Let me ask you something: How come the guys don't like Harry?"

"It's not that the guys don't like Harry," I said. "I think it's Harry don't like the guys."

"Jeez, I never thought of that."

Harry came back and Gerry sipped her beer. Pérez Prado's "Mambo No. 5" was blaring. Harry said, "You know I don't dance." And she turned to me. I looked at Harry, and he nodded okay, and Gerry and I pushed through the crowd to the dance floor in the back room. She danced furiously, amazingly, never losing the rhythm or the beat, but weaving a dozen complicated variations in and out of the basic steps. She made me feel as if I had a fire hydrant in each shoe.

Then the tune ended, and she laughed, and glanced out toward the bar, and then Tommy Edwards began to sing "It's All in the Game."

"Oh, I love this," she said, and took my hand again, and we began to dance slowly, the floor filling with other dancers. "Why do you think he doesn't like you guys?" she said. And I mumbled something about how hard it was to be an outsider around our crowd, how we had our own jokes and words and how we'd been together since grammar school. "Jeez, that could be trouble, couldn't it?" she said. But I never answered. I saw Harry Hansen under the arch that separated the dance floor from the bar. He looked bitterly angry. Gerry saw him, too.

"I better go," she said. "I'll see you down Sunset."

With that, she walked to Hansen, who said something I couldn't hear, turned away, and started for the door with Gerry behind him. I went back to the crowd. Miceli had flattened his opponent in seven rounds. Left hook, of course. Vito wanted to know if I was trying to break up the Mutt and Jeff Bandit Team. Duke was complaining to Betty Gahan that all the Irish girls he knew were plain-clothes nuns. Billy and Tim arrived from somewhere. The beer flowed. The smoke thickened. I danced with a dark-haired girl from Flatbush and went off with her into the night.

When I woke up, it was almost noon. I ate breakfast quickly and went up to the totes, but there was nobody around. I saw Colt, the cop, and asked him where every-body was. "The bums all went out to Sunset," he said. "To swim with the other bums." I went into the Sanders and sat in the cool Saturday afternoon darkness and watched *The Caine Mutiny* and then went home and took a nap. When I came back to the totes that night, everybody was sunburned. Gerry Grogan was not around.

"She isn't feeling too good," Betty Gahan said.

"Sound like a bad case of Harry."

"No," Betty said. "She really doesn't feel good."

By Tuesday, we knew that Gerry Grogan had polio. Of course. The news raced through the neighborhood, and it's difficult to explain now what the word "polio" could do to people in those days. The fear, the horror. Just the word. Polio. At the hospital, they wouldn't let us see her for a while, and her family seemed confused, as if possibly ashamed that this had happened to one of them. We sent flowers. We wrote notes. But I didn't get to see Gerry Grogan until the following Saturday afternoon. When I walked into the ward, she was alone in a bed against the far wall. She turned and saw me and started to cry. I tried to console her, feeling stupid and clumsy. But then I learned why she was crying. Harry Hansen had not come to visit her. Not even once.

"The son of a bitch, at least he could come and say good-bye," she said. "That's all I want. A good goddamned good-bye."

She never saw Harry Hansen again. But one chill night in autumn, after Gerry Grogan had left the hospital, and after we had thrown her a welcome-home party, and after she'd begun the exercises for her ruined legs, Colt, the cop, walked over to us at the totem poles. He wanted to know if we knew a Harry Hansen. Tall, red-haired, Colt said. He was in the Lutheran Hospital in Bay Ridge with both of his legs broken. No, nobody ever heard of him.

"He's not from around here," Duke said. And after Colt left, we went to pick up Gerry Grogan to take her down to the Caton Inn.

The Lasting Gift

THE BOY WAS COMING home from Coney Island one summer evening when he saw lights burning in the empty store. The store was across the street from the Minerva Theatre, where the gang called the Tigers lolled through all seasons in their zoot suits and pegged pants. The store had been empty all winter. Now the door was open, and the boy could see a one-armed man and an old Italian carpenter hammering away.

They were building a large slanted structure that filled the store, and the one-armed man held nails in his mouth, forced them into wood with his hand, then flipped a hammer that was tucked under his elbow and drove the nails into the wood. The boy, who was then twelve, watched this for a while, and then went home to climb into the bunk bed with his Brooklyn dreams.

The next day, the framework was covered with great sheets of plywood, and Seamus Grady, the one-armed man, was in business. He was a sign painter, and on the slanted plywood drawing table there were now large rolls of paper. Sheets of poster board were stacked on shelves under the tables, and a taboret was thick with jars of paint, cans of water, brushes of all shapes and sizes. The man worked with precision and delicacy, making signs for butcher shops and toy stores, bars and dry cleaners. Things for sale. Prices. The boy felt an odd excitement, watching the first artist he had ever seen.

A week later, while the Tigers were singing songs across the street, he saw that the shop window was now filled with some amazing things: large blown-up photostats, mounted on cardboard, of comic strips. *Flash Gordon, Prince Valiant.* And, most astonishing of all: *Terry and the Pirates,* the comic strip he loved more than any other. It was drawn by Milton Caniff, who the year before had given it up to begin *Steve Canyon.* Tentative, afraid, as if crossing this threshold might change his life, the boy walked into the studio of Seamus Grady.

The one-armed man turned and peered at him through thick glasses; he was wearing a sleeveless undershirt and a headband to hold back the sweat.

"Yeah?" he said. "Can I help you?"

"Uh, I was, uh, looking in the window, and I was wondering…well, you see, *Terry and the Pirates* is my favorite and I…"

"Yeah, that Milton Caniff, he's the best," Grady said. He

had a heavy Brooklyn accent and pronounced the name "Canipp." He flicked his brush, loaded with red paint, and made a dollar sign in front of a 29. "You know why? He's an *artist*. He tells stories, good as any movie. He got great characters, great dialogue. Everything. The best, the best... You take Alex Raymond. He draws *Rip Kirby* now, used to draw *Flash Gordon* before the war. Beautiful artist. But no *characters,* know what I mean? No *story*. Canipp, he does it all. Hey, kid, do me a favor, all right? Go over the deli, get me a Pepsi. Ice cold, tell 'em...."

So it began. That summer, the boy served a double apprenticeship: to Seamus Grady, who lived two blocks away, and to Milton Caniff, who lived in the distant world of fame and accomplishment. The boy learned that Grady had been a letterer for comic books all through the war and had to quit when his eyes weakened. And one night, he showed the boy his secret treasure, what he called the Collection, stored in an old wooden chest in the back of the store. These were original drawings, twice the size of a published comic book page, in black and white, with light blue pencil lines showing where the drawings had been roughed in. Grady had lettered these pages: some of them had been drawn by a nineteen-year-old named Alex Toth ("He might end up better than Canipp"), some of them by a master of the brush named Joe Kubert, and some by Will Eisner, who drew *The Spirit*. He also had photostats, and scrapbooks, and his own collection of comic books and newspaper strips. He also owned work by Roy Crane, the greatest master of the Benday grays, made of dots, and by Noel Sickles, who had helped Caniff when he was starting. He owned Alex Raymond's old *Flash Gordon* strips, and *Tarzan* pages drawn by Burne Hogarth. "These guys are the masters," Grady said. "Nobody ever did anything like these guys did before."

For three dollars a week, the boy delivered signs, swept the sidewalk, washed brushes, went for soda and sandwiches. He started showing Grady his own cartoons, copied from Caniff and Crane, and Grady fixed the drawings and showed the boy tricks with brushes. He let the boy pore through the Collection now, reading all the *Terry* strips from their beginnings in the 1930s. Soon the boy's head was teeming with characters: Connie and Big Stoop, the Dragon Lady and Burma, Tony Sandhurst and April Kane, and a weird character named Sanjak. They became part of the boy's life, following him to school in the fall, peopling his imagination just before sleep. The Dragon Lady made him feel funny, and he would look for a woman like Burma the rest of his life.

"What kind of a guy do you think he is?" the boy said one snowy Saturday afternoon that winter. Grady was working on a sign for Gutter's Shoe Store. "Milton Caniff, I mean?"

"I hear he's a great guy."

"You think if I write him a letter, he'd answer?"

"All you can do is try," Grady said. "Nothin' to lose, right?"

A month later, the boy came running into the store, waving a brown envelope, unable to get the words out of his mouth. Caniff had sent him an original drawing of Steve Canyon.

"Well, I'll be damned," Grady said softly, holding the drawing up to the light. "Isn't *that* something?"

That settled it; the boy would be a cartoonist. Caniff had sent him a little booklet, telling young cartoonists to read Robert Louis Stevenson, and Kipling, and Dumas. Grady told him that he would have to go to art school. "Learn to draw *everything!*" he said. Through the winter, the boy read his way through the local public library, and by the following spring was making large drawings on newsprint during the hours when Grady left him in charge of the sign shop, while the older man did big window signs in a downtown department store. He always kept the door locked when he was drawing. All the boy's women looked like the Dragon Lady.

Then one evening in that second summer, while Grady worked at the A&S department store, the boy was drawing in the store. The heat was wilting; great splotches of sweat fell on the newsprint, and the charcoal pencil cut holes in the paper. He opened the door to let a breeze in. About one hour later, two of the Tigers paused at the door. Junior and Cheech. Their faces were bleary, and each was carrying a quart bottle of beer. The boy was suddenly afraid.

"Well, lookit dis," said Junior. "An ahtist! We got ourself an ahtist, right here in da neighborhood. The boy ahtist!"

"Whyn't you draw *our* picture?" Cheech said. They moved into the store, and the boy couldn't bring himself to move. Then Cheech saw them open the top of the chest, revealing the treasures of the Collection.

"Well, how about this!" he said. "Comics! They got *comics* in here."

"Leave them alone," the boy said. "They're Mr. Grady's."

Junior switched to a singsong voice: *"They're Mr. Grady's. They're Mr. Grady's...."* They started tossing comics back and forth, over the head of the boy, who ran back and forth from one to the other. The more upset the boy became, the more they laughed. Then they started tearing pages out of the precious books, balling them up, pitching them to each other, while Cheech echoed the old radio show: "Ter-rrreeee an' da pirates!" They found the precious originals, neatly stacked on the bottom of the trunk, and started scaling them through the air. Then Cheech put his thumb over the top of his bottle, shook it up violently, and let the hot beer fly at Junior. The beer cascaded over Junior's head and spattered across some unfinished signs. The colors ran like blood.

The boy flew at Junior, frantically throwing small punches, crazy with rage and grief, and Junior shoved him toward Cheech, and Cheech kicked him, and then Junior knocked him down. They were in a snarling fury now, and they pulled over the taboret, spilling poster colors and water over the floor and onto the ruined comics. They sprayed the signs one final time with beer, and went laughing into the evening.

The boy sat there crying harder than he ever had before.

He was still there when Grady came in, and he tried to explain, but Grady exploded in injured anger: "Why'd you leave the *door* open? Why'd you *come* here, anyway? Lookit this place! You know how long it took me to save this stuff? Why'd you *come* here? Why? Why?"

The boy ran out to the darkening street. He never went back. That winter, he took another route to school because he couldn't look at the sign shop ever again without thinking of that terrible summer evening when he'd opened the door to blasphemy. He didn't become a cartoonist, either, but he had learned things in that shop that he carried with him for the rest of his life. In that place in the gardens of Brooklyn, a one-armed man had given him art.

The Man with the Blue Guitar

LATER, AFTER THE TERRIBLE thing had happened, people in the neighborhood remembered the day that Andreas Vlastopoulos had arrived among them. Marie from the dry cleaner's remembered that he wore faded jeans and a crisp white shirt, and that it was early summer and the sun gleamed on his yellow hair. Mrs. Caputo remembered that he asked her for directions to the Griffin house, and that his accent was thick and strange, because it wasn't a German or a squarehead accent and he was so blond. George, the bartender at Rattigan's, remembered seeing the young man staring up at buildings and street signs as if he were lost. Some remembered his blue eyes, others his battered brown canvas suitcase, tied shut with a rope. They all remembered the blue guitar.

"He finally went into Mary Griffin's," George said later.

"I remember thinkin' there was somethin' wrong with the way he looked. It wasn't just he was a big handsome guy; hell, there's lots of big handsome guys in this neighborhood. No, this guy was, I don't know how to say it. Beautiful?"

The young man—he was nineteen that summer—took a room in the back of Mary Griffin's house, which was the first building on the street below the avenue, one of two wedged between the tenements and a large garage. Since the tenements along the avenue had no backyards, their clotheslines stretched across the space above Mary Griffin's yard, and that of the Chinese house beside hers, to hooks drilled into the wall of the garage. The clotheslines were always full, blocking the sun. And on the top floor of one of the tenements, living alone with her six-year-old son, was the Widow Musmanno.

"She shouldn't live like that, alone," Mrs. Caputo used to say. "It ain't right. She married a bum and the bum got killed. But why should she pay the rest of her life? His family says she can't go out, she gotta wear black like an old lady. Hey, this ain't the old country. This is America. It ain't right. A young woman like that. A pretty girl like that…"

But for two years, Widow Musmanno had lived her sentence of solitude, worrying about her son as he played in the street, scrubbing the apartment, mumbling prayers in church each morning for her husband, and washing clothes. She ate too much. She added pounds. And then one day, that first week after the young man's arrival, she was hanging clothes on the line and glanced down into the yard and saw Andreas Vlastopoulos.

He was sitting alone on the wooden back steps and he was playing the blue guitar. The guitar was the blue of spring skies, the blue of postcard skies, the blue of the Aegean. The sounds he made were sorrowful and melancholy, and when he began to sing to himself, his voice ached with loss. Widow Musmanno did not understand the words, but she felt that somehow they were aimed directly at her and they made her ache, too. She stepped back from the window, and from the shadow behind the curtain looked down at the beautiful young man. She watched for almost a minute. And then she began furiously to scrub the table, to clean the refrigerator, to polish glasses and dust bureaus. When, a few hours later, her son came up from the street, he found her lying on her vast bed and when her eyes opened to look at him, they were sore and red.

"He'd come in every Monday morning," said Marie from the dry cleaner. "Always six shirts, medium starch, and a suit, always nice and polite. One day, one shirt. One week, one suit. He didn't flirt. He was the kind didn't know how good-lookin' he was. He told me he worked nights in a restaurant over New York, and he used to laugh at his bad English. He was a Greek, the kid. And tell the truth, it was hard to keep your eyes off him."

On the morning of her thirty-first birthday, after her son left for Coney Island with his Uncle Frank, Widow Musmanno was hanging wash while Vlastopolous played in the yard below. She heard the aching notes. Her thick body trembled. Suddenly, a piece of wash slipped from her hands and fell three stories into the yard. Vlastopolous glanced at the fallen piece, then up at Widow Musmanno, frozen in her window frame, and he smiled. He walked over and picked up the fallen piece. It was a woman's slip. He waved it like a wet silky pink flag at Widow Musmanno and explained with a gesture that he would bring it up to her. She shook her head no, almost desperately pointing to herself and then to him, meaning that she would come down. But Vlastopolous just smiled and went into the back door of the Griffin house with the wet woman's slip and his blue guitar. He went out into the street and found her building on the avenue and went up the hot dark stairs to the top floor and she came to the door, her hair swiftly brushed, her cheeks swiftly powdered, and she looked at him and that was the beginning of that.

There were few secrets in that neighborhood, and soon many people knew about Widow Musmanno and the beautiful young man with the blue guitar. They knew from the look on her face, the freshness of her color, and the way she began to dress again as she had before the death of her husband, in mauve and pink and yellow summer dresses. They knew when she stopped going to Mass. They knew from the drawn shades in the afternoon while the six-year-old was off at a ball game with his uncle. Somebody saw them in the hills above the Long Meadow in Prospect Park. Sitting under a tree, eating sandwiches while the young man played the blue guitar. And one hot night, Sadie Genlot climbed to the roof for air and saw them a few tenements away, leaning on a chimney, holding hands and staring at the glittering towers of Manhattan.

Of course, the old women gossiped about Widow Musmanno; it was too bad, they said, that she had gone "that way"; she sure wasn't showing proper respect for her poor husband. But most of the younger women approved, and a few were envious. There was nobody in any of their lives who announced himself with a blue guitar.

"The trouble was, how long could it go on?" Mrs. Caputo said. "It was the husband's brother was the problem. Frank. He took over when the brother died. He paid the bills. He was like a father to the kid. That was the trouble...."

Late one Saturday night, Vlastopoulos came out of Widow Musmanno's building. At the corner, as he turned toward Mary Griffin's house, he saw two men in gray hats sitting in a Cadillac. They were staring at him. A few days later, he came up from the subway and saw the same two men peering at him from behind the café curtains of a bar called Fitzgerald's. One of them nodded. Late that night, after the boy was long asleep, Vlastopolous mentioned the two men to Widow Musmanno.

"Oh, my God," she said, the words more prayer than exclamation. And then, after a long silence, she told the young man that it was all over between them and she could never see him again. He protested; she insisted. He said that she was grown up, she lived in a free country, she could do what she wanted with men. He said that if marriage was the problem, then they would get married. But Widow Musmanno turned her face and whispered that there were some things he would never understand. And Vlastopoulos answered that no matter what she said he would be around to see her again the following night. She took his beautiful face in her hands and kissed him on the mouth.

They found him the next morning on his back in the yard, as broken as the blue guitar beneath him. The police decided that he must have fallen from the roof of the tenement, and nobody in the neighborhood offered any other theory. But when the ambulance came from Kings County to take him to the morgue, Mrs. Caputo began to cry and so did Marie from the dry cleaner's and Mary Griffin, too. They waited around and after a while a short mustachioed man came to Mary Griffin's and said he was the uncle of Vlastopoulos and would pick up the young man's belongings. He was inside for about an hour, and came out with the brown canvas suitcase, and the broken pieces of the guitar. He put the broken pieces in a garbage can on the corner, sighed, and started trudging heavily toward the subway.

Late that night, when the bars had closed and the last buses had gone to the terminals and everybody in the neighborhood was asleep, Widow Musmanno came down to the street. She was dressed in black. She wore no makeup and her hair was blowsy. She pulled a shawl tightly over her shoulders, and then began to shuffle to the corner. The pieces of the blue guitar jutted from the wire garbage can. She looked at them for a long moment, and then removed them, all fractured wood and twisted wire strings. She held them to her breasts, the way a mother hugs a child, and then with a dry sob, she entered the country of the old.

The Hitter Bag

AT FORTY-EIGHT, SONNY MARINO lived with his wife and
three daughters in a small brick house up the block from
the Store. He wanted to live there until the end of his life.
In a way, the Store *was* his life. For more than twenty years,
starting in the Depression, the Store was his father's, and
from his first moments of consciousness, Sonny lived in that
plump, full world of tomatoes, cantaloupes, lettuce, pota-
toes, and garlic, inhaling the smell of fresh basil, or sum-
mertime apples, or ripe onions. When his father dropped
dead one morning, unloading a crate of watermelons, the
Store went to Sonny. There was no real choice: his mother
was long dead, his brother, Frankie, had been killed at the
Chosin Reservoir in Korea. If Sonny didn't take over the
Store, it would close.

So at nineteen, Sonny moved into the world of men. This was no easy matter, for Sonny was a leader of the Cavaliers. With Nit-Nat, Wimpy, Stark, and Midnight, he was one of the toughest street fighters in that part of Brooklyn, a defender of the holy neighborhood turf against the incursions of marauding vandals. When he was in what he called the hitter bag, he could beat you with his hands, cripple you in a wrestling match, or confront your ball bats with an iron pipe. In that neighborhood, his ferocity was legendary; so was his ability to absorb punishment.

"That's it, guys," he announced at his father's wake when the other Cavaliers came to console him. "I'm giving up the hitter bag. I got a business to run."

The Cavaliers did not long survive his retirement. Some went into the army, a few joined the police department, five fell to heroin. Most of the others married and moved away. And after a decade, Sonny Marino realized he was the last Cavalier left in the neighborhood. When he showed pictures of himself and the others to his daughters, they giggled at his "Duck's Ass" hairdo, his tight, pegged pants, his T-shirts rolled high on the shoulders with a cigarette pack tucked in the roll. They didn't understand how people could dress that way or do the things Sonny said they used to do when they were young and tough, feared and respected.

"Things aren't like that anymore, Dad," the oldest one, Rose, said to him. "The world is different now."

"I hope you're right," he said. "Go to college. Get a career. Maybe you're right. I hope so."

Occasionally, one of the old Cavaliers would show up in the neighborhood and Sonny Marino would be joyful. Nit-Nat saw his mother once a year, on her birthday. Stark drove in from Sayville with his kids to eat pasta at Monte's on Fifth Avenue. Midnight would come up out of the subway alone and pop a beer at the Store on his way to his sister's house. They always talked about old times, of course, the way soldiers do who once have shared danger and have survived. Sonny's wife, Maria, who was much younger than the Cavaliers, was amused; the girls always giggled. Sonny would turn to Nit-Nat or Stark and laugh at himself and say, "Hey, whatta they know?"

The neighborhood gradually changed, and so did Sonny. He had less hair and more paunch. He hired a Puerto Rican kid who could speak to some of the new customers. He learned a little Spanish himself. He added fresh *yames* to the vegetable section, cans of Goya beans to the shelves. He realized that the new people were not any different from his father's people, struggling with a language that was not their own, scrambling to make a living and raise their kids in a hard world.

Then a new gang began to form. They called themselves the Savage Lords and wore shiny black jackets and dungarees studded with metal. There were only a half dozen of them at first, but through one long, snowy winter they grew in numbers, and by summer there seemed to be fifty of them, maybe more. Most were Latinos, but there were some Irish in the gang, too, and the last of the Italians, and when Sonny Marino saw them moving together along the avenue, like some black-jacketed army, he felt uneasy, even afraid.

But he couldn't really judge them. He would look at the Savage Lords walking in their own version of the diddy bop, the weight heavy on one foot, the second swinging along loosely behind it, and he remembered the thrill of old summer evenings, the sense of power that came from being part of a large, hard group like the Cavaliers, afraid of nothing, makers of fear themselves. But looking at these young men, Sonny Marino, out of shape and growing older, couldn't rid himself of his fear. The Cavaliers were long gone, but this was the new guerrilla army of the neighborhood, and he knew that eventually he would have to deal with them. And he was alone.

"Did you hear what happened?" his wife said one morning. "They took over a building over Twel' Street. One of the abandoned buildings. They're movin' into the place. It's their headquarters, they say."

Almost every day after that, she would ask the same question of Sonny Marino: Did you hear what happened? The Savage Lords had wrecked Canavan's Bar, because the owner wouldn't serve them. They'd broken the doors off the emergency exit in the subway because the man in the token booth asked them to pay. A neighbor told them one night to stop playing disco music at two in the morning, and they set his car on fire. Harry Perez came into the Store, heartsick and desperate, to say that his daughter was forced to live with them in the headquarters, and when he came to take her home, they threw him down the stairs. The cops came around and made them move along in the evenings, but the cops couldn't watch them all the time.

In midsummer, Sonny Marino first heard about the "Lords Insurance Company." They were working their way through the neighborhood, explaining to the shopkeepers that for fifty dollars a month they could guarantee the safety of a store. "You know what that is?" Sonny Marino told his wife. "That's an old-fashioned protection racket." She looked at him gravely and said, "What are you gonna do about it? Go to the cops?" Sonny shrugged. He wasn't raised to call the cops.

The young insurance men came to the Store late one Saturday. Three of them: two were large, beefy, musclebound; the third was a short wiry kid with glasses. All wore black jackets. The short kid did the talking. "So that's the deal," he said. "Fifty a month and you're safe."

"Get out of here," Sonny Marino said, in a low, hard voice.

"Whajoo say?" the short kid said.

"I said get outta here before I break your head."

The short kid's face went blank, and then he turned on his heel and walked out, with the two muscle boys behind him. The short kid helped himself to an orange.

That night, it started. Three shots were fired from a car and shattered Sonny's plate-glass windows. A carpenter replaced the glass with plywood boards, and they came by again and shot out the glass pane in the door. Milk deliveries were smashed; stink bombs hurled into the Store;

a fire started in the cellar. Sonny broke his own code and called the cops; they explained about budget cuts, under-manning, asked him to press charges if he saw the kids who did it. After the cops left, Sonny went out to his car and found all four tires slashed. At the end of ten days, he got a phone call at home. A young voice asked: "You ready for a deal?" Sonny Marino screamed something into the phone about the young man's mother and hung up. That night, his daughter's boyfriend dropped her off, and then was grabbed on the stoop. They took him to the park, stripped him, tied him to a tree, and painted him with glossy red paint. Next time, they told him, they'd set him on fire.

His daughter cried, his wife talked about closing the Store and moving to Florida. But Sonny Marino said noth-ing. When they had all gone to bed, he sat alone in the kitchen, smoking a cigarette. And then he knew what he had to do. He reached for the phone.

Early on Sunday morning, before the rising of the sun, strange cars started appearing in the neighborhood. They had come from all over, from Long Island and Jersey, from the far reaches of Brooklyn, from the upper Bronx. One was driven all the way from Philadelphia. The drivers and pas-sengers were all middle-aged. They parked on the empty streets around the factories, and when they got out, they were hefting baseball bats, tire irons, slabs of metal. They embraced each other, patted their stomachs, laughed, smoked cigarettes.

Then, with Sonny Marino in front, the old Cavaliers started moving through the dark, empty streets. Ahead of them was the headquarters of the Savage Lords, the old tenement where the young hard guys slept. On the top floor, a light burned. In front of the building, Sonny looked at the others, at Nit-Nat, Stark, Wimpy, and the rest, feeling the old summer thrill, then turned and kicked in the front door. The Cavaliers came rushing in, and Sonny shouted up the stairs: "All right, tough guys! Let's rumble!"

The hospitals in that neighborhood had never before seen so many damaged people on Sunday morning. The fire department said later they could not save the old tenement and let it burn out. Sonny Marino opened for business as usual on Monday morning, his hands hurting, his body aching, a bandage across his left eyebrow. His wife murmured that maybe they should still sell and move to Florida. "Are you kidding?" Sonny Marino said. "I'm gonna live here the rest of my life."

Trouble

WHEN LIAM DEVLIN TRUDGED to the door of Rattigan's that Saturday night, the windows were opaque with steam. It was after midnight, and he was exhausted from a long shift delivering the fat Sunday newspapers. He hesitated for a moment. He could go and eat eggs at the Greek's, read the paper, then just collapse in bed. But he wanted a beer. One or two, really, and a little television, maybe some music on the jukebox. He opened the door. There were only three customers in the dark, warm saloon, but right away, Liam Devlin wanted to leave. The reason was simple. Jack Parker was drinking at the bar.

"That Parker is a real magician," the bartender, George Loftus, once said. "He opens his mouth and he makes customers disappear."

On this night, Jack Parker was drinking alone, facing

213

the beer taps, hatless, a thick mug in his fat pink hand. He didn't look up when Devlin came in. This was itself unusual. Jack Parker was a cop, and a bully; the bullying was done entirely with words, with wisecracks and scathing remarks. But when he had goaded people to the point where they wanted to break his face, Jack Parker retreated behind the gun. He never used it. But everyone knew he carried it.

"Fleischmann's and beer," Devlin said softly to Loftus. "You been busy?"

"Look around," the bartender said. "It's like the plague broke out here."

As always, Devlin started reading the Sunday *News* from back to front, absorbed in the stories from spring training. He sipped his Fleischmann's, and drank half the beer. Two old men drank in silence at the far end of the bar. The wind made a whining sound outside. Then Parker spoke.

"Who are you?" he said.

Devlin turned and saw Parker looking at him, a wet smile on his loose, florid face.

"Nobody," Devlin said. "I just walked in that door."

"George, you let anyone in here these days."

Loftus said, "Don't start, Jack."

"I mean, lookit this guy," Parker went on. "Those pants haven't had a crease in them since the Dodgers left Brooklyn. The jacket's like something outta Catholic Charities. And the shoes..."

"We can't all be fashion plates," Devlin said.

"And the hair," Parker said. "You let your hair grow down to your belt, I bet. Like Deanna Durbin."

Devlin said, "What are you? Fred Astaire?"

Loftus rubbed the back of his neck and leaned forward on the bar. "Hey, we don't need this, Jack. You understand? We don't need this. So Jack, leave the kid alone. And Liam, read your paper."

Parker downed his beer, nodded to Loftus to bring him another, and then stared for a while at himself in the part of the mirror visible behind the whiskey bottles. Devlin walked over to the jukebox. There were Irish songs by the Wolfe Tones and the Barleycorn, some tunes by Sinatra and Johnny Mathis, and a few rock-and-roll songs. He played "Sympathy for the Devil" by the Rolling Stones. The first chords boomed through the bar, and Parker spun around.

"Hey!" he shouted. "Shut that off."

Devlin ignored him and walked to the bar. He said to Loftus, "Hit me again."

"I said I don't want to hear that crap!" Parker said. "Turn it off!"

"He put a quarter in, Jack," Loftus said. "He can play the jukebox he wants to."

"I'm tryin' to *think!*"

"I could tell," Devlin said. "You got a real pained expression on your face."

"You wise bastid!"

He whirled, his eyes wild, while Mick Jagger and Keith Richards drove the Stones.

There was a gun in Parker's hand.

"You want noise?" Parker said. "I'll give you noise."

He walked over, very casually, and shot at the jukebox.

The glass face shattered, the record scraped and died. Then he fired again. The shots were very loud. At the far end of the bar, the two old men looked up. Parker turned to Devlin.

"There," he said. "How do you like that?"

Devlin didn't answer. His hand trembled.

"You want rock and roll? I'll give you rock and roll," Parker said, and walked back to the bar. "Didn't you read in the paper? Rock and roll is dead." He placed the gun beside his beer mug. Loftus gave Devlin a look that said: Don't move. Then he went to Parker.

"That's enough, Jack," Loftus said. "I think you oughta head home."

"Home? What home? What do I got at home? What's that mean, *home*? Answer me that, George."

"You got a wife at home," Loftus said. "A nice lady. You got kids. You got a nice warm bed. Go home."

"I had a wife," Parker said. He turned to Devlin again. "What are you lookin' at? This is none of your business, shmuck."

Devlin came at him in a rush, reaching for the gun, hurtling at the older man as quickly as he could. It was not quick enough. Parker grabbed the gun, spun, and slammed Devlin on the skull with the butt. Devlin fell, and then Parker kicked him. The two old men headed for the door.

"Stop right there!" Parker said. "You're not going nowhere."

They shuffled back to the bar. Devlin pulled himself up, climbing a stool rung by rung, as if it were a ladder. Parker faced him, an elbow on the bar. The gun was beside the beer mug.

"All right, punk. Now, I want an apology."

Devlin touched his head, and his fingertips came away red. "Apology for what?"

"For livin', punk."

"Go to hell," Devlin said.

Parker picked up the gun, his eyes wild now, and fired a shot into the ceiling.

"You better apologize, or you're a dead man."

Loftus leaned in. "Jack—"

Parker whirled and backhanded the smaller man.

"You shut up, George. This is between me and him. Me and this punk!"

Loftus said, "You're gonna get in trouble, Jack."

"Oh, yeah?" He waved the gun as if it were a toy. "Trouble, huh? *Trouble!?!*"

He fired at the TV set and missed. Then he stared at the mirror and the bottles, extended his arm, and fired two more shots. The mirror smashed and fell in huge jagged shards. Bottles broke, tipped over, bounced on the floor. The noise was ferocious. And then the bar was silent.

"Trouble," Parker said to himself in a flat voice. "Trouble."

His eyes were now blank. His body sagged. The gun hand hung straight at his side. He looked at Devlin as if he'd never seen him before, and then turned around and walked to the door, shoving the gun into his side pocket, and went out into the night.

"What the hell…" Loftus said. The two old men hurried to the door and left without a word. Loftus looked at the smashed mirror and started straightening the bottles.

"That guy should be in a nuthouse," Loftus said.

"Give me a dime, George," Devlin said. "That bum shouldn't be walking the streets with a gun."

"I don't have any dimes," Loftus said. "I don't have any nickels, either. The change is all gone. Go home, Liam."

Devlin went out. The wind was driving harder off the harbor. He went home for a while and then decided he couldn't sleep while Parker roamed the streets. He dressed again and walked to the precinct house, ten blocks away, his face frozen, his feet without feeling, the soft swollen patch on his skull beginning to throb. He hurried up the steps of the precinct house. He stopped at the desk and explained to the desk sergeant that he wanted to file a complaint against a cop. A cop named Jack Parker.

The sergeant looked at some papers. "Jack Parker? Forget it, sport. You're too late. They just found him on his wife's stoop, up there by the park. With a hole in his head." He shook his head sadly. "Seems like he eighty-sixed himself."

Devlin bounced a fist off the rail in front of the desk.

"That bum," he said. "He really did have trouble."

"The worst trouble of all, sport."

The Home Country

IT WASN'T A GOOD idea. Laverty was sure of that. But the girl had insisted, telling him that she couldn't have this New York week before college without seeing the place where he'd grown up. She could never go alone, she said, and she didn't know when they'd ever be together in New York again, and, so, after more of this, Laverty had agreed.

Now she was beside him in the rented car, three thousand miles from the house on the hill in Laguna; far from bougainvillea and surfboard summers and horse trails on the Irvine Ranch; far from the great blue lake of the Pacific. She was beside him, the map unfolded in her lap, her blond hair tossed by the river wind, and they were crossing the Brooklyn Bridge on a clear fall day and he was filled with dread.

"Now, this must be the East River, right under us," she said brightly. "Right, Dad?"

"Right. Except I'm not sure it's a river. I've read that it's an estuary but I've also read that it has been cut through at the top, and that makes it a real river. All I know is the water goes uptown and downtown at the same time."

"Amazing. And your house? Which way is it?"

"Away up there to the right. Where the green is."

He came down off the bridge, trying to get his bearings; there were government buildings on his right, new and ugly, and over to the left was Fulton Street, where the A&S department store was and Loew's Met and past them the Duffield and the RKO Albee and the Brooklyn Paramount and the Fox. They were probably all gone now; movie houses were vanishing all over the country, taking the balcony girls with them and the matrons and the gaudy dreams that filled the darkness. Namm's used to be down there somewhere, and Loeser's, too; I haven't pictured those stores in twenty-five years, Laverty thought. And remembered long aisles stacked with clothing, the elegant lettering on the Loeser's sign, the forbidden whisperings of the lingerie department, the sound of women's high heels on hardwood floors. And American Indians, all ironworkers, drinking around the corner in a place called the Wigwam.

The dread seeped through him anew. He had seen the photographs in the magazines, the documentaries on TV, showing the desolation of the Bronx and Brownsville, places where people like Laverty once had lived the plenitude of youth. He had long since imagined his neighborhood consumed by the summer fires. And he didn't really want to see the ruins.

"Now, what's that thing?" his daughter asked as they stopped at a light. He looked up at a huge glass-brick building on the corner of Atlantic Avenue. "I don't really know," he said, "but it's sure as hell ugly." And then she said, "Oh, it's a *jail*. Look, it has bars, and cops outside, and all those women waiting on line to get in. It's a *jail*, Dad!"

"You're right," he said, and remembered the time Shorty and Lahr were arrested for stealing a Pontiac, and everybody in the crowd went to the jail on Raymond Street and waited until they were released on bail; and how they'd all gone down to Coney Island that night to celebrate and they got drunk and started fighting with some South Brooklyn boys in a joint called McCabe's and Laverty woke up with skinned knuckles and no memory and knew that he wasn't going to live like this very much longer.

He remembered leaves burning everywhere that fall, in the yards of that neighborhood; and how when the other guys started to leave for the army, or for jail, or for swift, hot marriages, or for the murderous new joys of smack, he had stayed on at Brooklyn Tech, working late, sleeping with his head on the kitchen table, the books stacked around him, hungry for departure. And then when his father died, the dream of escape, of college, of the California he'd seen only in the movies, all of that wobbled, swayed, started to fall, and miraculously remained erect. He wanted to tell the girl, his daughter, about all of that, and maybe he would someday, but not now, not today.

"It's up ahead," he said, moving along Flatbush Avenue, passing the street where Diron's bar was and the Carlton movie house. He pointed to a bricked-up building. "My father used to drink right over there."

"Was he a drunk?"

"No," Laverty said, and laughed. "Not a drunk." He glanced again at the boarded-up place where the bar had been, with its noise, music, laughter. "He just worked himself to death."

"I wish I'd known him."

"So do I."

I wish I could have penetrated the Mayo silence, Laverty thought, the iron restraint. I wish I knew why he wore a hat after everyone stopped wearing them and why he always wore a suit on Sundays, and why he insisted on cloth napkins for dinner in what even he must have known was a slum. He worked for the Transit Authority, and for Bohack's on Thursday nights and all day on Saturday, and seemed always gray with exhaustion. He wouldn't move out of the neighborhood, even when at last he could afford to, and later Laverty knew why: the extra money went into the bank and when Laverty graduated with honors from Brooklyn Tech, the money was there waiting for him, the money that took him out of Brooklyn, away from home, and across America, the money that bought his escape.

Laverty had come back only twice: when the old man died, and when his mother followed seven months later. I wish I could have properly thanked him, Laverty thought. I wish I'd really thanked them both.

"Hey, this is nice here," his daughter said, and Laverty agreed, wondering if he'd made some wrong turn. There were restaurants along the avenue and boutiques and a bookstore and kids on bikes and trees in the side streets. Where were the empty lots, the gutted buildings? He drove on, moving steadily closer to the streets where he grew up. The streets of home. He crossed 9th Street and the hard light etched the buildings more sharply, and he began to fill with memories of a thousand mornings spent walking this avenue. A Spaldeen, he thought. I want to bounce a Spaldeen. Pink and powdery and fresh. Just that. Just a Spaldeen.

"This is it, sweetheart," he said, pulling the car into a spot beside a bodega. "That house, right there, on the corner. That's where I grew up. Second floor. Where that fire escape is."

"Wow," she said, and got out, and he told her to lock the door, and then he stood alone for a moment on his side of the car. In a way, everything had changed. Rattigan's was gone, and the old Kent cleaners, and Semke's meat market, and Mr. B's candy store, and Our Own bakery, and Sussman's hardware store. There were no longer any trolley tracks, no electric wires suspended over the avenue, and the Greek's coffee shop had gone, too, and Bernsley's heating oil and the variety store. But the buildings were intact. The names had changed, the people had changed. A lot of them were speaking Spanish here, not Yiddish or Italian. But it was here. The neighborhood. Laverty felt his blood coursing through him, the dread gone, excitement lifting him along.

"This looks pretty rough, Dad," his daughter said. "You think we should—"

"It's all right. It is. Let's look around."

He went into the vestibule of the house where he'd lived his youth. The inside door was locked. The mailboxes were wrecked. He rang the bell of the old apartment, but nobody answered. "Just as well," he said. "It wouldn't be the same anyway."

Then the door jerked open suddenly, and a middle-aged man with watery eyes stared at him. The man wore soiled clothes, and needed a shave, and the girl backed up in fear. Then the man's face softened.

"Is that you, Jimmy?" the man said. "Jimmy Laverty?"

"Frankie D'Arcy..."

They hadn't really been close; they'd just been boys in that neighborhood. But they embraced, and stepped into the bright sunlight, talking quickly, names and events and places coming in a stream as they went out into the street. Cubans now lived where the Lavertys had lived, but they were on vacation. "They're good people," Frankie said. "Hard workers..." Joe Fish had died, Eddie Gregg too. Joe Dee had four grandchildren now and lived out on the Island...

The girl backed away as the men moved along beside her, speaking a kind of code. She noticed that her father had begun to walk differently, his weight falling heavier on his right foot. He was gesturing with his hands, too, and his words were clipped now, his mouth pulled back tighter against his teeth. Laverty turned to her at one point and saw the abandoned look in her eyes.

"I'm sorry," he said. "It's just…"

D'Arcy hurried into a candy store. She shrugged and said, "Maybe we—"

And then D'Arcy was back. "Here you go," he said. He handed Laverty a Spaldeen. Laverty held it in his hand as if it were something precious, and squeezed it, then rubbed it against his face, and then bounced it. Once. Again. And then he turned, and threw it against a stoop, thinking: I'm home. I'm home. I'm home.

The Waiting Game

EVERYBODY AGREED THAT THE best fruit and vegetable store in that neighborhood was run by Teddy Caravaggio. In the summer, the stands and bins outside the store were plump with the products of the earth: oranges, grapes, apples, and melons, tomatoes, lettuce, onions, and leeks. The garlic was moist and thick; the basil was always fresh. Teddy's array of greens and reds and purples seemed lavish and extravagant on that avenue of redbrick old-law tenements.

His customers arrived from the farthest reaches of the neighborhood and some even came back after they had moved to Flatbush and Bay Ridge. When the A&P opened its giant store, Teddy continued to flourish, six days a week, from eight in the morning until eight at night. His prices were a little higher than they were in the supermarkets, but his goods had been chosen by a human hand, not hauled to market by a corporation. All the women of the neighborhood knew this and shopped at Teddy's with a certain passion. All except Catherine Novak.

"The tomatoes at Teddy's are beautiful this week, Catherine," her neighbor, Mrs. Trevor, would say. "Jim would love them."

"Thanks, Mrs. Trevor," Catherine would say. "But the A&P's more convenient."

Nothing was made of this. In that neighborhood of working people, the few who took time to notice simply dismissed Catherine Novak's little boycott as a mysterious failure of taste. They all kept going to Teddy's. One reason for his excellent reputation was that Teddy gave his produce the kind of attention that could only be called love. Some of the women remembered coming into the empty store and hearing Teddy whispering to the tomatoes or the melons. And he gave the store his total attention. Altar boys, rising for the six o'clock Mass, could see Teddy arriving at the store in his old Plymouth to unload the boxes of produce. He'd already spent two hours at the market. Arguing, haggling, choosing. The store had his complete fidelity. He lived alone in one large room in the back, where he listened at night to opera on the Italian radio station while hand-lettering the small signs that he would place in the morning among his beloved parsley, plums, celery, and artichokes.

Nobody ever asked why Teddy Caravaggio lived alone; it was his choice, after all, like the priesthood, and his choice had certainly granted benefits to the neighborhood. In fact, nobody really knew Teddy Caravaggio outside the store.

He was a thickset, blocky man, with black eyebrows and thinning hair. He never went to church, and had been too old for World War II and so was not a member of the American Legion or the VFW. Teddy existed only in the context of his wonderful store; he was what he did.

Then one morning in the fall of the year, Catherine Novak's husband, Jim, fell over at his desk in a Wall Street brokerage house. He was dead on arrival at Beekman Downtown Hospital, and the news shocked the neighborhood. He was, after all, only forty-three, a tall, good-looking Swede. Cops, firemen, ironworkers, and longshoremen might die young, victims of the risks of their trades. Wall Street guys were supposed to die in bed. Even the low-level guys. The wake at Mike Smith's funeral parlor was packed with mourners; the funeral filled the church; and everyone said that Catherine Novak and her three children faced the ordeal with courage and dignity. If they cried, they did not cry before an audience.

A month after the funeral, the VFW and the American Legion combined forces to throw a beer racket at Prospect Hall for the benefit of Jim Novak's wife and children. The great hall was filled early, the beer flowed, whiskey bottles and setups crowded the tables, and the band played old songs. Catherine Novak sat with her neighbors at a table near the front of the hall. And then, a few hours after the racket had begun, Teddy Caravaggio appeared at the door. He was wearing a new blue suit and new black shoes. His face gleamed. His thinning gray hair had been freshly cut.

He entered the hall hesitantly, even shyly, and eased over

to the crowded bar. The men didn't know him very well, but the women started coming over, happy to see him. A few were surprised, because they knew that Catherine Novak didn't patronize Teddy's store, but they were pleased that he had come in a show of neighborhood solidarity with the grieving widow. He said his hellos, murmured his regrets, sipped a beer. And all the while, he looked through the gathering nicotine haze at Catherine Novak.

Just before midnight, he walked down the length of the hall, staying close to the walls, and came over to her.

"Hello, Catherine," he said.

"Why, Teddy," she said. "How nice of you to come."

"Like to dance?"

She looked around uneasily, her hands moving awkwardly. The tables were empty as dancers moved to a tune called "It's All In the Game." She smiled, tentatively, and said: "Well, sure."

They went out to the crowded floor and began to dance. Teddy moved gracefully, but maintained a discreet distance.

"I'm sorry what happened, Catherine," he said. "If there's anything I can do, you know, give a holler."

"Thanks, Teddy."

There was an uneasy moment. Then Teddy said: "I never thought I'd dance with you again. It's hard to believe."

"I never thought you'd talk to me again."

"Me, neither."

"You're not angry with me?" she said.

"Yeah, yeah, I'm a little angry," Teddy said. "But not too much. Not like I was." He paused. "A long time ago."

"Yes," she said. The band ended the first tune, and started playing "Because of You."

"I'm sorry Jim died," Teddy said. "But you know, while he was alive he was the luckiest guy in the neighborhood."

"Teddy, please don't talk like that."

"It's what I believe, Catherine," he said. "Sometimes I used to come home from the market in the morning, and I'd go out of my way just to pass your house. Sometimes I'd stop at the corner, and I'd look up. And the lights'd be on, and I'd say to myself, look, there's a real life up there. They live a real life, Jim and Catherine, with kids making noise in the morning and bacon frying and the radio on and everybody getting dressed. I'd see Jim go past the store sometimes in the summer with the kids, and they'd have a baseball bat and gloves, and they'd be going to the park to play ball, and I'd want to cry. Sometimes I'd see you go by, too, with a baby carriage, or on the bus at Christmas, or in the car with Jim and the kids going to the beach. And I'd be sick for a day, or a week, or a month."

She squeezed his hands. "Teddy, I—"

"Why didn't you ever come to the store?" he said. "All those years, you never came, even once."

"I thought that would make it worse. I didn't want to hurt you, Teddy. I did it once. I didn't want to do it again."

"Well, maybe you were right. 'Cause you hurt me real good, Catherine. Worse than a punch. Worse than a bullet."

"I know," she said. "And I'm sorry. I thought I was doing the right thing, and it was wrong for you."

*   *   *

The ballad ended; an uptempo Lindy began. Catherine disengaged her hand from Teddy's and started to walk off the suddenly jumping, pulsating dance floor. He followed behind her. At the table she turned to him.

"Well, thank you, Teddy, for the dance," she said, forcing a smile. Her features had thickened in twenty-five years; her hair was scratched with gray. Teddy faced her, started to say something, then abruptly stopped. He looked around, as if certain that everybody was watching him; but the beer racket was roaring now, and nobody was looking their way.

"Will you at least come in the store once in a while?" he said.

"Of course," she said. "I know it's a wonderful store. Everybody knows that."

"I gave it everything I had."

"I'll come by," she said, and smiled. Looking directly at Teddy's aging, decent face.

"Well," she said. "Thanks again."

He started to leave, then turned and took her hand.

"I told you I'd wait for you the rest of my life," Teddy Caravaggio said. "And I did."

"I know."

His face trembled, he squeezed her hand, then released it and said, "I'm still waiting."

Then he turned and walked away, his back straight, looking proud, easing his way through the crowd to the door.

The Home Run

At 4:20 in the afternoon of October 3, 1951, Frankie Bertinelli took to his bed in tears and sorrow, and was not seen again in our neighborhood for more than thirty years.

On that stunned autumn afternoon, Frankie was nineteen, a thin, sickly young man who had pulled some terrible numbers in the lottery of childhood. Scarlet fever weakened his heart. Measles ruined his eyesight. Acne gullied his face. When Frankie was fourteen, his father was killed in an accident on the pier, and since Frankie had no brothers or sisters, he was left alone with his mother. She was a pale Irish woman named Cora. Sometimes, in the evenings of those Spaldeen summers, she would arrive at the corner, looming in a ghostly way, and order Frankie home, saying: "Remember, you got a bad heart." And Frankie would go.

When the Korean War broke out, most of us started the

long journey out of the neighborhood by going into the army or navy. Frankie, of course, was rejected by all the services, and soon was the only one of the old crowd left along Seventh Avenue. He took a job in a brokerage house as a clerk (his handwriting was superb and he was taking typing at Lamb's business school) and lived his friendless, womanless life with one intense and glorious passion: baseball. Specifically, baseball as played by the Brooklyn Dodgers.

"The whole calendar is wrong," he said to me one Christmastime. "The real year doesn't begin on January first. I mean, what's the difference between January first and December thirty-first? Nothing. They are the same kind of a day. The real year begins the day Red Barber starts broadcasting from spring training."

He was right, of course; the year did begin in the spring, and nothing was more beautiful than baseball. In his apartment, Frankie Bertinelli had compiled immense scrapbooks about all the Dodgers, and even about the prospects in the farm clubs at Montreal and Saint Paul and other towns peopled by Branch Rickey. He had saved every scorecard from every game he'd ever seen at Ebbets Field. On the walls, he had pictures of Reese and Robinson, Hodges and Furillo and Reiser. His bureau drawers were crammed with baseball cards. He had composition books filled with mysterious statistics of his own devising, stacked copies of the *Sporting News,* back pages from the *News* and *Daily Mirror.* When childhood ended and his friends went away, baseball was all that Frankie Bertinelli had left.

"I love the Dodgers," he once said, forcing a smile after a girl turned him down at a dance. "I don't need nothing else."

But then it was October 3, 1951, the third game of the playoffs against the Giants. On this chilly gray day, Frankie Bertinelli did not go to work. Frankie Bertinelli was genuinely sick. He had been sick for months. In July, Charlie Dressen said, "The Giants is dead," and everybody thought the Dodgers manager was right. But on August 12, the Giants started their ferocious run for the pennant under the leadership of the turncoat Leo Durocher. They had won thirty-seven of their previous forty-four games, sixteen in a row at one time, the last seven in a row enabling them to catch and tie the Dodgers. It was as if everything Frankie Bertinelli knew about certainty, even justice, was eroding. Leo Durocher had been the greatest Dodgers manager of all time and then defected to the Giants; it was as if Benedict Arnold could end up a hero. It was wrong. It was awful.

"This can't be," Frankie said after Jim Hearn pitched the Giants to a 3–1 victory in the first game at Ebbets Field. Frankie Bertinelli got so mad that day he threw his radio across the room. When he turned it on, half the stations were missing, including WMGM, which broadcast the Dodgers games. The next day, the Dodgers came roaring back at the Polo Grounds. Labine pitched a six-hitter; Rube Walker hit a home run over the right-field roof. The Dodgers slaughtered the Giants, 10–0. That night, Frankie Bertinelli was elated. But on the morning of October 3, he looked out at the gray, overcast sky and was filled with dread.

That afternoon, he sat in the kitchen, listening to the horrible Giants announcers on WMCA, while his mother made coffee and tried to get him to eat something, anything. Sal Maglie was pitching for the Giants, and Frankie Bertinelli could picture his face: lean, mean, shrewd, hard. Newcombe was pitching for the Dodgers, big and strong, but always something wrong, never quite what he should be. First inning: Reese and Snider walk. Robinson singles to left, scoring Reese; 1–0 Dodgers. This weird Russ Hodges says the lights have been turned on at 2:04. Lights! In a *day* game! Frankie Bertinelli sat on the floor. Newcombe is pitching great, but then in the last of the seventh, Irvin doubles, and Lockman moves him to third with a bunt single. Irvin scores on Thomson's sacrifice fly; 1–1. Frankie Bertinelli's stomach knotted, churned, flopped around. Then, top of the eighth, the Dodgers score three runs, and in the last of the eighth, Newcombe strikes out the side; 4–1 Dodgers! Justice! Certainty! Beauty!

And then it's the last of the ninth. Newcombe still pitching. Alvin Dark singles through the right side. Okay. So what? Keep the ball down. Get a double play. But no…Don Mueller singles to the right of Hodges, who for some insane reason is holding Dark tight on first with a three-run lead. Dread. Then Newcombe gets Monte Irvin to pop up a foul ball to Hodges. One out, two to go…And then here comes Whitey Lockman. *Walk him.* Load the bases, get the double play! Something about Lockman…and then Lockman slices a double down the left-field line. Dark scores. Mueller slides like a crazy man into third and breaks his ankle!

They're carrying him out through center field, all the way to the clubhouse. In the Dodgers bullpen: Carl Erskine and Ralph Branca are warming up. And Bobby Thomson is the batter....

"Bring in Erskine," Frankie Bertinelli shouted, while his mother moved around the kitchen. "Not Branca. Please not Branca. Thomson hit a homer off Branca in the first game! Into the upper deck! Please not Branca..." But Dressen calls in Branca. Clint Hartung goes in to run for Mueller at third. And it's Branca. "Walk Thomson!" Frankie Bertinelli shouted. "Walk Thomson and pitch to the kid, to that Willie Mays. He's a kid, he won't handle the pressure, he—"

And then Frankie went silent, and listened to Russ Hodges:

Bobby Thomson...up there swinging...He's had two out of three, a single and a double, and Billy Cox is playing him right on the third-base line....One out, last of the ninth...Branca pitches...and Bobby Thomson takes a strike called on the inside corner....

Frankie Bertinelli got up, walked around, leaned his forehead on the wall. He could hear other radios from open windows.

Bobby hitting at .292...He's had a single and a double and he drove in the Giants' first run with a long fly to center. Brooklyn leads it, 4–2....Hartung down the line at third, not taking any chances...Lockman with not too big of a lead at second, but he'll be running like the wind if Thomson hits one....Branca throws...There's a long drive...it's gonna be, I believe...THE GIANTS WIN THE PENNANT! THE GIANTS WIN THE PENNANT! *THE GIANTS WIN THE PENNANT!*...Bobby Thomson hits into the lower deck of the left-field stands....THE GIANTS WIN THE PENNANT! THE GIANTS WIN THE PENNANT AND *THEY'RE GOING CRAZY!*

That was at 3:58 p.m. At 4:20, Frankie Bertinelli got undressed, put on a pair of blue pajamas, and went to bed. Two days later, some kids found bags full of baseball cards in the garbage cans downstairs, along with old copies of the *Sporting News,* shredded photographs, torn scorecards. Cora continued to move in her dim way around the neighborhood, shopping at Jack's, picking up fish at Red's and meat at Semke's, and black-and-whites at the Our Own bakery. But nobody saw Frankie.

"He's not feeling well," she would say if anyone asked. "He's got the bad heart, you know, from the scarlet fever...."

After a while, nobody asked anymore. The years went by. Cora got old. Delivery boys from the grocery stores said that the apartment was very strange. A man was always sleeping in the bed off the kitchen. There was no sound in

the place, no radio, no TV. The shades were drawn. Sometimes, late at night, neighbors in the building could hear a
man weeping.

More than thirty years later, Cora Bertinelli died. She
was waked at Mike Smith's, and late on the first night of the
wake, I dropped by the funeral parlor. The large room was
empty. Cora Bertinelli was dusty and white in the coffin.
There was no sign of Frankie. I went out to the sidewalk
and a small, fat, bearded man was standing there, staring at
the church across the street. It was Frankie. He looked at
me blankly, and I introduced myself, and said I was sorry
about his mother. He looked tentative and lost.

"What about you, Frankie?" I said. "How've you been?"

He looked at me, and blinked, and said, "They shoulda
walked Lockman."

I followed him back into the funeral parlor.

Up the Roof

SHAWN HIGGINS, AGE SIXTEEN, 5 feet 11 inches and still growing, stepped into the kitchen of the railroad flat on the top floor right. He laid two wrapped sandwiches on the table. It was about six o'clock and he was finished with his deliveries from the corner grocery store, where he worked. The source of free sandwiches and tips. He could hear a voice coming from the new television set in the living room. He hurried in to see his Uncle Jimmy, who was parked in a ratty armchair, staring at the solemn black-and-white face of an announcer. The news was, of course, about Korea. That was all anybody talked about over the last two weeks. The new war. More guys being drafted. Others being called back, five years after the last war. The war was on the front pages of the *Daily News* and the *Brooklyn Eagle*. The war was on the radio each evening.

"'Lo, Uncle Jimmy," Shawn said.

"Yeah," Jimmy said, curling the fingers of his good right arm, but staring at the small set. Patting the white-haired man's stooped back, Shawn saw tears running down his face. They had to be tears about the war. The new war. The old one. The boy didn't know what to say and so said nothing. On the mantelpiece behind the television set, down at the left, there was a picture of Shawn's father, killed at Anzio in 1943, when his only son was eight. He was smiling, wearing his army uniform. Beside it was a second framed photograph, this one of his father with his mother, all dressed up at their wedding. She was gone now, too.

Shawn eased into his room, the only one with a door, the tiny room where his sisters shared a bunk bed until each got married, three months apart, and vanished into Long Island. The room was tiny and hot and smelled of his own dried sweat. The shade was drawn to keep out the heat. Beyond the shade was the rusting iron fire escape. His clothes were hanging off the rack below the top bunk, his shirts and underwear and socks folded on the old unused mattress. His books were stacked on the floor, beside his comics. A *Daily News* color photograph of Jackie Robinson and Pee Wee Reese was Scotch-taped to the wall. Two days earlier, the *Eagle* said that even some of the ballplayers could be called up for the new war.

Shawn removed his sneakers, khaki trousers, and underpants, then pulled on a gray bathing suit. He was tying his sneakers again when he heard Uncle Jimmy say "oh" once, then again, and he wanted to hug him. Out at the VA hospital in Bay Ridge, the doctors told Shawn last year that his uncle was okay, except for the shell shock. Christ. When Shawn's mother died just after the war, of heartbreak, his sisters said, he and his sisters had moved in here with Uncle Jimmy, who would take care of them. They learned quickly that they had to take care of Uncle Jimmy. One sandwich in the kitchen was for him.

Shawn dug out his hand weights from under the bed, a pair of eight-pounders that had once belonged to his father. Now the news was finished in the living room, and he could hear gunshots and horses galloping, as his Uncle Jimmy entered the Wild West. And thought: I have to get us out of here. Leave high school. Get a real job, not just delivering groceries, but real work. And make real money. Get a place on the first floor of some new building. Let Uncle Jimmy sit in a garden, and smell grass or roses, or go walking without help. Gotta do that. Gotta do it soon.

He inhaled deeply, exhaled slowly, told Jimmy he was going up the roof. Then climbed the stairs two at a time.

Shawn loved the roof in summer. The tenements were on the avenue between 11th and 12th Streets. They had no backyards. No gardens right outside a door. But on the roof, there was always a breeze blowing from the harbor, and he could stand there and see the skyline of New York, off to the right, and remember that night in 1944 when the lights came on again, on D-day, when the armies landed in France to kick Hitler's ass. All the women of the block seemed to be on the roof, and their kids, and a few old men, and someone began singing "The White Cliffs of Dover" and he heard those words about peace and laughter and love ever after. Something like that. Knowing it was already too late for his father. Knowing that Uncle Jimmy was there in that France and guys from all over the neighborhood were with him. Not one of them was up the roof that night. They were fighting the war. Shawn didn't know until a few years later how many of them did not come home.

He took off his T-shirt and faced west. The sun was slowly descending into New Jersey, and the sky was full of new colors, blue and purple and red, all mixed together, changing every minute. Beautiful. He did fifty curls with the hand weights. Paused. Did fifty more. Then faced the remains of the abandoned pigeon coop, where the birds once fluttered and murmured behind wire walls and now were gone forever. He did moves he had seen the boxers doing at the gym on 8th Street. Jab, jab, jab, bend, left hook. Jab, right hand, hook. The rooftops of the block's six tenements were all different. Different kinds of chimneys, some bare, some cowled. Some had clotheslines, some did not. Some were covered with gray pebbles, a few with raised wooden planks, others with tar paper. In the summers, they called those rooftops Tar Beach. People would get home from work, too late to grab the trolley to Coney Island, and try to spend an hour or two in the fading sun. On weekends, some of them would spread blankets and cover themselves with suntan lotion, all the while drinking iced tea or soda or beer. Tar Beach. For Shawn, it was just the roof. All of it.

Now he turned to face north, beginning his bends, touching his left ankle with his weighted right hand, the right ankle with his left. Doing each bend very hard. Grunting. Feeling the sweat on his face and shoulders and back. Feeling muscles tightening in his gut. Turning from north to east to south.

Then he saw a woman on the roof of the last house on the 11th Street end. A woman with long black hair, wearing a pink bathrobe. She was smoking a cigarette.

When she saw him staring, she smiled.

When Shawn first met Marilyn Carter on the roof, he was a virgin. Three weeks later he was not.

She lived in the apartment just below the roof and went down to fetch him a glass of cold water, introduced herself, and just started talking. That day, and on the afternoons that followed. She wasn't some beautiful kind of movie star. In the real world, who was? She was on the chubby side and her hair was often tangled in a frantic kind of way. But she had a beautiful smile, and good white teeth, and talked very clearly, without an accent. She definitely wasn't from the neighborhood.

"I grew up in New Jersey, way down, below Atlantic City," she said one afternoon that first week. "Whatever you do with your life, Shawn, never move to New Jersey."

He learned that she was a teacher at PS 10, the public school six long blocks away, teaching English. In the mornings now, she taught summer school. One afternoon she asked Shawn the name of the last book he had read, and he told her *The Amboy Dukes,* by a guy named Shulman.

"Hey, Shawn," she said with a laugh. "You could do better than that."

And brought him a copy of *The Red Badge of Courage,* which he read across three nights on the bottom bunk in his room. A book about a young soldier who was afraid. He wondered if his father had been afraid when he landed at Anzio. He wondered if Uncle Jimmy felt fear, too, but didn't ask. Uncle Jimmy never talked about his war.

On the evening he returned the book, they talked about the characters and the writing, and what it was like in the Civil War, and then her voice abruptly dropped and her face darkened.

"My husband, Danny, is in the army," she said softly. "In Japan." She turned her head and stared at the darkening harbor. "I'm real worried now," she said. "Korea's right up the block."

She turned away from the harbor, looking now at nothing.

"I can't call him," she said. "He can't call me. We write every day, but the letters take forever.... I *told* him not to go in the army, but no, he knew better. He wanted to go to college, get the GI Bill, get a degree. Like I did. That was a year ago. He—"

She turned to Shawn and smiled in a thin way. "Why am I telling you all this? Don't worry. I'm okay." A pause. "I just hope my husband's okay."

That evening she invited him down to her place for a cup of tea. They sat facing each other at the kitchen table, and in the muted light he thought she looked beautiful.

Her husband watched them from the photographs on the walls. His name was Danny Carter. Blond and handsome in the photographs from civilian life. Looking like a soldier in the photographs from Fort Dix, where he did his basic training. Marilyn saw Shawn stealing looks at the photographs.

"Danny's such a wonderful man," she said. "A man with a good heart. A *very* good heart. My parents wanted me to marry, oh, I don't know, a doctor, a lawyer, a school principal, at least. They barely talk to me anymore." She looked again at Danny Carter in his soldier's uniform. "I can't imagine him killing anyone."

She stood up and started into the other rooms, flicking on lights as Shawn followed her. There were paintings and photographs on most walls. One room had two walls packed with books. He had never seen so many books in a person's house.

"Let me find you another book," she said.

Two days later, on a Saturday morning, a pair of uniformed soldiers came to her building.

Shawn was in the basement of the grocery store, unpacking cans of Del Monte peaches, when he heard her screaming.

He didn't see her leave, and didn't see her, or hear her voice, for five more days. He rang her bell. No reply. He tried the roof door. Locked from the inside. At night, no lights ever burned in her top-floor apartment. As he worked at the grocery store, leaving with deliveries, then returning, he watched her front door. Other tenants came and went. But there was no sign of Marilyn Carter.

On the sixth day, Shawn brought Uncle Jimmy two slices of pizza for dinner, and then went up the roof with his hand weights. He worked out with a kind of fury. Then, his bare hands gripping his knees, facing the sunset, breathless, he heard a door creaking open. When he turned, she was there. She looked forlorn. She gestured for him to come to her.

He did. An hour later, they were in bed. She was his teacher, helping him to do what he had never done before. He entered her wet, gasping warmth, into a kind of grieving heat and closeness he had never known until then. And then she rose to a pitch, gripping him tightly, digging fingers into his flesh, erupting into a deep, aching moan. One prolonged name.

Daaaaaaannnnnyyyy…

After that night, and for a dozen nights afterward, Sean was there with her. She cooked him small meals, even preparing food for him to bring to Uncle Jimmy. She told him about books he must read and gave him copies from her own library. She told him he should never drop out of high school and should try to get into City College, where there was no tuition. She urged him to buy a notebook and when he saw a word he didn't understand, he should look it up in a dictionary and write it down. "Just writing it down," she said, "will help you remember it." She even gave him an extra dictionary. And he started writing down many words from the newspapers. Mortars. Casualties. Shrapnel.

She never mentioned her own future. When he told her

the latest jokes he'd heard at the grocery store, she laughed out loud. Sometimes, lying in bed, they watched a movie on her television set, but never looked at the news. She said nothing at all about Danny and how he had been killed in Korea.

Above all, their time was devoted to the joys of the flesh. They pleasured each other in every part of the flat, in darkness or lamplight. In bed. In the bathtub. On hard wooden kitchen chairs and the soft couch and armchair in the living room. On a dark blue exercise mat on the floor beneath the cliffs of books.

Each fleshy embrace ended the same way: with the moaning of her dead husband's name. Full of regret, longing, desire, and memory.

Then one Saturday afternoon in late August, as the skies darkened with the threat of a storm, Shawn arrived from the roof. Marilyn was in her pink bathrobe. The exercise mat was draped over a chair. There was an urgency in her eyes, and then in her voice.

"Let's go up the roof," she said.

"It's blowing hard up there," he said. "Someone at the store said there might even be a hurricane."

"I know," she said, and grabbed the mat and led the way to the roof.

She laid the mat on the roof and told him to get undressed.

"Here? What if—"

"In this storm, Shawnie, nobody's heading for the roof."

The first fat drops of rain began to fall. Trembling with urgency, Shawn pulled his shirt over his head and tossed it away. Marilyn removed her bathrobe and laid it upon the mat. She was naked. Then she kneeled, her body trembling, her arms stretched to Shawn. He squatted beside her. They kissed gently. She pulled away and smiled.

Then the rain came at them angrily, in huge, powerful drops, and they lay out flat, side by side, holding hands, facing the angry sky. Rain poured upon their bodies as they surrendered to the howling power of the storm. And then it changed to hail. Small, fierce pellets of ice. Like shrapnel. The waves of hailstones hammered the rooftops, creating a wordless roar. Shawn turned to protect her body with his own. He heard her making sounds, but not words, held her hair with both hands, kissed her fiercely, felt her amazing warmth, while the endless rounds of ice stabbed at his own flesh.

Then she pulled away from his mouth, her eyes closed, and he heard her high-pitched voice, rising into the roar of the storm. Screaming one long extended name.

Shaaaaaawneeee…Oh, Shaaaaaaawnneeeeee…

He woke late on Sunday morning. Flashes of the storm scribbled through his mind, and he rose, dressed quickly, gazed out the window, and saw that the storm was finished and gone. He quickly prepared some cornflakes and a sliced banana for Uncle Jimmy. And headed to the roof. The door to her house was locked from inside. He went home, then downstairs, and hurried to 11th Street. A small battered moving van was being stuffed with furniture that he knew. Chairs and a couch and cardboard boxes heavy with books. His heart was pounding as he entered the open front door and hurried up to Marilyn Carter's top-floor apartment.

She was not there.

"She left this morning," one of two burly moving men said. "Early. Said she had to go someplace. Already paid us, plus the tip."

"Where are you taking her stuff?"

"Somewhere in Jersey," the man said with a shrug.

Shawn turned away. He went down the stairs slowly, then out into the street. He noticed bands of small kids scampering in all directions, splashing puddles beside the curbs. Trash cans were overturned on every corner. A tree had fallen on 11th Street, its smashed limbs now blocking traffic. He counted three wrecked umbrellas outside the grocery store. A flowerpot had been blown off a fire escape. Yes, Shawn thought: there really had been a storm. He didn't dream it.

For more than an hour, he walked around the neighborhood, looking at damage, and trying to make his mind blank and empty. Like the mind of Uncle Jimmy. Men waited for the corner bars to open. He saw a crowd outside Saint Stanislaus Martyr church on 14th Street, but he did not go in. He saw a fallen tree that had crushed the top of a car. When he arrived home, Uncle Jimmy was facing the TV set, with the sound turned off. Shawn told him he was going up the roof.

When he stepped out the door, he saw that the old pigeon

coop was smashed flat. Some clotheslines were down. Then he looked the other way, toward her rooftop. He saw something pink and his heart stopped. He hurried to the small, soaked bundle jammed against the base of a chimney and lifted it. He shook the bathrobe open, and then held it to his chest. Then, at last, he began to weep.

The Book Signing

CARMODY CAME UP FROM the subway before dusk, and his eyeglasses fogged in the sudden cold. He lifted them off his nose, holding them while they cooled, and saw his own face smiling back at him from a pale green leaflet taped to the wall. There he was, in a six-year-old photograph, and the words READING and BOOK SIGNING and the date and place, and he paused for a moment, shivering in the hard wind. The subway was his idea. The publisher could have sent him to Brooklyn in a limousine, but he wanted to go to the old neighborhood the way he always did, long ago. He might, after all, never come this way again.

The subway stairs seemed steeper than he remembered and he felt twinges in his knees that he never felt in California. Sharp little needles of pain, like rumors of mortality.

He didn't feel these pains after tennis, or even after speed-walking along the Malibu roads. But the pain was there now, and was not eased by the weather. The wind was blowing fiercely from the harbor, which lay off in the darkness to his right, and he donned his glasses again and used both gloved hands to pull his brown fedora more securely to his brow. His watch told him that he had more than a half hour to get to the bookstore. Just as he had hoped. He'd have some time for a visit, but not too much time. He crossed the street with his back to the bookstore that awaited him and passed into the streets where he once was young.

His own face peered at him from the leaflets as he passed, some pasted on walls, others taped inside the windows of shops. In a way, he thought, they looked like "Wanted" posters. He felt a sudden...what was the word? Not fear. Certainly not panic. *Unease.* That was the word. An uneasiness in the stomach. A flexing and then relaxing of muscles, an unwilling release of liquids or acids, all those secret wordless messages that in California were cured by the beach and the surf or a quick hit of Maalox. He told himself to stop. This was no drama. It was just a trip through a few streets where once he had lived but that he had not seen for decades. After seventeen novels, this would be his first signing in the borough that had formed him. But the leaflets made clear that here, in this neighborhood, his appearance was some kind of big deal. It might draw many people. And Carmody felt apprehensive, nervous, wormy with...unease.

"How does it feel, going back to Brooklyn?" Charlie Rose had asked him the night before, in a small dark television studio on Park Avenue.

"I don't know," Carmody said, and chuckled. "I just hope they don't throw books at me. Particularly my own books."

And wanted to add: I've never really left. Or, to be more exact: those streets have never left me.

The buildings themselves along the avenue were as Carmody remembered them. They were old-law tenements, with fire escapes on the facades, but they seemed oddly comforting to Carmody. This was not one of those New York neighborhoods desolated by time and arson and decay. He had seen photographs of the enrubbled lots of Brownsville and East New York. There were no lots here in the old neighborhood. If anything, the buildings looked better now, with fresh paint and clear glass instead of hammered tin on the street-level doors. He knew from reading the *New York Times* that the neighborhood had been gentrified, that most of the old families had moved away, to be replaced by younger people who paid much higher rents. There was some unhappiness to all of that, the paper said, but still, the place looked better. As a boy he had walked these streets many times on evenings like this, when most people retreated swiftly from the bitter cold to the uncertain warmth of the flats. Now he noticed lights coming on in many of those old apartments, and shadows moving like ghosts behind drawn shades and curtains. He peered down a street toward the harbor and saw a thin scarlet band where the sun was setting in New Jersey. That was the same, too. The day was dying. It would soon be night.

If the buildings were the same, the shops along the avenue were all different. Fitzgerald's bar was gone, where his father did most of his drinking, and so was Sussman's hardware and Fischetti's fruit and vegetable market and the Freedom meat store and the pharmacy. What was the name of that drugstore? Right there. On that corner. An art supply store now. An art supply store! *Moloff's*. The drugstore was called Moloff's, and next door was a bakery. Our Own, they called it. And now there was a computer store where a TV repair shop once stood. And a dry cleaner where men once stood at the bar of Rattigan's, singing the old songs. All gone. Even the old clock factory had been converted into a condominium.

None of this surprised Carmody. He knew they'd all be gone. Nothing lasts. Marriages don't last. Ball clubs don't last. Why should shops last? Wasn't that the point of each one of his seventeen books? The critics never saw that point, but he didn't care. Those novels were not literature, even to Carmody. He wasn't Stendhal, or Hemingway, or Faulkner. He knew that from the beginning. Those novels were the work he did after turning forty, when he reached the age limit for screenwriting. He worked at the top of his talent, to be sure, and used his knowledge of movies to create plots that kept readers turning the pages. But he knew they were commercial products, novels about industries and how they worked, his characters woven from gossip and profiles in *Fortune* or *Business Week*. He had started with the automobile industry, and then moved to the television industry, and the sugar industry, and the weapons industry. In each of them the old was destroyed by the new, the old ruling families decayed and collapsed, the newer, more ruthless men and women taking their places. The new book was about the food industry, from the farms of California to the dinner plates of New York and Los Angeles. Like the others, it had no aspirations to be seen as art. That would be pretentious. But the books were good examples of craft, as honest as well-made chairs. In each of them, he knew, research served as a substitute for imagination and art and memory. Three different researchers had filed memos on this last one, the new one, the novel he would sign here tonight, in the Barnes & Noble five blocks behind him. He hoped nobody in the audience would ask why he had never once written about Brooklyn.

To be sure, he had never denied his origins. There was a profile in *People* magazine in 1984, when his novel about the gambling industry went to number one on the *New York Times* bestseller list and stayed there for seventeen weeks. He was photographed on the terrace of the house in Malibu with the Pacific stretched out beyond him, and they used an old high school newspaper photograph showing him in pegged pants and a T-shirt, looking like an apprentice gangster or some variation on the persona of James Dean. The article mentioned his two ex-wives (there was now a third woman enjoying his alimony checks), but the reporter was also from Brooklyn and was more intrigued by the Brooklyn mug who had become a bestselling author.

"You went west in 1957," the reporter said. "Just like the Dodgers."

"When they left, I left, too, because that was the end of Brooklyn as I knew it," Carmody said. "I figured I'd have my revenge on Los Angeles by forcing it to pay me a decent living."

That was a lie, of course. He didn't leave Brooklyn because of the Dodgers. He left because of Molly Mulrane.

Now he was standing across the street from the building where both of them had lived. The sidewalk entrance then was between a meat market and a fruit store, converted now into a toy store and a cell phone shop. Molly lived on the first floor left. Carmody on the top floor right. She was three years younger than Carmody and he didn't pay her much attention until he returned from the army in 1954. An old story: she had blossomed. And one thing had led to another.

He remembered her father's rough, unhappy, threatening face when Carmody first came calling to take her to the movies. Paddy Mulrane, the cop. And the way he looked when he went out in his police uniform for a four-to-twelve shift, his gun on his hip, his usual slouch shifting as he walked taller and assumed a kind of swagger. And how appalled Paddy Mulrane was when Carmody told him he was using the GI Bill to become a writer. "A writer? What the hell is that? I'm a writer, too. I write tickets. Ha-ha. A writer...how do you make a living with *that*? What about being a lawyer? A doctor? What about,

what do they call it now, *criminology?* At least you'd have
a shot at becoming a lieutenant...." The father liked his
Fleischmann's and beer and used the Dodgers as a substitute for conversation. The mother was a dim, shadowy
woman who did very little talking. That summer, Molly
was the youngest of the three children, and the only one
still at home. Her brother Frankie was a fireman and lived
with his wife in Bay Ridge. There was another brother:
what was his name? Sean. Seanie. Flat face, hooded eyes,
a hard, tanklike body. Carmody didn't remember much
about him. There had been some kind of trouble, something about a robbery, and Seanie had moved to Florida,
where he was said to be a fisherman in the Keys. Every
Sunday morning, father, mother, and daughter went to
Mass together.

Now, on this frozen night, decades later, Carmody's unease rushed back. Ah, Molly, my Molly-O... The fire escapes still climbed three stories to the top floor, where the
Carmodys lived. But the building now looked better, like
all the others on the avenue. On the top floor right on this
frozen night, the shades were up and Carmody could see
ocher-colored walls and a warm light cast by table lamps.
This startled him. In memory, the Carmody flat was always
cold, the windows rimed with frost in winter, he and his
sisters making drawings with their fingernails in the cold
bluish light cast from a fluorescent ceiling lamp. His father
was cold, too, a withdrawn, bitter man who resented the
world and the youth of his children. His mother was a
drinker, and her own chilly remorse was relieved only by

occasional bursts of rage. His parents nodded or grunted when Carmody told them about his ambitions, and his mother once said, in a slurred voice, "Who do you think you are, anyway?"

One Saturday afternoon in the Mulrane flat, he and Molly were alone, her parents gone off to see Frankie and his small child. Molly proudly showed him her father's winter police uniform, encased in plastic from the Kent dry cleaners, and the medals he had won, and the extra gun, a nickel-plated .38-caliber Smith & Wesson, oiled and ready in a felt-lined box. She talked to him about a book she was reading, by A. J. Cronin, and he told her she should read F. Scott Fitzgerald. She made him a ham-and-Swiss-cheese sandwich for lunch. They sipped sweet tea thick with sugar. And then for the first time, they went to bed together in her tiny room with its window leading to the fire escape. She was in an agony, murmuring prayers, her hands and arms moving to cover breasts and hair, trembling with fear and desire. "Hold me tight," she whispered. "Don't ever leave me."

He had never written any of that, or how at the end of his first year of college, at the same time that she graduated from St. Joseph's, he rented the room near New York University to get away from his parents and hers, and how she would come to him after work as a file clerk at Metropolitan Life and they would vanish into each other. He still went back to Brooklyn. He still visited the ice house of his parents. He still called formally at the Mulrane apartment to take Molly to the Sanders or the RKO Prospect. But the tiny room in Manhattan had become their true place, their gangster's hideout, the secret place to which they went for sin.

Now on this frozen night he stared at the dark windows of the first floor left, wondering who lived there now, and whether Molly's bones were lying in some frozen piece of the Brooklyn earth. He could still hear her voice, trembling and tentative: "We're sinners, aren't we?" He could hear her saying: "What's to become of us?" He could hear the common sense in her words and the curl of Brooklyn in her accent. "Where are we going?" she said. "Please don't ever leave me." He could see the mole inside her left thigh. He could see the fine hair at the top of her neck.

"Well, will ya lookit this," a hoarse male voice said from behind him. "If it ain't Buddy Carmody."

Carmody turned and saw a burly man smoking a cigarette in the doorway of a tenement. The face was not clear in the muted light but the voice told Carmody it was definitely someone from back then. Nobody had called him Buddy in forty-six years.

"How *are* ya?" Carmody said, peering at the man as he stepped out of the doorway. The man's face was puffy and seamed, and Carmody tried to peel away the flesh to see who had lived in it when they both were young.

"Couldn't stay away from the old neighborhood, could ya, Buddy?"

The unease was seething now. Carmody felt a small stream of fear make its move in his stomach.

"It's been a long time," Carmody said. "Remind me, what's your name?"

"You shittin' me, Buddy? How could you fi'get my name?"

"I told you, man, it's been a long time."

"Yeah. It's easy to fi'get, for some people."

"Advanced age, and all that," Carmody said, faking a grin, glancing to his left, to the darkening shop windows, the empty street. Imagining himself running.

"But not everybody fi'gets," the man said.

He flipped his cigarette under a parked car.

"My sister didn't fi'get."

Oh.

Oh, God.

"You must be Seanie," Carmody said. "Am I right? Seanie Mulrane?"

"Ah...you remembered."

"How are you, Seanie?"

He could see Seanie's hooded eyes now, so like the eyes of his policeman father: still, unimpressed. He moved close enough so that Carmody could smell the whiskey on his breath.

"How am I? Huh. How am I...Not as good as you, Buddy boy. We keep up, ya know. The books, that miniseries, or whatever it was on NBC. Pretty good, you're doing."

Carmody stepped back a foot, as subtly as possible, trying to decide how to leave. He wished a police car would turn the corner. He trembled, feeling a black wind of hostility pushing at him, backing him up, a wind that seemed to come from the furled brow of Seanie Mulrane. He tried to look casual, turned and glanced at the building where he was young, at the dark first floor left, the warm top floor right.

"She never got over you, you prick."

"It's a long time ago, Seanie," Carmody said, trying to sound casual but not dismissive.

"I remember that first month after you split," Seanie said. "She cried all the time. She cried all day. She cried all night. She quit her job, 'cause she couldn't do it and cry at the same time. She'd start to eat, then, *oof,* she'd break up again. I was there, just back from the Keys, and my father wanted to find you and put a bullet in your head. And Molly, poor Molly... You broke her fuckin' heart, Buddy."

Carmody said nothing. Other emotions were flowing now. Regret. Remorse. Mistakes. His stomach seethed.

"And that month? Hey, that was just the start. The end of the second month after you cut out, she tells my mother she's knocked up."

"No...."

"Yes."

"I didn't know that."

"Don't lie, Buddy. My old man told your old man. He pulled a gun on him, for Chrissakes, tryin' to find out where you was."

"I never heard any of this."

"Don't lie, Buddy. You lie for a livin', right? All those books, they're lies, ain't they? Don't lie."

"I didn't know, Seanie. I swear."

"Tell the truth: you ran because she was pregnant."

No: that wasn't why. He truly didn't know. He glanced at his watch. Almost time for the book signing.

"She had the baby, some place in New Jersey," Seanie said. "Catholic nuns or something. And gave it up. Then she came home and went in her room. She went to Mass every morning, I guess praying to God to forgive her. But she never went to another movie with a guy, never went on a date. She was in her room, like another goddamned nun. She saw my mother die, and buried her, and saw my father die, and buried him, and saw me get married and move here wit' my Mary, right across the street, to live upstairs. I'd come see her every day, and try talkin' to her, but it was like, 'You want tea, Seanie, or coffee?'"

Seanie moved slightly, placing his bulk between Carmody and the path to Barnes & Noble.

"Once I said to her, I said, 'How about you come with me an' Mary to Florida? You like it, we could all move there. It's beautiful,' I said to her. 'You'd love it.' Figuring I had to get her out of that room. She looked at me like I said, 'Hey, let's move to Mars.'" Seanie paused, trembling with anger and memory, and lit another cigarette. "Just once, she talked a blue streak, drinkin' gin, I guess it was. And said to me, real mad, 'I don't want to see anyone, you understand me, Seanie? I don't want to see people holdin' hands. I don't want to see boys playin' ball. You understand me?'" He took a deep drag on the Camel. "'I want to be here,' she says to me, 'when Buddy comes back.'"

Carmody stared at the sidewalk, at Seanie's scuffed black shoes, and heard her voice: *When Buddy comes back.* Saw the fine hair at the top of her neck.

"So she waited for you, Buddy. Year after year in that dark goddamned flat. Everything was like it was when you split. My mother's room, my father's room, her room. All the same clothes. It wasn't right what you done to her, Buddy. She was a beautiful girl."

"That she was."

"And a sweet girl."

"Yes."

"It wasn't right. You had the sweet life and she shoulda had it with you."

Carmody turned. "And how did she... When did she..."

"Die? She didn't die, Buddy. She's still there. Right across the street. Waiting for you, you prick."

Carmody turned then, lurching toward the corner, heading to the bookstore. Thinking: She's alive? Molly Mulrane is alive? He was certain she had gone off, married someone, settled in the safety of Bay Ridge or some suburb. In a place without memory. Without ghosts. He was certain that she had lived a long while, had children, and then died. The way everybody did. And now he knew the only child she ever had was his, and he was in flight, afraid to look back, feeling as if some pack of feral dogs was behind him, chasing him across some vast abandoned tundra. He did not run. He walked quickly, deliberately, but he did not run and did not look back. And then he slowed: the signing itself filled him with another kind of fear. Who else might come there knowing the truth? Hauling up the ashes of the past? What other ancient sin would someone dredge up? Who else might come for an accounting?

He looked back then. Nobody was following. Not even Seanie. A taxi cruised along the avenue, its rooftop light on, looking for a fare to Manhattan. I could just get out of here. Just jump in this cab. Call the store. Plead sudden illness. Just go. But someone was sure to call Rush and Molloy at the *Daily News* or Page Six at the *Post* and report the no-show. BROOKLYN BOY CALLS IT IN. All that shit. No.

And then a rosy-cheeked woman was smiling at him. The manager of the bookstore.

"Oh, Mr. Carmody, we thought you got lost."

"Not in this neighborhood," he said. And smiled.

"You've got a great crowd waiting."

"Let's do it."

"We have water on the lectern, and lots of pens, everything you need."

As they climbed to the second floor, Carmody took off his hat and gloves and overcoat and the manager handed them to an assistant. He glanced at himself in a mirror, at his tweed jacket and black crewneck sweater. He looked like a writer, all right. Not a cop or a fireman or even a professor. A writer. He saw an area with about a hundred people sitting on folding chairs, penned in by walls of books, and more people in the aisles beyond the shelves and another large group standing at the rear. Yes: a great crowd.

He stood beside the lectern as he was introduced by the manager. He heard the words "one of Brooklyn's own..." and they sounded strange. He didn't often think of himself that way, and in signings all over the country that fact was seldom mentioned. This store itself was a sign of a different Brooklyn. *Nothing stays the same. Everything changes.* There were no bookstores in his Brooklyn. He found his first books in the branch of the public library near where he lived, or in the great main library at Grand Army Plaza. On rainy summer days he spent hours as a boy among their stacks. But the bookstores—where you could buy and own a book—they were down on Pearl Street under the El, or across the river on Fourth Avenue. His mind flashed on *Bomba the Jungle Boy at the Giant Cataract.* The first book he'd ever finished. How old was I? Eleven. Yes. Eleven. It cost a nickel on Pearl Street.

During the introduction, he peered out at the faces, and they were different, too. Most were in their thirties, lean and intense, or prepared to be critical, or wearing the competitive masks of aspiring writers. About a dozen African Americans were scattered through the seats, with a few standing on the sides. He saw several men with six or seven copies of his books: collectors, looking for autographs to sell on eBay or some fan website. He didn't see any of the older faces. Those faces still marked by Galway or Sicily or the Ukraine. He didn't see the pouchy, hooded masks that were worn by men like Seanie Mulrane.

His new novel and five of the older paperbacks were stacked on a table to the left of the lectern. He began to relax. Thinking: It's another signing. Thinking: I could be in Denver or Houston or Berkeley.

Finally, he began to read, focusing on words printed on pages. His words. His pages. He read from the first chapter, which was always fashioned as a hook. He described his hero being drawn into the mysteries of a grand Manhattan restaurant by an old college pal who was one of the owners, all the while glancing up at the crowd so that he didn't sound like a professor. The manager was right: it was a great crowd. They listened. They laughed at the hero's wisecracks. Carmody enjoyed the feedback. He enjoyed the applause, too, when he had finished. And then the manager explained that Carmody would take some questions, and then sign books.

He felt himself tense again. And thought: Why did I run, all those years ago? Why did I do what I did to Molly Mulrane?

I ran to escape, he thought.

That's why everybody runs. That's why women run from men. Women have run from me, too. To escape.

People moved in the folding chairs, but Carmody was still. I ran because I felt a rope tightening on my life. Because Molly Mulrane was too nice. Too ordinary. Too safe. I ran because she gave me no choice. She had a script and he didn't. They would get engaged and he'd get his BA and maybe a teaching job and they'd get married and have kids and maybe move out to Long Island or over to Jersey and then—*I ran because I wanted something else. I wanted to be Hemingway in Pamplona or in a café on the Left Bank. I wanted to make a lot of money in the movies, the way Faulkner did or Irwin Shaw, and then retreat to Italy or the south of France. I wanted risk. I didn't want safety. So I ran. Like a heartless, frightened prick.*

The first question came from a bearded man in his forties, the type who wrote nasty book reviews that guaranteed him tenure.

"Do you think if you'd stayed in Brooklyn," the bearded man asked, "you'd have been a better writer?"

Carmody smiled at the implied insult, the patronizing tone.

"Probably," he answered. "But you never know these things with any certainty. I might never have become a writer at all. There's nothing in the Brooklyn air or the Brooklyn water that makes writers, or we'd have a couple of million writers here...."

A woman in her twenties stood up. "Do you write on a word processor, or longhand, or on a typewriter?"

This was the way it was everywhere, and Carmody relaxed into the familiar. Soon he'd be asked how to get an agent or how he got his ideas and how do I protect my own ideas when I send a manuscript around? Could you read the manuscript of my novel and tell me what's wrong? The questions came and he answered as politely as possible. He drew people like that, and he knew why: he was a success, and there were thousands of would-be writers who thought there were secret arrangements, private keys, special codes that would open the doors to the alpine slopes of the bestseller lists. He couldn't tell them that, like life, it was all a lottery.

Then the manager stepped to the microphone and smiled and said that Mr. Carmody would now be signing books. "Because of the large turnout," the manager said, "Mr. Carmody will not be able to personalize each book. Otherwise many of you would have a *very* long wait." Carmody thanked everybody for coming on such a frigid night and there was warm, loud applause. He sat down at the table and sipped from a bottle of Poland Spring water.

He signed the first three books on the title page, and then a woman named Peggy Williams smiled and said, "Could you make an exception? We didn't go to school together, but we went to the same school twenty years apart. Could you mention that?"

He did, and the line slowed. Someone wanted him to mention the Dodgers. Another, Coney Island. One wanted a stickball reference, although he was too young to ever have played that summer game. There was affection in these people for this place, this neighborhood, which was now their neighborhood. But Carmody began to feel something else in the room, something he could not see.

"You must think you're hot shit," said a woman in her fifties. She had daubed rouge on her pale cheeks. "I've been in this line almost an hour."

"I'm sorry," he said, and tried to be light. "It's almost as bad as the motor vehicle bureau."

She didn't laugh.

"You could just sign the books," she said. "Leave off the fancy stuff."

"That's what some people want," he said. "The fancy stuff."

"And you gotta give it to them? Come on."

He signed his name on the title page and handed it to her, still smiling.

"Wait a minute," she said, holding the book before him as though it were a summons. "I waited a long time. Put in, 'For Gerry'—with a *G*—'who waited on line for more than an hour.'"

She laughed then, too, and he did what she asked. The next three just wanted signatures, and two just wanted "Merry Christmas," and then a collector arrived and Carmody signed six first editions. He was weary now, his mind filling with images of Molly Mulrane and Seanie's face and injuries he had caused so long ago. All out there somewhere. And still the line trailed away from the table into a crowd that, when viewed without his glasses, had become a multicolored smear, like a bookcase.

The woman came around from the side aisle, easing toward the front of the line in a distracted way. Carmody saw her whisper to someone on the line, a young man who made room for her with the deference reserved for the old. She was hatless, her white hair cut in girlish bangs across her furrowed brow. She was wearing a short down coat, black skirt, black stockings, mannish shoes. The coat was open, showing a dark, rose-colored sweater. Her eyes were pale.

Holy God.

She was six feet away from him, behind two young men and a collector. A worn leather bag hung from her shoulder. A bag so old that Carmody remembered buying it in a shop in the Village, next door to the Eighth Street Bookshop.

He glanced past the others and saw that she was not looking at him. She stared at bookshelves, or the ceiling, or the floor. Her face had an indoor whiteness. The color of ghosts. He signed a book, then another. And the girl he once loved began to come to him, the sweet, pretty girl who asked nothing of him except that he love her back. And he felt then a great rush of sorrow. For her. For himself. For their lost child. He felt as if tears would soon leak from every pore in his body. The books in front of him were now as meaningless as bricks.

Then she was there. And Carmody rose slowly and leaned forward to embrace her across the table.

"Oh, Molly," he whispered. "Oh, Molly, I'm so, so sorry."

She smiled then, and the lines, like brackets, that framed her mouth seemed to vanish and Carmody imagined taking her away with him, repairing her in the sun of California, making it up, writing a new ending. Rewriting his own life. He started to come around the table.

"Molly," he said. "Molly, my love."

Then she took the nickel-plated revolver from the leather bag, the sweet smile frozen on her face.

Carmody thought: *Oh, God. Oh, yes, God. Oh, yes. Do it.*

She shot him four times in the chest, while women

screamed and men shouted and many simply ran. She dropped the revolver on the floor beside Carmody and began to weep. One of the collectors said later that as the bullets tore into Carmody, he smiled and looked relieved.

Acknowledgments

Acknowledgment is made to the following publications, in which the stories in this collection first appeared, some with different titles or in slightly different form. New York *Daily News:* "The Christmas Kid," "The Price of Love," "A Death in the Family," "A Christmas Wish," "The Love of His Life," "Good-bye," "Changing of the Guard," "Footsteps," "A Poet Long Ago," "The Car," "Just the Facts, Ma'am," "6/6/44," "The Trial of Red Dano," "Leaving Paradise," "Lullaby of Birdland," "The Boarder," "The Radio Doctor," "The Challenge," "A Hero of the War," "The Final Score," "Gone," "You Say Tomato, and…" "'S Wonderful," "The Warrior's Son," "The Second Summer," "The Sunset Pool," "The Lasting Gift of Art," "The Man with the Blue Guitar," "The Hitter Bag," "Trouble," "Home Country," "The Waiting Game," "The Home Run." *Brooklyn Noir,* edited by Tim McLoughlin: "The Book Signing." *Ellery Queen's Mystery Magazine:* "The Men in Black Raincoats" (reprinted in *Brooklyn Noir 2,* edited by Tim McLoughlin).

About the Author

PETE HAMILL is a novelist, journalist, editor, and screenwriter. He is the author of twenty-one previous books, including the bestselling novels *Tabloid City, Forever,* and *Snow in August* and the bestselling memoir *A Drinking Life.* He lives in New York City.

READING GROUP GUIDE

The Christmas Kid

And Other Brooklyn Stories

by

Pete Hamill

Pete Hamill's Christmas Book Bag

Think of Pete Hamill and you think of Brooklyn. Perhaps it's time to add Christmas to that association. The author of *The Christmas Kid: And Other Brooklyn Stories* tells us what he's been reading—you should curl up with these books during your Christmas nights, too.

Winter Journal by **Paul Auster**
More than simply a memoir by one of the finest American novelists. This is also a reflection on time, age, mistakes, work, the closing of some doors, and the opening of others. For me it's a perfect book in a season usually marked by reflection, regret, and, yes, hope.

The Greater Journey: Americans in Paris by **David McCullough**
Not another rehash of the Lost Generation. This rich book is about an earlier time, when American doctors could not perform autopsies on the corpses of American women, when female models appeared fully clothed in the few American art schools, when the legacy of American Pu-

ritanism created an intellectual and artistic prison. Some young Americans, men and women, went to Paris. They returned with the gifts of reason, science, art, and vision. McCullough tells the story as a triumphant human tale about individuals. His prose is fluid and detailed, never abstract, never pedantic. The result is marvelous.

Human Chain by **Seamus Heaney**

The most recent volume of poems by the 1995 Nobel Prize winner, this should not be read cover-to-cover. Take the book to bed before sleeping, read one poem each night, like a prayer. Then turn off the lights. If you're like me, you will awake each morning charged with the music of what happens. Heaney's music. Now part of yours.

Rome: A Cultural, Visual, and Personal History by **Robert Hughes**

This is at once a celebration of one of Europe's essential cities and a detailed exploration of the things that truly matter about its past. Hughes was, of course, one of the finest writers of his day, an art critic for *Time,* an author of several books of history. In this, his final work, he reminds us again that all empires inevitably fade but their truest legacies are almost always works of art. He tells us that part of the Roman tale, too, and what happened during the many centuries that followed the fall. Every man or woman who reads this book will be wiser when they finish.

The Story of Babar by **Jean de Brunhoff**

This brilliant book (published in 1931) was the first I ever read, at age five, my eyes following my mother's finger as she touched each precious word. I remember weeping the first time I understood that the little elephant's mother had been shot dead by a hunter. I must have read the tale another thirty times before I was six, weeping each time, hating that hunter, but loving the city Babar went to from his jungle home. The place called Paris. I still read it every year in this season. And no, it never did make me a defender of French colonialism.

"Pete Hamill's Christmas Book Bag" originally appeared in the *Daily Beast* on December 25, 2012.

Questions and topics for discussion

1. What do these stories say about the immigrant experience? What has changed since the time in which these stories took place, and what has stayed the same? Does your family's history include similar stories?

2. In "The Christmas Kid," how did Lev's experiences in the Holocaust influence his reactions to his new life in Brooklyn? Why do you think the neighborhood boys need to look out for him? Why is Lev called "The Christmas Kid"?

3. How does Hamill describe the sense of community in Brooklyn's neighborhoods? Do you think this kind of community still exists in today's cities? Why or why not?

4. What do you think will happen in the aftermath of "The Price of Love"? Do you think it's "worth a try" (page 30)?

5. In "A Death in the Family," do you think Joe Tooks got what he deserved? Why or why not?

6. In "Wishes," in what ways has Uncle Roy's accident altered the course of his life? Do you think things will change for

Uncle Roy, or is he already too set in his ways? Based on his nostalgia, do you think he has regrets about the year 1949? Is there a year in your life that you feel particularly nostalgic for?

7. Like Hugo in "The Love of His Life," do you believe in love at first sight? Why or why not? What do you think happened to Daria Stark?

8. In "Good-bye," why do you think Mitchell makes the decision he does?

9. What do you think it means to Sanno and Carlos to have "everything" (page 60) in "Changing of the Guard"?

10. Who do you think is responsible for what happens to Ira in "Footsteps"?

11. Do you think Sonny's life as described in "A Poet Long Ago" would have been different had he been born at another time? Was he right to make the decision he does? Why or why not?

12. Do you think Cavanaugh overreacts to what he learns about Kelly's Chevy in "The Car"? Would you have reacted similarly? Why or why not?

13. In "Just the Facts, Ma'am," what do you think makes Mercedes different from other women? What do you think she likes about Facts?

14. What role does Helen play in "6/6/44"? What do you think triggers this memory for Harry so many years later?

15. Do you think Dano feels he deserves his fate in "The Trial of Red Dano"? Why or why not?

16. In "Leaving Paradise," Gillis feels very self-conscious that he wasn't "part of that college crowd" (page 104). What does the "college crowd" stand for in Gillis's mind? How do you think this affects his attitudes and actions toward Cathy and the man she's with?

17. What do you think the men in the blue Plymouth want with Mr. Macias in "The Boarder"?

18. Do you agree with the logic of "The Men in Black Raincoats"? Why or why not? Do you think there is a statute of limitations on Brendan's actions? Did he have a choice?

19. Do you agree with Dr. Ambler's assessment of Tommy in "The Radio Doctor"? Why or why not? What advice would you have given Tommy?

20. In "The Challenge," why do you think Shank is so reluctant to give up what he's earned for the safety of his family? Could Shank have changed the outcome of his meeting with Rojo if he had acted differently? Why or why not?

21. In "A Hero of the War," Paulie Fitzgerald tells his son Billy, "War is hell, kid. War is hell" (page 143). Does the truth revealed about Paulie Fitzgerald's past support this statement? How does this differ from Soldier Dunne, who in "The Warrior's Son" believes that "a real man's greatest glory was war" (page 173)? Do other characters' experiences of war throughout the collection support one view or the other?

22. In "Gone," do you think Hirsch's paranoia is well-founded? Does Hirsch represent a larger societal fear of strangers and crime? If so, do you think this fear has increased or decreased in recent decades?

23. What do these stories say about the nature of love? Why do you think so many of the relationships in this collection are ill-fated? How does Hamill play with these ideas in "You Say Tomato, and…"?

24. What, if anything, is the moral of "'S Wonderful"? Can you draw any parallels between Wonderful Kelly and contemporary true-life figures? What do these men have in common?

25. In "The Second Summer," Dotty Haddam says, "Love is for children" (page 184). Do you agree with this statement? Do you think Dotty herself agrees with it? Why or why not?

26. In "The Sunset Pool," why do you think Harry Hansen doesn't go to visit Gerry Grogan? Do you think Harry's fate is deserved? Who do you think is responsible?

27. Why is Widow Musmanno in "The Man with the Blue Guitar" not allowed to move on with her life? Why do you think widows were treated as they were? Do you think any element of the "old country" attitudes about women still exists in the modern day?

28. In "The Hitter Bag," Rose tells her father, "The world is different now" (page 207). How is Rose's world different

from that of her father? Is the world for you significantly different from what it was for your parents' generation?

29. What kind of "trouble" (in the story of the same name) do you think Jack Parker was in that made him act the way he did?

30. What does the Spaldeen ball represent for Laverty in "The Home Country"?

31. In "The Waiting Game," do you think Catherine Novak will ever shop at Teddy Caravaggio's store? Why or why not?

32. At the end of "The Book Signing," why do you think Carmody "smiled and looked relieved" (page 271)?

Also by Pete Hamill

Tabloid City
A Novel

"Murder and mayhem...a ticking time bomb of a novel."
—Susan Salter Reynolds, *Los Angeles Times*

"A suspenseful tale, set in the present day, that captures the grit and smell and pulse of Gotham's sidewalks and subways....Hamill's sentences are short and pack a punch."
—John Darnton, *New York Times Book Review*

"Engrossing....A gritty tone-poem in prose on New York City life—and death."
—Alan Cheuse, *San Francisco Chronicle*

"Exciting to read....Thoughtfully crafted and written with care and cutting caricature."
—Adam Rathe, NPR

Back Bay Books • Available wherever books are sold

Also by Pete Hamill

Snow in August
A Novel

"A tender novel.... When it comes to evoking the sights and sounds of postwar Brooklyn streets, Pete Hamill has no peer.... When you finish that roller-coaster last chapter you'll wonder if the shade of Isaac Bashevis Singer whispered in his ear."

—Frank McCourt, author of *Angela's Ashes*

"Strong and soulful—a wonderful addition to a compelling body of work. Few are as good at evoking New York City's life and heart as Pete Hamill."

—Oscar Hijuelos, author of
Mambo Kings Play Songs of Love

Also by Pete Hamill

Forever
A Novel

"A swashbuckling, ribald tale told with flair and, sometimes, unbridled emotion. At the same time it is a serious look at what makes a city more than just bricks and mortar."
— Tom Walker, *Denver Post*

"Hamill's knowledgeable love for the city and his writerly exuberance explode here into a New York fantasy: big, extravagant, untrammeled, and as hugely readable as it must have been hugely entertaining to write….*Forever* is old-fashioned storytelling at a gallop."
— Frances Taliaferro, *Washington Post Book World*

"A grand, dark, swashbuckling, yet essentially simple tale about a man's lifelong journey from revenge to mercy, hate to love." — Jodi Daynard, *Boston Globe*

"A tabloid epic in a folkloric American style….*Forever* is fueled by the cruel dictates of history — corruption, exploitation, murder — but it wholeheartedly celebrates human goodness at every turn." — Troy Patterson, *Entertainment Weekly*

Back Bay Books • Available wherever books are sold

Also by Pete Hamill

North River
A Novel

"A wonderfully old-fashioned, big, wet cinematic kiss of a novel."　　　　　—Tim Rutten, *Los Angeles Times*

"*North River* might be the best book Hamill has written since *A Drinking Life*. It is about New York, and the '30s, about parents and children and grandchildren and friendship and love and honor. Buy it as soon as you can."
　　　　　—Mike Lupica, *New York Daily News*

"Hamill tells a good yarn and has a knack for drawing empathetic portraits of rogues and rule benders."
　　　　　—Michael Hill, *San Francisco Chronicle*

"An elegiac, beautiful novel.... Hamill's most assured piece of fiction to date."
　　　　　—Scott Stephens, *Cleveland Plain Dealer*

Also by Pete Hamill

A Drinking Life

"Energetic, compelling, very funny, and remarkably—indeed, often brutally—candid....*A Drinking Life* is much more than the story of Pete Hamill and the bottle. It's also a classic American tale of a young person's struggle to expand his horizons without doing violence to his personal identity."
—*Entertainment Weekly*

"A vivid report of a journey to the edge of self-destruction. It is tough-minded, brimming with energy, and unflinchingly honest. Mr. Hamill may lament what drink did to his memories, but to judge from this account he never lost the best of them." —*New York Times*

"Magnificent....*A Drinking Life* is about growing up and growing old, working and trying to work, within the culture of drink." —*Boston Globe*

"Pete Hamill's thirty years of writing come to fruition in *A Drinking Life*. It is constructed seamlessly, with the pacing and eye for telling detail learned as a novelist and the hard, spare prose of a fine journalist." —*New York Times Book Review*

Back Bay Books • Available wherever books are sold